HACKNEY LIBRARY SERVICE

THIS BOOK MUST BE RETUR
BEFORE THE LAST DATE ST/
CHARGED IF IT IS LATE. AVO
BOOK.
(SUBJECT TO IT NOT BEING F

D0545742

PEOPLE WHO ARE OVER 60, UNDER 17 OR REGISTERED
DISABLED ARE NOT CHARGED FINES.

PS.6578

THE COMMUNITY LIBRARY SERVICE
Stoke Newington Library
Church St., London N16 0JS
0181 356 5238
Mobile Library: 0378 963 800

COMMUNITY LIBRARY SERVICE
DEPOSIT COLLECTION

55

66

COMMUNITY LIBRARY SERVICE
DEPOSIT COLLECTION

LONDON BOROUGH OF HACKNEY

3 8040 01481 2962

Sea Stories

A collection of new stories from
from the National Maritime Museum

LONDON BOROUGH OF HACKNEY LIBRARIES	
PBK FICTION	
Bertrams	16.03.08
SEA	£7.99

First published in 2007 by the National Maritime Museum
Greenwich
London
SE10 9NF
T: +44 (0)20 8858 4422

www.nmm.ac.uk/publishing

ISBN: 978-0-948065-80-4

The Shoals © Sam Llewellyn
Devonia © Desmond Barry
The Doldrums © John Williams
Getting There is Half the Fun © James Scudamore
The King's Daughter of Norroway © Margaret Elphinstone
Omar's Island © Robert Minhinnick
Fresh Water © Chris Cleave
Bathyspheres © Niall Griffiths
In Time: A Correspondence © Erica Wagner
Something Rich and Strange © Charles Lambert
The Island © Roger Hubank
The Convalescent's Handbook © Evie Wyld
The Boy © Tessa Hadley
The Anniversary © Martin Stephen
A Snow Goose © Jim Perrin
The Museum of the Sea © Nick Parker

The moral right of the above to be identified as the authors of this
work has been asserted in accordance with the Copyright, Designs and
Patents Act of 1988.

All rights reserved. No part of this publication may be reproduced,
stored in or introduced into a retrieval system, or transmitted, in any
form, or by any means (electronic, mechanical, photocopying, recording
or otherwise) without the prior written permission of the publisher.
Any person who does any unauthorised act in relation to this publication
may be liable to criminal prosecution and civil claims for damages.

Cover by Poise Design

Contents

The Shoals

by Sam Llewellyn

Alexander Rourke was born in a place with no name close to Stiffkey in the county of Norfolk. The baby had a full set of teeth. Those who knew him later laid his nature at the door of his first meals having been of blood and milk mingled.

It is remembered that Alexander Rourke when six would sit on the wooden shedding of the creek, fishing. David Jordan from the cottage next door would be there too, running around catching gilly crabs on bits of mussel so he could put them in a bucket to watch them fight. Alexander (he suffered no abbreviation, no dear little Sandys or good old Alexes, not even then) was different. Alexander had scrounged himself a hook and a line and some rabbit guts, and what he was catching were the fat eels that lived in the holes under the pilings. These he would put in a bucket of his own and sell to the man on the fish cart. As time went by, David made himself a rod and went after the sea trout that streaked into the river in the black of the night. Rod fishing was too slow and stupid for Alexander. Alexander got himself an old herring net, studied its construction, mended it carefully and cut it down to six foot deep and fifty yards long. This net he used to seine up the sea trout, thirty and forty fish in a night. David complained that Alexander had caught all the fish, leaving none for him. Alexander broke his nose for him. He knew that this was a stupid explanation, depending on imagination, not logic. Alexander knew that there were infinite numbers of fish in the sea. It was just that by the time lazy David got to the river the shoals had moved on.

The father of Alexander Rourke was a gamekeeper, and for that reason detested in the parish. He built up the wall of his cottage more than head high, and cemented thick bars into the windows, and laid down a floor of stone slabs set in concrete so that in all the enclosure there was no bush nor other plant behind which an enemy could hide.

One day in his thirteenth year Alexander was bowling a barrow of mussels across the marsh. By the creek he met a party with a stretcher. On the stretcher under a sack was a man in a green velveteen livery. The man was his father. They had found him face down in the sea pool, the common theory being that he had fallen in while carrying a net he had found staked in the river, and become tangled, and the leads had sunk him.

There was no grand outpouring of sympathy, not even when word got round that the net that had drowned William Rourke had been his son's. His Lordship made a donation, and so did other worthies of the region. None of this touched the widow, who sat looking at her stone yard until one morning she got up early, unfastened the five locks between her and the world, and walked through the spring-green fields into the grey sea.

On which her son was by then floating, having bought a boat – rotten, crank and small, but the best that could be had with the donations of the worthies, which he had stolen immediately after the funeral.

Alexander proved to be a good fisherman, for he had no other object in his ice-clear mind but the getting of money, which rather than the catching of fish is the successful fisherman's goal and aim.

Yes, indeed. Alexander's mind was a busy one. It took him off to Lowestoft, where he studied the new gear, notably the trawling apparatus just coming into use, great socks of net held open by baulks of weighted timber that tore from the seabed every weed, fish and invertebrate that thereon lived.

And one morning David Jordan, eighteen now, unmooring his little crab boat in the Freshes ready to go longlining for cod, looked over the grey-green marshes at the blue horizon, and saw against that blue sails the colour of dried blood: a trawler, creeping across the rim of the world. Every day for three months it trawled. And when David hauled his lines there were fewer and fewer fish, smaller and smaller. So one day David went out and hove to by the trawler's endless tar-black side. For a moment he watched the main and the mizzen and the jib and the tow foresail forward of the mainmast with its forward-raked topmast, and the jib topsail firing air over the gaff topsail, a cliff of heavy canvas trudging across the sea. He heard the creak of the trawl warps bar-taut over the port side, the scream of the gull cloud diving over the trawl's wake. He found he was trembling with rage.

A man in a dark suit and a bowler hat was glaring at him over the rail. David recognized Alexander. 'What do you want?' said Alexander, as if he owned the sea and all that therein was.

'You are buggering up the grounds,' said David. 'You and that damned Godless machine of yours.' There were other faces at the trawler's rail now, strange to David, cold.

'Christ fished Galilee,' said Alexander, clamping his jaw.

'Christ said, cast your nets over the right-hand side of the boat. But your gear is over the port side, which is an affront to God and bloody man, so go you away, boy, and do not come back.'

'Before you ask, I fish on Sundays,' said Alexander. 'So no doubt I will go to hell. But you can go to the devil first. Now do you keep clear, boy, because some on us has work to do before the shoals move on.'

David got married and had a son. By the time the son was a year old, he was an enthusiastic promoter of gilly-crab fights. By the time he was two he had caught his first creek eel. David was sure he would be a fisherman. Which was a ground for worry, of course. Because the new trawlers had made it just about impossible to make a living longlining inshore. David was a kind man, but not a very enterprising one. The crab boat was mortgaged, then sold. He was seen hoeing turnips with the child, now eight, at his side, and the horizon blurred with icy drizzle. Then he was seen no more. Not that Alexander was looking for him. Alexander was far away, looking after himself, making a name for himself on the Silver Pits and the Dogger Bank. He was a man in a hurry. You had to be in a hurry.

A hurry for what? said the man from the *Eastern Daily Press*, sent to interview the rising star.

A hurry to develop the British fishing industry, said Alexander.

A hurry to eat the world and turn that into shit, said the inshore men, casting an uneasy glance at the workhouse looming grim over Walsingham.

Naturally Alexander had no time to listen to this sort of nonsense. Not with the shoals moving, and being captain of the *Perseverance*, and owner of the rest of the fleet, and General Director of Rourke and Rourke, the second Rourke being imaginary, having been invented to give an impression of long establishment and solidity to the backers. Alexander had become an innovator in his industry. Obviously it was a dismal folly for his boats to be off the grounds while he landed his fish. So, according to the latest practice, he caused to be built some fast smacks with big fish holds and big sails, that would hustle the fish back to the railhead and return with provisions and gear; so the trawlers could stay out there in the grey North Sea, reaching back and forth, back and forth, snow, frost, rain and shine, three months at a time, until even the gulls were glutted with guts and wrack.

Difficulties were there to be solved. Lowestoft was too far from the grounds, so Alexander moved his fleet to Grimsby. Ice was hard to come by, so Alexander bought a frost-pocket lake in Norway. The biggest difficulty of all was manning. Crews needed paying. Naturally, Alexander hated giving away money. Equally naturally, no one wanted to spend their lives in the fleet, three months at a time for seven bob a week. Even miners had lives and wives. Strangely, it was this that led to Alexander's reacquaintance with David Jordan.

This was a time when the inshore fishery was bad and farming was worse. So the workhouses were shockingly overcrowded, and Walsingham was no exception. When Alexander arrived in front of the overseers, neat and grim in his blue suit and his bowler and a watch chain the thickness of a medium conger, the overseers gave him a cup of tea and made flattering remarks while the paupers were assembled. Then they followed him down the carbolic-smelling hall, and stood him on the dais, and let him get on with it.

'Look here, you paupers!' cried Alexander Rourke, his voice echoing from the painted brick. 'I am Alexander Rourke of whom you will have heard. I am here to offer you a chance to learn a trade. Diligent apprentices may rise. Lazy apprentices will sink. I refer to the sea trade, and in particular to that noble branch of it known as fishing. Six shillings a week, all found. No one over fourteen need apply. Step forward now, my lads.'

Forward they shuffled, whey-faced and dirty, made their marks in the ledger in front of two attendant Justices (both drunk) and slouched out to wait in the cold yard. Alexander became aware of a scuffle. He looked up. A man aged somewhere between twenty and fifty was wrestling with a beadle. 'Let him go,' said Alexander, with a face of stone. 'David Jordan, is it? You're too old.'

'Not me,' said Jordan, with that mild, dazed air of his. 'My boy.' He drew forward a puny youth in the canvas workhouse uniform. The boy's arms were thin, but the eyes were freezing with hatred. Alexander was impressed.

'Alexander, that is, Mr Rourke,' said Jordan, pale with emotion. 'Please take him. Only I had to stop fishing when the grounds… that is, when the boat went, and my wife died, and the boy's got fishing in him, so if you could give him a chance?'

'I do not give, I take,' said Alexander. 'So I'll take the boy, ha, what?' A sly, bullying thought occurred to him. 'And I'll take you too.' Pause, while he watched the smile start on Jordan's feeble face. 'Separate boats, of course.'

The smile went. Highly satisfactory. 'All out,' said Alexander. 'Hurry.'

And to Lowestoft the paupers marched, forty-five miles without food or rest to save money – a hard twenty-four hours, but one upon which they would look back with tender nostalgia when they were on the boats. Alexander went ahead in his carriage. As always, he was in a hurry. He needed to get back to sea.

The shoals might move on.

The night after he had put his mark in the ledger, young Jordan – nobody used his Christian name from that day forward, and pretty soon he forgot he had one – found himself shivering on a quay. Gas globes hissed in the rain. They shone on the leaf-shaped decks and oiled masts of three enormous boats. 'That's huge,' he said.

'God bless you, that's only a smack,' said his father. 'Do you wait till you see a trawler.' He squeezed his son's hand. 'Here goes,' he said.

A burly man with shining oilskins and a list said, 'Jordan, boy, *Marigold*. Jordan, David, *Sibylla*.'

'Take good care of him,' said David.

'Take care of yourself,' said the man in oilskins. 'Because this is not a fucking boarding school for the children of the clergy.'

'Watch your tongue,' said David, among whose kindly faults was a tendency to generous wrath.

The burly man picked him up and threw him off the quay and onto the deck of the smack eight feet below. He lay there groaning in the gaslight. Jordan wanted to help his father, but something hit him on the head and the head was ringing like a gong and he was on a deck and someone was making him haul on a rope. There was a flap and boom of canvas. Something happened to the deck under his feet, as if it had been dead and was now living. He saw the gas globes reflected in black water between the bulwark and the quay. The stripe grew wider. He heard the roar of the ebb in the pilings, saw the pilings slide by, the staysail flop and fill against the rain weeping out of the sky. The tide carried the smack out of the harbour and into the coal-sack night. Someone thrust hard manila into his hard workhouse hands, and said here, workus, two, six, *heave*, so he heaved, and got his feet stamped on by the man on the fall in front of him. Under the gas globes back in the harbour another smack, tiny now with distance, was hoisting her staysail, backing it to pull her nose off the wall, moving into the night. That's my dad, he thought, tasting salt that was not sea salt in the rain on his face. He's coming too. We'll be close together.

They were out of the lee of the town. The true breeze bumped the mainsail. There was a groan of shrouds and partners. The *Marigold* dug her lee rail into the inky sea and began to tear north-east. Jordan lay down in a wet wooden room that stank of fish and heard the sea drum against the larch planking three inches from his ear and thought: out there I will see my dad again. But the feeling was oddly muted. The future had started, and it was taking him into the dark, where his real life waited for him.

A boot kicked the air out of his ribs. The workhouse reflex

brought him upright before he was awake. He stumbled up on deck.

The sea was steel-blue with ice-white teeth. The smack's mast was drawing huge scribbles in the sky. Her mainsail was scandalised, gaff-peak dropped, tricing line made up, so the mainsail was shrunk to a clattering tan bundle. The staysail was taking her down on a huge black boat with two masts. The black boat's mainsail was backing and filling, her mizzen hard in, staysail aback.

'Jordan, Dyke, Cotman,' roared a voice hoarse as gravel. The two boats came together. The trawler seemed as long as an express train. The bulwarks hovered a foot apart. 'Go!' cried the gravel gargle.

Jordan found himself hauled onto a wet deck. People were cursing him and kicking him and hauling bundles past him. Someone screamed at him to clap on, and reinforced it with a kick. Jordan clapped on. Parcels came across from the smack. A net. A trawl beam. Ice in sacking. Potatoes, already foul. Deal boxes in the other direction, wet, cold; cod. He saw the smack's gaff-peak go up, her mainsail luff come down, the boom sheeted in so the sail filled, saw her streak away towing a cream road across the steel-blue. 'Oi,' said the gravel voice. 'You. Go and stow the fucking ice.'

'Ice?' The light was too bright. There was no horizon.

A stony hand gripped his ear. 'I am the mate,' whispered the voice, raw as blood. 'Now fuck off into the hold before I kill you.'

'Dear oh dear,' said a man with no teeth, hauling a spare trawl across the hold floor. 'Welcome to the rest of your life, workus. Which will be short, unless you learn to move faster. You got to move fast in this hair game unless you want to get yourself killed. Move fast, catch fish. Before the bloody shoals move on. Now we will show you what the capstan is for and we will shoot and you can cook us our fucking scran.'

'Cook?'

'Or die,' said the man with no teeth. 'We don't care which.'

It was a matter of neither interest nor regret to Alexander that David Jordan was drowned rowing boxes of cod from a trawler to a smack a month after his arrival at the fleet – though he probably regretted the loss of fish. There is no record of the younger Jordan's feelings on the subject, or indeed any other. Successful apprentices did not make a habit of allowing their feelings to be legible, and young Jordan was showing early signs of success. The signs seemed amplified after his father's death. He passed through his apprenticeship swiftly, cook, deck-boy, third hand, mate in six years, losing in the process the end of one finger and most of his scruples.

Which was the moment Alexander noticed him again.

It had been a busy six years for Alexander. The fish were coming ashore in a silver flood, out of the smacks and into the markets and onto the trains and away to wherever people would pay for them. The shareholders pushed hard. And so did the God-botherers, because if you were in a hurry and you wanted to keep your costs down, people got hurt, and it was nobody's fault if a lot of them were workus brats. Nobody swift and decent would end up in the workus, stood to reason. The way Alexander saw it, if your degenerates had accidents or ran away, that improved the condition of the population and hence the fleet or the industry.

Oh, yes, said Alexander. You could not build a strong fishing industry without knowing how Nature conducted herself. Look at the fish. The inshore fishery was long gone. The Silver Pits were full of boats. The Dogger Bank was thick with them, too, and your fish sizes were down. It was time to look further afield. Which was not a thing you could do with the old boats. Steam was the ticket now. Bigger boats and fewer of them. Fewer boats meant you had to take a hard look at your skippers and separate your sheep from your goats, winners from losers, survivors from lazy animals.

Which was what Alexander was doing now, this evening in the dark mahogany study of his good house overlooking the Humber, dark mahogany everywhere, thinking about Jordan. Outside, a blood-red portlight was reflected in the black river – one of his boats bound for the grounds. There was a murmur from across the hall: his wife having the Bishop to tea. It was all a mile or two from a hamlet with no name near Stiffkey. A good mile or two. Oh yes, thought Alexander, unstoppering the square decanter. That was what you did, in life as in fishing. Follow the shoals when they moved on.

This Jordan, though. Feeble father, useful son. All those years the workus apprentices had been squealing beatings, buggery and drowning, never a peep out of Jordan. He had stood his watches and gutted his million cran in the *Black Maria*, and hauled his trawls and done Alexander neither knew nor cared what with his liver money.

Then there had been that December, four years ago.

That had blowed a rum 'un. The spring tide racing north, the breeze howling down from Iceland and the North Sea standing on end. When the tide turned it had knocked over the sea wall at Cley and torn Spurn Point loose from the mainland. Half the fleet had masts down, and bad skippers had paid for their badness with their lives. More than a hundred men lost, Alexander reckoned. He pursed his lips at the statistic and reached once more for the decanter. By that time the *Black Maria* had a hold full and about to spoil, and the markets had seen no fish for most of a week. Jenkins of the *Marigold* had been out there, but he wouldn't move, wouldn't take the *Maria*'s fish, claiming stress of weather, and by the time the *Maria* would have got home all the other boats would have been home too, and the price would have been gone.

So Jordan, the *Maria*'s mate in those days, told his skipper to tell the *Marigold* to run up alongside. It was too rough for a punt, so they lashed the boats together with big fenders in between and slung over the boxes as best they could, the wind wailing and the *Maria*'s mizzen keeping them head to wind. And all the time they were moving fish and dodging splinters Jenkins was yelling that he wasn't going, until Jordan said if Jenkins was shy he would take the bloody fish his own self, and Jenkins said, on your head be it. Then Jordan asked for the punt and a couple of spars and a hand, just one, who would volunteer for five pounds. So a hand stepped across, and Jordan had to ask *Maria* three times to cast the smack off on account of nobody could hear him over the howl of the breeze.

And suddenly from the deck of the *Black Maria* the *Marigold* was no more than a rag of staysail sliding off towards a rain squall, white water all around her.

'Never,' says Jenkins. 'They're dead men.' But perhaps he had inside him a sort of hollow sensation, the kind you get if you have saved your life but lost your job and it is dawning on you that this is not the right way round but it is too late to do anything about it now. 'The boxes'll shift and she'll lie down and she'll fill and—'

'They're putting up the main,' said Wally Hitter, the skipper, who had the glasses.

'Dead men,' said Jenkins, hollower.

Hitter kept his glasses on the *Marigold*. He saw the main go up. He saw *Marigold* take a wild broach that buried first her lee side, then, as she lost the wind in her sail and counter-rolled, the other. He said, 'My goodness me.' A man less Chapel would have sworn.

Because something had happened on the starboard side. The

spars were lashed flat, so they stuck out to windward like outriggers. And lashed under the outriggers was the *Marigold*'s punt, which the weather roll had filled with water, so it now acted as a three-ton counterweight to the heeling force of the mainsail. Out of which the hand was even now, in this screaming tempest, shaking out the second reef.

The smack became a white blur of water tearing towards the Humber, seventy miles across the wind. The white blur winked out in the rain squall.

'Jenkins,' said Wally Hitter, solemn as the pulpit, 'you will be needing a new boat.'

This prophecy Alexander had caused to come true by sacking Jenkins and putting Jordan on *Marigold* in his place. And when Wally Hitter had slowed down to the point where he could not keep up with the shoals, Alexander had sacked him and moved Jordan onto the *Black Maria*.

And in the three years since then, Jordan had done the job. He had kept his gear down. He had kept the sails pulling in weather that sent the rest of the fleet scuttling for home. As relief skipper of a steam trawler he had followed the shoals further and further north, and fought Icelanders in plain sight of their own nasty black shore. Give him a steam trawler of his own, thought Alexander. The *Gloria*. Now. He wrote the note, and signed it, and felt dissatisfied.

He was fishing with his pen, nowadays. He had bought out his shareholders years ago. He owned twelve trawlers and half a dozen steam drifters. He had been one of those who had changed fishing from something people did outside their back doors to a great industry. He was forty-five now, and he understood everything there was to be understood.

Except why the shoals moved on.

And why women wanted to have tea with Bishops.

He reached for the decanter again.

Next morning he ordered a small but luxurious suite to be built for his personal use abaft the wheelhouse of the *Minnie*, newest of his steam drifter fleet. To the consternation of her skipper, he would appear in the wheelhouse and spend hours in stone-faced contemplation of the jiggling line of net corks stretching away from the *Minnie*'s bow. Soon, his steam trawlers, heading in from the northern North Sea, would come within range and salute with a dip of the basket. Alexander pretended not to notice, but anyone watching could see he liked it.

Another source of gratification were the tuna who pursued the herring into the North Sea at that time. Perhaps Alexander felt a vague kinship with them as fellow shoal hunters. The North Sea was not obvious tuna grounds. So how did these great silver torpedoes locate the shoals and predict their movements? Naturally, Alexander's curiosity made him want to kill them, and he embarked on the only fishing of his life that had as its object the catching of fish rather than the making of money – telling himself that he was getting soft, like Denis, no, David Jordan, silly bugger, all that time ago with his longlines.

The next time the sea started to boil and churn with clown heads and scimitar tails, Alexander had a boat launched from the drifter, an elegant little punt with a gaff mainsail. Into the punt he climbed while the drifters lay to their nets, and away he sailed with a short, thick rod, a tub of herring for bait and a lout of a boy to drag the tuna aboard. This he did all through the summer, catching from time to time a fish. One September afternoon when clouds were brushing sharp bristles of rain across the sea, Alexander, the boy and the boat disappeared into a rain squall.

And were seen no more.

What was seen was the sail of the punt, but not the punt itself. The sail was found wrapped tightly round the starboard anchor of the *Gloria*, Captain Jordan, pride of the Rourke trawler fleet. The *Gloria* had been hurrying north to the new grounds off Tromso – a long way north, true. But fish sizes were small in the southern North Sea nowadays, and the job of a steam trawler was to follow the shoals when they moved on.

It emerged at the inquiry that the *Gloria* had altered course on passage to the grounds to give the now customary salute to the *Minnie*. It seemed likely that Alexander's punt had been run down as Captain Jordan, hurrying, had steered the *Gloria* through the rain squall at twelve knots. It was also assumed that Captain Jordan's silence and unchanging expression masked a sincere sadness at this shocking accident, which by a tragic irony left him (it was discovered, when Alexander's will was read) in control of the second biggest fishing fleet in the North Sea. These things were assumed in the same way that it was assumed that beneath the impassive surface of the sea the shoals were infinitely numerous, but given to moving on.

There were those who wished to investigate further. But the year was 1914, and the world soon had other things to think about. Five years of war followed, and the North Sea cod fishery came to a dead halt. On the resumption of fishing after the five-year pause, large numbers of gigantic cod were caught.

It was assumed that the shoals had moved back.

Devonia

by Desmond Barry

I've never been on a trip away from home before. Not like this. Abroad. Out of the country. My father's driving me and Charlie Williams to Swansea Docks. Charlie Williams is in the back seat. He's in the next class up because he's fourteen. I'll be thirteen the week after the ship gets back. A couple of girls from my class are going. Vanessa Francis, Elizabeth Jennings and Jane Phillips. I quite fancy Jane Phillips but she doesn't fancy me at all. She likes older boys. I look young for my age.

The sky is a sort of green and black because we're going down the dual carriageway by Jersey Marine next to the oil refineries. The air stinks. An orange flame waves around at the top of a gantry. They're burning off gases. All that oil comes into Port Talbot Dock, thick and black from Saudi Arabia or somewhere, and they turn it into petrol and stuff over here. Cracking oil. We learned about it in geography. We're off to Alicante, Gibraltar and Lisbon. We were supposed to go to Tangier but the Six-Day

War broke out and they didn't think British kids should go to an Arab country.

Howard Schwartz reckoned that the Third World War would have broke out if the Israelis hadn't beaten the Arabs. I couldn't see it happening myself. But Schwartz said the Americans would step in because of the oil. There isn't any oil in Israel but the Arabs got plenty and the Russians support the Arabs and so the Americans support Israelis. So there might be something to it. Schwartz is the only Jew I ever met. He's in our class but he isn't coming on the cruise with us. His dad is an optician so they must have had the money. My dad works in a factory and my mam in a shop. About ten months ago they gave me ten pound to take to school for the deposit and a pound a week every Monday to pay for this cruise on the *Devonia*. It cost forty-two pound altogether. Charlie's dad doesn't work in a factory. He's a drummer in a band. He plays in the clubs. He likes old rock and roll…Bill Hailey and Buddy Holly and that. He's too old to be in a band like the Beatles or the Stones or The Who. The Stones went to Tangier. For the drugs, I think. We're going to Gibraltar instead. So the Arabs have got all the oil and all the drugs. The Israelis just have Israel, which is just as well after what the Nazis did to them. Except they threw out the Palestinians to get the land. Anyway, the Six-Day War screwed up our trip to Tangier. I don't know who to blame really. I don't think the Stones cared very much about the Six-Day War or who's on whose side. They just wanted the drugs. It would have been great to go to the

Casbah. Down all them alleyways with blokes in burnouses and selling carpets and smoking hookahs. That's all me and Charlie Williams talked about for months. It's a bit connected with the music. The Beatles are playing these incredible songs with Indian music on them, and that's all a bit druggy, too, to tell the truth. I don't know what the problem is supposed to be with drugs, except that you can go to jail for having them. They can also make you think you can fly and you might jump out of a window or something. Anyway, we're going to Gibraltar instead of Tangier and I don't think they have any drugs in Gibraltar. It's too British.

After the Jersey Marine, the air is clear and it's sunny and it doesn't stink of oil any more. We turn off the dual carriageway, left, into Swansea Docks. At the gates, there's a bloke in a boiler suit waving his arms around to show us where to park. My dad pulls up in the car next to a big building and we get out. Kids are everywhere. We're down by these huge customs sheds and I can see Neddie Seagoon with the other kids from our school. His real name is Mr Morgan and he teaches History but he looks like Neddie Seagoon off the *Telegoons*. Miss Cooper is with him. She teaches Latin. Miss Cooper is really beautiful. Blonde hair and big boobs. I bet Neddie wouldn't mind getting off with her. I don't think he's got a chance, to tell the truth. Miss Cooper is pretty strict. I reckon all Latin teachers have to be a bit strict because you got to do all that conjugating and it's pretty boring really. *Amo, amas, amat, amamus, amatis, amant. Ero, eris, erit, erimus, eritis, erunt.* I wouldn't mind getting my hands on Miss Cooper either but I've got about as much chance as Neddie.

Are you ready, boys? my father says.

Yeah, I say.

I'm ready, Charlie says.

Charlie is really nervous. He laughs. His eyes are pretty narrow anyway and they get narrower when he laughs. I'm probably nervous, too, but I don't show it. We get the cases out of the back. My dad is smiling but he's nervous as well.

Come on, boys, Neddie calls.

Go on, son, my dad says.

The case is a bit heavy and I swing it, using my leg to help. It's got clean pants and socks and shirts for every day we'll be away. I also got a copy of *Moby-Dick*. It's really thick. I don't know if I can get through it in two weeks on the boat. I just started. The first few pages are brilliant but then it slows down a bit. I've seen the film so I know what happens. But the book is better. Parts of it anyway. I don't know what Charlie's got in his case. But he definitely hasn't got a copy of *Moby-Dick*. He doesn't read much. My dad is letting me carry the suitcase by myself. Charlie is carrying his, too, and he's trying to drag it along with two hands. He's pretty skinny and his face is all red.

Neddie shakes hands with my dad.

We got to go in now, he says.

My dad gives him my passport. It's a one-year passport, folded cardboard, sort of fawn colour with my picture in it, and my details and a stamp. Neddie has everybody's passport in his hand. Miss Cooper is with the girls. She got these great curves on her. I think I mentioned that before.

Bye, son, my dad says. See you in a fortnight.

Bye, Dad.

I wave and then I follow Charlie and Michael Powell, and Ian Jones and them, with Neddie in front, and we go into one of the Customs sheds and it's huge. It's echoing with the noise of all these kids talking. Kids from all over the Valleys and Cardiff and Swansea, and there's some kids from England: Liverpool and Manchester and Birmingham. And Miss Cooper is over at the other table with the girls, showing the bloke their passports. And then they let us out of the big doors at the other end of the shed and we're right on the dock now, with these massive white-painted capstans with ropes around them as thick as Neddie's leg, and he's fat, and the boat is just huge. You're not supposed to call it a boat, it's a ship, but anyway, it's all painted white and the ropes come down off it onto the dock and around the capstan, and there's a gangplank coming down onto the dock and into a door in the side of the ship. And then we're walking up the gangplank. It's creaking and moving and this is just amazing. And there's this tall, thin bloke with greasy hair who looks like the ship's head-master or something, he can't be the captain, looking like that. He gives me the creeps, to tell the truth, the way he's looking at us.

Welcome aboard, he says. Follow Officer Stevens down to your cabin.

Officer Stevens looks about seventeen. He fancies himself, to be honest. He's ordering us about like we're in the Navy. We go down these iron steps and into the cabin. There's about twenty bunks in there.

I bags a top one, I say.

I already got *Moby-Dick* out of the case and I throw it up onto my bunk so everyone can see it's mine. Michael Powell slings his case onto the bunk underneath mine. Charlie Williams bags the top one opposite me. I don't know where the girls are. Not in here anyway.

Here are your cabin badges, the officer says. All cabins are named after British explorers.

The badge is yellow, with 'Burton' written on it.

In the reference library in school there are about six volumes of the *1001 Nights*. They've got drawings of half-naked women in them. Burton translated that. He also translated the *Kama Sutra* and *The Perfumed Garden*. Carl Ponting bought both them books off a stall in Ponty market. We read bits of them out loud in the woods behind the school. My mother would kill me if she found out. It's funny they put his name on the badge for schoolkids. I'm glad I seen his books, though.

Back on deck, the officer says. Report to the muster station.

We follow him up the steps and we get to a place on the foredeck which is Burton's muster station. I like that name. Muster station.

This is where you come in case of an emergency, he says. If the siren goes off. The life jackets are in here.

He shows us where the life jackets are in a kind of wooden box on the deck. Then he shows us how to put them on, then he shows us where the lifeboats are. We haven't even moved off the dock yet.

All right, that's it for now. Dismiss.

We all look around at each other and you can tell everyone is thinking the same thing. What a twat… So now we know where to come if the ship is sinking and we know how to get the life jackets on and how to get into the lifeboats. Just in case there's a storm or something and we hit a rock. No chance of an iceberg where we're going. The Mediterranean is supposed to be hot. I just hope that twat is not going to be ordering us about for two weeks.

A hooter goes off and we can hear the engines rumbling below. I run over to the ship's rail to look at the dock. We're casting off. They've unloosed the ropes around the capstans. The crew, most of them look Indian to me, are winding in the ropes on the fore-deck. I expect they're doing that aft as well. I look down at the dock and all the parents are there and I can see my dad and I wave at him and the ship reverses away from the dock, and swings out of it faster than I thought it could. We're out into Swansea Bay and looking back at the town and I can see Mumbles Pier and the lighthouse and the ship's prow is cutting through the water and we're really on our way now. No turning back. No parents. It's really good, that.

Where we're going the sea is supposed to be blue but this is the real sea. The Atlantic Ocean. Grey. Like a battleship. Like in the war films with Hayley Mills's dad. I've got an Airfix model of HMS *Hood* and the *Bismarck*. It took ages to make them. Both of them got sunk in the war. You can just imagine them steaming around in the fog and the grey sea blasting away with their 15-inch guns. But off the coast of Swansea the sky is clear and the sun's rays slant across from the horizon and now the whole surface of the sea shimmers like a mirror. It's so calm. The ship's prow cuts straight through the water and churns it up all white. We're not supposed to whistle. Neddie told us that. The sailors reckon it'll bring a storm. Makes you *want* to whistle, someone telling you that. Me and Charlie Williams walk about the decks having a whistle. Colonel Bogey. We stop when we see Neddie.

I can hear Liverpool accents. It must be brilliant to be from Liverpool because the Beatles come from there.

Then this girl shouts out.

Hey, you're that boy, aren't you? The one who was with Robin.

Hiya, Rosie, Charlie says.

The girl is skinny. She's acting like she knows me, but I don't know her. She obviously knows Charlie. She's got short hair and a yellow sundress and you can see the strap of her bra. She's Charlie's age, I think, or a bit older.

Robin? I say. I don't know any Robin.

It's weird, though. I can tell she's sure she knows me.

It was you. Definite, she says. Under the bridge. Down Abercanaid way.

No, I say, I don't know any Robin.

Him and that other boy, she says.

And then I remember. But she didn't look like this. Not so skinny. Not with those curves. And her friend was a lot younger than her. And we all told each other the dirtiest jokes we'd ever heard. And started talking about what boys did with girls.

I don't know any Robin, I say again.

And I can feel myself go beet red. But I can't turn back now, can I? I just said I don't know any Robin. That's true. She's talking about Robert Wells. He brought me down there with Peter McKenzie, because I was supposed to know a lot about what boys did with girls. And I did... But how I found out... She knew more than me, anyway. This Rosie. I couldn't remember her being called Rosie, could I? Or her friend's name. And I think they both done some of the things she talked about. With boys she knew. And all I'd done...

I'm sure it was you, she says.

What you up to, Rosie? Charlie says.

There's this gorgeous Liverpool boy, she says. Started chatting me up, right away.

Fast off the mark, Rosie, Charlie says.

I hope he is, she says.

She laughs. She looks at me again because she's sure it's me and I look away because I've already said I don't know her and

I can't back down now. I don't want to. I can feel the deck shift under my feet.

A bell rings three times like in school.

That's the galley bell, Charlie says.

I'm gonna find the girls, Rosie says.

She gives me one more look and then she's gone down the deck.

She'll do anything, she will, Charlie says.

I laugh. It's a bit forced.

I don't know any Robin, I say.

We go down to our cabin and this Officer Stevens leads the way down into the galley. I hold on to a bulkhead as the ship rolls and the stair tilts. It stinks like school dinners below deck. Stevens shows us the door to the galley and I get a tray and an Indian bloke puts meat and potatoes and green beans into the little compartments on it. I carry it to the table, keeping my balance. The tables have got a rail around them so the trays don't slide off when the ship lurches about in a storm. We'll see if the whistling did any good.

I don't want to see a lot of Rosie, but the ship isn't that big, is it? The engines are drumming underneath my feet. Black oil. She knows more about me than I'm willing to admit. I wonder what Robert Wells told her. If she'd tell the others like Charlie, or other kids, what they'd say about me. But I was only seven when it happened. How I found out all that stuff I knew. I don't think Robert Wells knew. Unless John Broderick told him. How he wanted to try things out with me. I thought it was all right because they were older but now I know better. I wish it hadn't happened. But Rosie would have said about that anyway, if she knew, wouldn't she? I'm not telling anyone. They'll think I'm queer.

The food's not much cop but it's all right. It's still light outside because it's summer. They say we have to be in bed by half past nine and lights out is at ten. We'll see. I don't mind. Right now, I want to read a bit of *Moby-Dick* lying in the top bunk. Look for a good part. Something with a bit of excitement in it. Harpooning a whale. I wouldn't mind having a go at that. Or bullfighting in Spain. There's nothing in *Moby-Dick* like the *Kama Sutra*. At the beginning, the Indian harpooner gets into the same bed with Ishmael, the hero of the book. They don't know each other. They don't do anything. They don't try anything out. Is it ten o'clock yet? The lights go out. I put *Moby-Dick* under the pillow and try to sleep on it. I don't know any Robin, though. That wasn't a lie.

Swansea has disappeared. Off to port somewhere is the coast of France but we can't see it. We're in the Bay of Biscay. We're in the middle of the sea and we can't see any land. It's brilliant: just the ship and these huge waves lifting us up and dropping us down. Neddie is up on deck. His face is green. Like the sky over Jersey Marine. You can tell he's thrown up. And I feel pretty dizzy myself but I don't throw up. Other people are vomiting over the rail, making sure they don't puke into the wind. This is the real sea and it's grey and it's not going to make me sick. I'm not going to do any more whistling, though. I wouldn't mind seeing a whale. No chance of that though, I reckon. It's a long way across the Atlantic to New Bedford, where the *Pequod* set sail, and it would take about three weeks for us to get there, I reckon. It takes a day to cross the Bay of Biscay. Neddie has a quick puke over the side. I feel a bit sorry for him, to tell the truth, and I can tell he's a bit embarrassed because he can see that I'm not going to throw up like that. I'm not. But I got to admit I'm glad it's over when we reach the other side. We must be out of range of the shipping forecast down here, I reckon.

Dogger, fair to middling, force eight.

Francis Drake sailed this way in the *Golden Hind*. He sailed down here and he singed the King of Spain's beard. In Cadiz. Set their ships on fire. We've always been fighting the Spaniards. They still want Gibraltar back and we're not supposed to say anything about Franco when we're in Spain, and not supposed to give any cheek to the Guardia Civil. Neddie doesn't want us to all end up in jail. A lot of Welsh people went off to fight against Franco in the Spanish Civil War, but we lost. Franco is a bit like Hitler but not quite as bad. I don't know how the Spanish put up with him for so long. Neddie reckons no one can say anything about him because of the Guardia Civil. I imagine they must be like those Mexicans you see in the cowboy films: fat with drooping moustaches and big guns, and they don't like gringos. So we better shut up. I have to admit I'm a bit scared about them. I don't think they care much about how old you are; if they don't like you they take you to jail, and that's it. They do some awful things to you in there. That's what they reckon. I don't want any of that. Don't even want to think about it.

It's all sunny now. The beaches and cliffs are all white. Neddie reckons we're just about to sail into the Mediterranean. First stop Alicante. There's a fort there where there was a battle in the Spanish Civil War. The good guys lost. As usual. Not like in the films. I want to meet some Spaniards. And Portuguese. I'm not so fussed about Gibraltarians. They're probably like the people back home. I don't mind. I just like being on the ship, going somewhere. We're on the deck most of the time playing deck hockey with a rope puck and cane hockey sticks, or deck cricket in the nets, or swimming in the pool that's aft. There's a DJ on board. He plays the Beatles and the Stones and The Who and he's started playing the Monkees, now and then, when he gets requests. Bubblegum shit. Right in the middle of 'Last Train to Clarksville' Alison Taggart comes up to me by the side of the pool.

Hey, will you meet Trish Mooney on the foredeck about eight o'clock?

Trish Mooney? Who's she? I don't say that. Charlie Williams has got a big grin on his face. He knows who she is. I can't back down even if I don't know who she is. She must be all right or Charlie wouldn't be grinning like that.

She woke up in the night, Alison says. She said, I got an urge for Tommy Peters.

Tommy Peters. That's me. She got an urge for me. I'm glad she did even if I don't know who she is. It sounds like some kind of swelling. An urge. That's great.

Yeah, I'll meet her, I say.

I'm going to wear my jeans and a decent shirt.

And when me and Charlie get to the deck, there's Rosie.

You sure you don't know any Robin, she says, I been thinking about it.

I shrug my shoulders.

How's it going, Rosie? Charlie says.

I got that Liverpool boy up here on the foredeck last night, she says. He hardly touched me. He's really slow.

Charlie laughs. And Rosie spins away in her yellow sundress, and I'm glad she's gone but I can't help thinking how I really like her and how she laughs.

And then Alison is on deck with Trish Mooney. And Trish Mooney is in a white cotton sports shirt and shorts and tennis shoes. And she has long brown hair, and big brown eyes, and she's quite skinny and really nice-looking and I'm so glad she had an urge for me. For me? I mean. What have I ever done for her to have an urge for me? She never even met me. Or me her. And we haven't even reached Alicante yet. And then Charlie and Alison go away and I'm left with Trish and we walk along to the foredeck.

I wanted to go out with you, she says.

You're nice, I say.

Sounds a bit lame but she don't seem to mind. I stand with my back to the rail and step up onto a pipe that's running around the deck, which is the only thing that makes me taller than her. And then she tells me where she lives and some other stuff about liking the Monkees, which is definitely not a plus in my book, but I don't mind a few of their songs as long as you understand that they aren't a real band, like the Beatles or the Stones, although I don't say that to her. And then I kiss her. Or she kisses me. On the mouth. I don't know who starts it. And then I've got my arms around her. And her arms are around me. And the sun is going down over the Atlantic and it's really warm down here close to Africa and it doesn't matter about all that with Robert and Rosie or how I found out about all this stuff between boys and girls because none of it is anything like this, and I can't believe it, even if I know that the bridge and Robert and Rosie will all come back to haunt me some day, just as the ship is sailing back into Swansea Dock, or the car going back up the dual carriageway under the green skies of the Jersey Marine, or sheltering from the rain under the bridge in Abercanaid, but not now. I can forget about it now because this girl, this beautiful girl, had an urge, just as our ship is about to sail out of the Atlantic Ocean and into the Mediterranean Sea. Trish Mooney had an urge for me. Not for anyone else, but for me. I just can't believe it. And all over the foredeck are other kids just like us, backed up to the rails and the sea going up and down behind us, with Spain off to port and Africa off to starboard, and there must be about forty to fifty kids on the foredeck, I reckon, twenty-odd couples. And I'm in one of them. And I can see Rosie necking that boy from Liverpool over Trish's shoulder, and then I can't see anything, because my eyes are closed, and I can smell Trish's hair and her breath and taste her lips and this is the best thing that's ever happened to me. The best thing ever in my life. And I know it's only going to get better because right now, Trish Mooney is in my arms and my back is against the rail, and I just know I will never, ever, want to go back home.

The Doldrums

by John Williams

Kenny Ibadulla had never had much of an enthusiasm for the sea. His father had been on the boats and, from what Kenny had seen, it was a hard life and a dangerous one. Growing up, he'd resolved to do anything rather than find himself on some beat-up old hulk crawling its way to Barbados to pick up a load of bananas. And so he had. Done whatever it took, that is. He'd had dealings with the boats, all right. Used them to import products from the West Indies and so forth. Not bananas, Kenny wasn't exactly a greengrocer. Kenny specialised in what you might call unofficial imports. Stuff that got measured in kilos, grams and ounces, not container-loads.

That was all in the past, though. These days Kenny Ibadulla was a respected member of the community, more or less. Between the clubs and the security business, looking after all the building sites around town, he was doing fine. Doing more than fine, in fact. So fine that his accountant had been telling him for a while he should be putting some money into investment projects. Which was kind of how this whole situation had come about. The whole yacht situation.

It had crept up on him, really; it wasn't like he'd grown up doing all that Sunday afternoon pottering about in boats stuff. There hadn't been a lot of it around when he was a kid. What with the tide and the docks being so run down, hardly anyone went sailing for fun. A few posh folk over Penarth, no doubt, and one of his mum's cousins had a little fishing boat and offered to take him out once or twice, but that was about it. Recreational sailing never crossed his mind really, not till they built the Barrage and the docks turned into a bloody marina all of a sudden.

It was his new brief who finally got him interested. The brief was a feller called Deryck Douglas. Funny bloke, been a copper for a while before they kicked him out after a bit of a scandal involving police officers looking the other way when the unofficial-type imports were coming into the docks. Far as Kenny knew, and he knew quite a lot about this particular subject, Deryck had had nothing to do with it: he'd just been the scapegoat. Usual shit: blame everything on the black copper.

He'd had some kind of a pay-off, though, and he made a hell of a brief: knew his stuff and really hated the coppers. He was a man after Kenny's own heart, in that respect, at least. Anyway, Deryck was well into his sailing and he'd been going on at Kenny for ages to have a go until finally one Sunday afternoon – beautiful sunny day, Mel trying to persuade him to go over IKEA with her – he'd said yeah, why not, what the hell.

He hadn't exactly loved it right away, but there was something that appealed to him about it, getting away from people, mostly. Deryck wasn't much of a talker and Kenny appreciated that. Most of the time people were on his case 24/7, calling him up for favours, asking stupid questions, all the crap that went with being a legitimate businessman.

So, a couple of weeks later, he went out again and after a few months it had settled into pretty much of a regular thing: Sundays he went out sailing with Deryck. Wasn't too exciting for the most part, just pottering about in the Bay, learning how it all worked and, now and again, if the wind and the tides were right, heading out through the Barrage and into the Channel. First time he'd done it, that had been a blast, like taking the stabilisers off your bike when you were a kid. Suddenly it got serious and you felt the possibility of disaster.

Risk, that's what it was. Kenny had always thrived on risk and lately it seemed to have vanished from his life. Everything was going so smoothly. It was all too easy, the security business making money hand over fist, and it didn't feel natural. Out there on the Channel, getting buffeted by the wake from some tanker heading over to Avonmouth, he realised how much he missed that risk.

'So, Del Boy,' he said one of these afternoons, sitting on the boat, halfway through the lock system that took you through the

Barrage, waiting for the water to rise. 'How far could you go in this little tub?'

Deryck shrugged. 'Well, as far as you like in a sense, all the way round the coast if you wanted. Take a couple of weeks, you could sail down the Bristol Channel, round Land's End and along the south coast. You fancy doing that sometime?'

Kenny shrugged back. 'Sounds all right,' he said, 'but couldn't you take it over to France or something like that?'

'Could do, Ken, but you'd be taking a chance; it's not exactly a yacht, you know what I mean.'

Kenny looked at the boat. It was pretty basic, about fifteen foot long with a sail and a rudder. A dinghy, Deryck called it, though Kenny had always been under the impression that a dinghy was a little rubber boat you had on the side of a car ferry.

'So,' he said, 'say you wanted to take a big trip down to the Canaries, or across to the Caribbean. What kind of a boat would you need for something like that?'

Deryck gave him a look. 'Jesus Christ, Ken,' he said, 'you've been out to Steep Holm once or twice, and now you want to cross the Atlantic?'

Nevertheless Kenny found himself thinking about it a fair bit over the next few weeks. Sailing across the Atlantic – he could end up in the Caribbean, potter round the small islands, even go over to Trinidad. He had a few business associates there from back when he was in the import–export game. At least he did if they were still alive.

Before long it was less an idea and more an obsession. When Kenny had an idea he liked to carry through with it. That was what had always made him different from the rest of the layabouts he grew up with. They were all still sat on the sofa watching *Deal or No Deal*, shouting at the missis to bring them their tea, talking a good game. Kenny got on and did things.

It was time he had a challenge, a real challenge. That was what he'd thrived on all along – when he was a kid playing rugby, when he was a junior bad boy making his rep, when he was a senior bad boy rewriting the rulebook by going legit – challenges. And this would be a physical challenge too. That was what he was really missing. Sure, when he'd been coming up he'd had physical challenges all the damn time. These days, though, the challenges were all the wrong way round – like he'd had to learn not to get into a fight, not to hang some tosser from the WDA out of a tenth-floor window the way he would have done to some wannabe dealer who moved in on his turf. It was all about restraint these days, and Kenny had had enough of it. He wanted to be out there on the ocean, steering through the fifty-foot waves, going mano-a-mano against the elements.

It was just a matter of figuring out how to go about it, starting with buying a boat. Deryck gave him a couple of magazines with boat ads in them, but Kenny didn't really know what he was looking at. Wasn't like any of his other mates were much help either. They just looked at him blankly, as if he'd said he was thinking of buying a space shuttle or something.

The first person who actually had something useful to say was Bernie Walters. They were sitting in Bernie's office on St Mary Street puffing on Cohiba Esplendidos and sorting out the security arrangements for one of Bernie's shows at the Hilton, talking about how far things had moved on since Kenny'd been hiring Bernie's strippers for a Wednesday night down the Dowlais. Both of them had done more than all right out of Cardiff's upturn. Bernie still had the agency, but nowadays the strippers were hidden way down the list. His speciality these days was providing reality TV contestants. South Walians seemed naturally suited to those shows. Bernie'd represented that girl from *Big Brother* who used to go on about how she loved burping, and it had all kicked off from there.

Anyway, there they were, sat in Bernie's office, smoking cigars like a pair of old gits, when Kenny mentioned the sailing across the Atlantic thing. 'Oh yeah,' said Bernie. 'My youngest boy – you know, Jerry? – he loves sailing. Got this nice boat, yacht, what have you. He sailed it down to the Canaries last year. Took the family.'

'Yeah?' said Kenny. 'Did it go all right?'

'Sure,' said Bernie. 'His missis was going nuts beforehand but it all went fine. Here, I'll show you.'

Bernie fiddled with his computer then turned it round to show Kenny some photos, running on one of those slideshow things. Kenny put his glasses on, came over to have a look. Loads of pictures of Jerry, who Kenny had met a few times over the years, and his wife, this Indian girl was a doctor over Dinas Powis or somewhere, and their two kids, all posing around on this great big fuck-off yacht in assorted harbours.

'Nice,' said Kenny.

'Yeah,' said Bernie, 'and I dunno for sure, but I think he might be open to offers for it if you're serious?'

'Why's that, then?'

'The missis wants them to buy a place in France instead. Don't think she's all that mad on the sailing lark, to be honest.'

'Oh right,' said Kenny, who hadn't even contemplated taking Mel and the kids on a boat with him. Couldn't imagine Mel would be interested for a second. Not unless there were some shops on board.

So he took Jerry's number and the next weekend there they were, Kenny, Jerry and Deryck, who'd come to offer a bit of vaguely expert advice, all stood around in the flash bit of the marina, admiring Jerry's boat, something called a Warrior 40.

And there was plenty to admire. Jerry was reeling off the spec: forty foot long, Volvo engines, glass-fibre hull, folding prop, solar panels, all teak interior. Most of it went over Kenny's head, of course, but Deryck looked impressed. Then, when Del Boy started getting technical, asking about the satnav and the radar and stuff, Kenny climbed on board and had a bit of a poke around. Couldn't make too much sense of the on-deck stuff. There was a bloody big mast and some sails. He supposed the principle was the same as on Deryck's dinghy, but you'd have to be careful with this one, he reckoned, a bit of a misjudgement and one of these poles could have your head off.

He ducked down inside. Christ, it wasn't bad. Little cabin on the left, little cabin on the right. Sizeable main area with a kitchen and a lounge area. He heard the others coming down the stairs after him. The Jerry feller started pointing out all the features, storage space, folding beds and so on, then led the way through the main room to a decent enough cabin at the back with a bathroom attached. That'd be his room, Kenny figured, already determined to own the boat, whether he knew how to sail it or not.

Six months later Kenny did know how to sail it. He'd spent every weekend on it with Deryck. First just sitting in the marina learning the basics, then, step by step, taking it further and further afield. He'd had to, really, after the shit Mel had given him for spending 100K on a boat without even asking her. He'd pointed out it was an investment, tax deductible, blah, blah, and that they could easily afford it – that was the amazing thing, all he'd had to do was sell off one of his investment properties over Grangetown, a place that had only cost him 40K three years ago, and there it was, cash in hand. But it was more the principle, she said; she wanted to be consulted.

Wasn't much point in telling her that the reason he hadn't consulted her was he knew she'd have said no, so Kenny let her rant and rave and threaten to go over her mum's for a bit, and then got on with learning how to sail the damn boat, show her it wasn't just a midlife crisis, like she kept saying it was.

That was one pain in the arse thing about owning a yacht, the grief he got from Mel. Another was everyone else he knew making assumptions about why he'd bought it. 'Going to be running it down to Morocco, are you, Ken?' 'Over to Ireland maybe?' As if the only reason Kenny Ibadulla would have a boat was to run drugs. He'd tried explaining that there was a lot more money these days in buying houses in Grangetown than sailing round the Med with a ton of Moroccan black on board, but they weren't having it. He was the victim of stereotyping, if you asked Kenny.

And as if all that wasn't enough, there were the exams. Kenny had not exactly taken school seriously, so he'd been horrified when Deryck told him he ought to pass a bunch of exams if he wanted to take his own boat out on the sea, at least he did if he wanted Deryck to come too. And not just practical exams either, but theory too. Two nights a week he'd head back over the office and study online. First couple of weeks he'd felt like jacking it in but after a while he'd got into it, and Deryck had started doing the same course too, which helped. They'd be out there on the boat at weekends testing each other like a pair of nerds. Christ, if certain people could see him now.

Every now and again, once he'd got the basic idea of how to sail the thing, he'd asked Mel if she wanted to go for a little jaunt. Wasn't like he really wanted her to, to be honest, it was more like he was making a point: the boat was for all the family, not just his own personal indulgence. Course Mel wasn't buying that for a second; every time he mentioned it she'd just roll her eyes and get off some cheap shot about boys and their toys. And naturally the same went double for his girls. The three of them were all total teenagers now and he couldn't see any of them getting into it in a million years.

Still, six months in and he was really getting the hang of the boat. Another couple of months and, all being well, he should have his yachtmaster exam in the bag. Meanwhile, he got on with planning the big trip. He had all the charts laid out in his office and before long he and Deryck had agreed on a route: down to the northern coast of Spain, round to the Algarve, then start heading out into the ocean. Stop off in the Canaries somewhere, then go for the big push across the Atlantic, head for Cape Verde, then over to the Caribbean, maybe Barbados. He figured the time to set off would be in the late autumn, so that he could get down to the Canaries in November and cross the Atlantic in December, once the hurricane season was out of the way, allowing himself three months for the whole trip.

It was weird thinking about it, hard to believe he was serious. He felt half excited, half terrified in a way he hadn't in years.

By September it was all coming together. Both Kenny and Deryck had passed their exams and were now fully accredited yacht guys. Somewhere along the way it had become accepted that Deryck was coming along on this adventure, which was fine. There weren't a lot people Kenny could imagine spending three months on a boat with, without chucking them overboard, but Deryck was one of them. Didn't say anything that didn't need saying, that was what Kenny liked about him. Both of them had sorted out taking the time off work. Kenny wasn't exactly totally comfortable with that, being a control freak at heart, and knowing all too well what a bunch of dodgy bastards he had working for him. Still, Mel would be there to keep an eye on things.

He was talking to her about all that one evening, running through the stuff needed looking after, when out of the blue she said:

'But what about if I come with you?'

'Jesus Christ,' said Kenny, 'you're joking,' unable to keep the note of panic out of his voice

'Am I now?' she said, giving him a smile.

'Well, you never shown any interest up to now, apart from giving me a hard time about it.'

'Well, maybe I've seen the error of my ways.'

Kenny didn't get it: this wasn't like Mel at all, this teasing thing. He decided to play along, just take what she said at face value.

'C'mon, love,' he said. 'How could you come too? Who'd look after the girls?'

Mel laughed. 'The girls, Kenny, in case you haven't noticed, and you probably haven't, seeing as every minute of the day you're either working or on your damn boat, the girls are actually grown up. Keisha is eighteen years old, she's at sixth form college. You remember Keisha? The short one with the braids? Lauren – you know, the tall one – she's sixteen, and Hannah, little baby Hannah, is fifteen. Yes, I think they can manage. 'Sides, my mother's here and so's yours.'

Kenny nodded, still bewildered by this turn of events. 'Look, Mel,' he said after a bit of a pause, 'are you serious or are you winding me up? Because, honest to God, I can't tell.'

Mel let out a long sigh and sat down at the breakfast bar, her smile evaporating, to be replaced by a frown. 'I dunno, Ken. Started off I was winding you up, making a point about you swanning off like this, leaving me to sort everything out. But you know what? You know what, just saying it to you now, I'm thinking, yeah, I would like to go. I'd like an adventure and all. I've been sitting here thinking my girls need me, I can't possibly go, but maybe it would do them good if I did go, teach them to look after themselves. And it would do me good too. So what d'you think about that then, Ken?'

Kenny didn't know what to think, but he had a definite sense that his plans were about to change.

And so it came to pass. On November 10th, Kenny was right where he'd hoped to be: anchored up in Tenerife. Deryck was on shore sorting out a supply of petrol for the big crossing, much as planned. And Mel was in the galley, which was a long way from his original conception and was causing him considerable grief right now.

What had happened was they'd come to a compromise. Deryck and Kenny would sail down to the Canaries. Mel would join them there for the big sail across the Atlantic, then she'd fly back home from Barbados. She'd be on the boat for about one month out of the three.

The sail down – or rather the passage, that's what all the boat people called sailing from A to B, a passage – through the Bay of Biscay, round Spain and Portugal and all that, had gone great. There'd been some hairy moments, but Kenny and Deryck were really acting like a team. It had been excellent, no other word for it. But now here they were anchored up in the Canaries. Mel had flown in the night before and Kenny couldn't help suspecting that things were about to go to hell. It wasn't that he didn't love Mel. It was just that, well, they had their own lives. The whole point of this trip had been to get away from domesticity and the work grind and all that, and already her presence – asking if they'd got this, that or the other in the galley – had begun to drag him back into that world. And now they were about to spend three weeks on the water together. Jesus.

Straight away, once they were out at sea, Kenny could see all his fears confirmed. It should have been a fantastic passage, going round the western Canaries, La Gomera and La Palma, feeling like Christopher Columbus heading off to the new world. Deryck had tried pointing out that his ancestors had done the trip in chains but Kenny wasn't playing, reminding him that his own ancestors hadn't been on no slave ship, they'd been the ones selling Deryck's ancestors. They'd just been having a laugh about it, winding each other up a bit, but then Mel joins in and it becomes some serious debate about roots and culture. Jesus.

And then she starts turning dinner into a major production: where's the this, where's the that? What was wrong with opening a couple of tins of tuna and eating them up with a few crackers, like they had on the way down. And then at night she'd been all what's that noise and what's that and I can't sleep and then expecting him to have sex with her, which he didn't feel remotely like because he was up to here with resentment, and anyway Deryck was about six feet away, up above them, keeping the night watch.

'Look,' he said, 'why don't we get some sleep? I'm due up on deck in three hours.'

'Okay, sorry, love,' she said, throwing her arm round him, and in minutes she was asleep while Kenny lay there thinking bad thoughts.

The next day was more of the same. What should have been a perfect day's sailing, bowling along with a nice little wind behind them, spinnaker up, heading out into the unknown, was ruined by Mel's constant questions: how does this work, and that, how do you take the sail down, how do you put it up, what does this do? Thankfully, Deryck fielded most of that stuff. Kenny just spent the day rooted to the wheel or poring over the satnav. When Mel came up and asked him how it worked, it was all he could do not to tell her to fuck off. Jesus Christ, didn't she understand? This was not how their marriage had operated all these years, getting in each other's business like this.

That evening, they'd just finished supper – some kind of stew Mel had made, very nice and everything, but he'd still sooner have had a tin of corned beef on his own – and it had gone dark all of a sudden, the way it does when you're this far south, when the sea starts to get up. First sign something was going on came when Mel's stew began to slide off the table. She just managed to catch it before it splattered all over the floor, and Kenny had to stop himself from telling her she'd have been better off opening a few tins of corned beef because at least they don't spill everywhere. Next thing, Deryck stood up, said, 'Shit, we'd better get the spinnaker down pronto,' and Kenny followed him up on deck.

Mel began to get up from the table. Kenny turned to her. 'It's rough out there, love; why don't you stay in the cabin?'

'Bollocks to that, Ken,' said Mel, 'I'm here to help,' and followed him up onto the deck.

Deryck was at the front of the boat trying to bring the spinnaker down. There was a kind of rope-operated sock that was meant to pull down over the sail and gradually bring it under control. On the flat, in the Bristol Channel, it had always worked fine. Right now, though, in what was suddenly a fair old gale with waves to match, Kenny could see that Deryck was struggling.

A big part of the problem was that the boat was getting increasingly side-on to the waves, and the wind was billowing out the spinnaker and starting to make the boat list alarmingly. As if to illustrate the point, the next wave had the boat momentarily at what had to be 60, even 70, degrees.

Kenny yelled at Mel to get her harness on, then turned to see that she already had.

He signalled to her to stay where she was at the back of the boat, and began to make his way forward. This was a lot easier conceived of than done, but Kenny was strong and determined and he'd always had great balance, so eventually he got there, soaked to the skin and frankly scared. He pointed to Deryck, then to the wheel, indicating that his sailing partner should try and get them pointing in the right direction while Kenny, who had more brute strength going for him, wrestled with the spinnaker.

Deryck understood immediately and waited till the boat was momentarily upright to make his tortuous progress over to the wheel. As he finally did so, Kenny grabbed the rope, pulling the sock down over the spinnaker. He had it halfway down and Deryck had the boat straightened, and both of them were starting to relax fractionally, when a super-powered gust of wind came from a new direction and made the spinnaker balloon back up and out.

Kenny's arms were wrenched off the rope and as he staggered backwards, trying to regain his balance, he saw the spinnaker pole swing back round at him, looking to take his head off and/or knock him into the water, where he would surely drown, seeing as he hadn't put his fucking harness on like he'd told Mel to do, had he, because he was an idiot, and there was absolutely no time to duck, and oh shit.

Kenny went down like a big old tree hit by an axe. The moment he realised he was actually all right was when he felt something soft underneath him. Something soft that was screaming for him to get off her.

What had happened, he pieced together later, once the spinnaker had been stowed and the wind and waves had died down a little and Deryck was securely at the wheel, was that Mel had seen Kenny buggering things up and she'd rugby-tackled him, taking him off at the knees, just before the moment of impact, saving him from injury at best, death at worst. She'd always been a sporty girl, Mel, now he came to think about it, and of course she went to the gym three or four days a week, though he'd always assumed that was more to talk to her mates than actually do any serious exercise. Well, clearly he was wrong; she'd taken him down like a pro.

The bad thing was he didn't feel grateful. He actually felt resentful, was having to work hard not to blame the whole thing on her. Like if they hadn't been eating her nicely cooked meal, and had just had a tin of corned beef, then they would have noticed the wind getting up, and they'd have had the spinnaker down ages before.

The next day they hardly spoke to each other. He could see

that Mel was tamping but he didn't care. Had he asked her to come? No he had not. He was kind of glad that the weather was choppy and changeable all day and most of the night. There was always stuff to do and he made sure he was doing it, not giving her an opening to tell him what a bastard he was.

So he made it through day three okay, but the following morning, after a couple of hours of pretending to sleep, he got up on deck to discover that the night's wind had disappeared completely, the sea was flat as the proverbial and the boat was just sitting there.

He found Deryck up at the wheel as usual. Kenny said they might as well get the engine going. Deryck, of course, responded by suggesting they should wait and see if the wind got up before using up precious petrol, but Kenny wasn't having any, he was in no mood to just sit around doing nothing, going nowhere.

'What did you expect, butt?' said Deryck. 'We are in the doldrums, you know.'

'Fucking right,' said Kenny, 'and the sooner we get out of them the better.'

These words came back to haunt him over the next three days, as they alternated between guilty hours spent motoring, and frustrating hours spent checking the weather forecasts over the internet. Oh yeah, the boat had the internet, all right, satellite connection, cost a fortune, but Kenny could afford it.

Actually, it was another thing Kenny was beginning to hate: here they were, meant to be on this big adventure, and instead he was stuck on a fucking floating Barratt home with an internet connection and a load of DVDs to watch on the laptop and his bloody wife sat next to him on the sofa, and the bloody kids calling up every ten minutes on the bloody satellite phone.

It was just like being at home, only worse. It was like being locked in his bloody living room. He was tempted to say it was worse than being in prison; at least in jail you could go and exercise a few hours a day, and your cellmate generally shut it if he knew what was good for him. Course he realised he was probably exaggerating here, it was a long time since he'd been banged up and he had absolutely no desire to experience that again, but still... Jesus, he was fed up.

It all came to a bit of a head sometime on the afternoon of... day six, he thought it was, maybe it was day seven, he was going nuts enough not to know for sure. Anyway, he was sat on the edge of the boat, where he'd taken a bit of the guard rail down so he could sit with his feet over the side and pretend to fish, like he had done for most of the past however many days it was. He'd actually caught a couple, but it was mostly just another excuse not to talk to anyone. Deryck was at the wheel, feet up, working his way through a book of sudokus, when Mel came down and sat next to him and she started in on him, asking where the hell he got off on the not talking to her shit, and just like that he pushed her overboard into the sea. It was only a few feet below and it was calm as a millpond, the whole thing no more outrageous than tipping someone into a swimming pool, but even so, just for a moment,

God help, he caught himself hoping the boat would magically start moving along, leaving her behind in its wake.

Instead, of course, he saw Mel six feet below him in the water, looking first astonished then angry, and he was just wondering how to react when he felt a shove in his own back and suddenly he too was in the water. Once he came up and spat the seawater out of his mouth, he saw Deryck grinning down at him and Mel, and as one they all decided to play along with the notion that this was just a bit of horseplay between friends.

Mel swam over to Kenny and tried to duck him under again, and Kenny pretended to fight her off, and later on, when they were all back on deck, he pretended to laugh about it, and pretended to enjoy the fresh fish Mel grilled up for their dinner, and later still he pretended to enjoy having very quiet sex with Mel. But he can't have done much of a job because afterwards, even though she'd enjoyed it – he was sure she had – she'd turned to him and said, 'You really are a miserable bastard, Kenny, you know that,' and he was just wondering what to say when something wet and wriggling slapped him in the face.

He sat up in bed and turned the light on, and discovered that they were having an impromptu threesome with a flying fish, and first Mel screamed, then both of them tried to grab the fish and chuck it back out, and both of them missed and missed again, and then Kenny did his 'I'm the man' bit and waved Mel out of the way. He set himself and dived at the fish like he was a number eight breaking from the scrum and heading for the try line. And missed it completely. Hurt his bloody shoulder and all and, to make matters worse, when he turned round he could see Mel laughing at him. He was about to blow up then, ready to give vent to all the frustrations of the past days, when Mel stopped laughing, put a finger to her lips, then crept up on the fish, which was still flopping around on the floor, crept up like it was a sleeping baby, and then flopped down on it. A scuffle and a squeal and Mel was back on her feet, the flying fish caught by the tail. With a deft flick of the wrist she lobbed it out of the window, turned to Kenny and said, 'Ta-da.'

And, try as he might, Kenny couldn't keep from laughing, at her and at himself, and then both of them were laughing, faintly hysterical, holding on to each other for support, and it struck him that there he was in the middle of the ocean, miles of water beneath him, with this woman who was as much a part of him as his heart, and that he was in the wrong, and that it had taken a slap across the face from a wet fish to tell him so, and he laughed some more, even harder now, and then, when they were finished laughing and they were both lying back down in bed, he turned to her and said one word that didn't come easy, never had come easy.

And it was probably a bit of an exaggeration, but he was sure afterwards that it must have been right then that the wind picked up, and began to carry them out of the doldrums.

Getting There is Half the Fun

by James Scudamore

The voice of an imaginary female passenger was kicking up a fuss in Rachel's head:

—*To be honest, this isn't exactly the kind of ship I was expecting.*

Another figment, this one a salty sea captain, gruffly replied:

—*Ach, she's a fine vessel; stop whining and come aboard. You'll get your journey to remember.*

The Maiden of the North, a huge, sparkling passenger ferry, looked sleek and modern against the granite cliffs of Aberdeen harbour. Everything about her slanted white lines screamed forward motion. Rachel had plenty to look forward to, so she was only slightly disappointed to find that her mother had been right: this was not the kind of ship that would have a figurehead. She had repeatedly pestered her parents for the name of the ferry that was taking them to their holiday on the islands, and had been satisfied when 'The Maiden of the North' came back. She had pictured a strong-jawed, winged figure breasting the waves at the prow of a magnificent sailing ship. This reality was considerably less romantic, but Rachel wasn't about to let that diminish her excitement.

Her father hated water – he felt queasy on the rowing boats in the park – but her mother had insisted on keeping the promise she had made to Rachel that they would take the ferry.

'We're going *north*,' her mother said. 'You can't do that for the first time on a plane. I want to feel it happening.'

Her father stared. 'You want to feel what?'

'You know. How did that cruise line advert go? *Getting there is half the fun.*'

'And what does that mean?'

'It means that all the romance has gone out of travelling,' her mother said. 'And this is a way for Rachel and me to get some. You can keep your one-hour flight: we'll be tucked up in our cabin, with rain lashing at the portholes.'

'For *twelve hours*,' reminded her father. 'And there's nothing romantic about requesting extra sick bags. But fine – if that's what you want, you have your night of hell, and I'll take the plane. I'll meet you green-gilled at the other end.'

'You're on. We're going to sleep like babies, aren't we, Rachel?'

'Babies don't sleep. They spend the night screaming and throwing up,' said her father.

There had been something about the bitterness of the exchange that Rachel couldn't quite comprehend; something to do with her mother trying to prove to her father that she was better at living life than he was – almost that he was boring, but not quite that exactly. She also knew that her father prided himself on knowing what was best for all three of them, and got stroppy when anyone else thought they had a better idea. Nevertheless, she thought her mother was onto something: Rachel *was* excited about the voyage – the fact that they were travelling by sea made it a voyage rather than a journey – and she hoped there would be rough weather. She wanted to lose her balance, and fly up into the air.

But before they set sail she had to spend a tortuous afternoon sitting in the tea room of their hotel waiting for the departure time to come. Now that the question hung in the air of whether or not her mother would sleep on the crossing, her parents sat together in silence, too locked into the challenge to pay attention to Rachel. Her mother, wrapped in a big belt-up cardigan, did a crossword in the paper with a cold cup of coffee at her side, while her father sipped water, read his birdwatching book and studied maps of the islands. Not for the first time, Rachel wondered why she had to get the outward-bound parents – the ones who packed hiking boots instead of beach towels. The room stank of stale smoke, stewed tea and spilt beer. She watched ribbons of multicoloured light rippling across the face of a fruit machine, and then stared out of the window, watching the city's cold-looking buildings sink into the winter night. When she asked if she could go for a walk round the hotel, her father told her to stay where she was.

Finally, he shut his book. 'It's half past five,' he said. 'We should get you two on board.'

In the taxi on the way to the harbour, he turned cheerily to Rachel and her mother, and said, 'Last chance to back out. You can have a vomit-free evening with me in the hotel tonight and we'll all hop over on the plane in the morning.'

'No chance,' said her mother, forcing a smile. 'We're seafarers, aren't we, Rachel?'

'Well, yo-ho-ho then,' said her father. 'And *bon voyage*,' he spat.

At the ferry terminal, a porter flung their luggage into a green wagon on wheels that would be stowed in the hold. Rachel and her mother followed the signs out of the ticket office and onto a caged walkway that led up to the main deck. Cold air bit through the gap in Rachel's jacket as they climbed.

Her mother's mood improved the minute her father stopped waving and turned back to the taxi rank. 'Isn't this exciting?' she said. 'Stupid old Dad. Doesn't know what he's missing.'

Rachel had started to notice the gap that often existed between what her mother said and what she was actually feeling, but thought that in this case she might mean it: there was a definite spring to her step as they boarded the ferry, which added to Rachel's own sense of anticipation. In fact, *everyone* seemed to be in a good mood. Rachel had expected that for most of the passengers the night ship would just be their way of getting home; that nobody else would be as thrilled by it as her.

But as they passed the souvenir shop and the bolted-down tables and chairs of a bar, then descended the stairs to the sleeping decks, Rachel felt the tingle of people going home; of heading north; of escaping the heavy tug of countries, and heading for *islands*.

'Have you got Benson?' said her mother. 'We won't see that luggage again till morning.'

Rachel nodded. 'He's in your rucksack. Don't worry, he's all bagged up.'

Benson was Rachel's rabbit. She had made him herself, with her mother's help. He had silver buttons for eyes and was stuffed with red lentils, some of which had begun to leak out, which was why he was made to travel in a freezer bag. Benson had been around for a while, and Rachel knew she was getting too old for toys. But there was a big difference between being seven and being eight and, at least until next year, Rachel had decided that she was going nowhere without him.

She held her mother's hand. They walked together down a narrow corridor lit canary yellow, her mother scanning the numbers on the doors and then peering back at the tickets in her hand. It smelt down here of cleaning products and air freshener, with the faintest tang of puke underneath. Rachel was looking forward to getting seasick. She had been warned it might happen, and resolved to be upset if it didn't.

'Here we are,' her mother said, finding their cabin. They stepped inside over a high step. All the doors had thresholds like this – to stop water coming in, Rachel supposed, although she'd watched *Titanic* enough times to know that things would have to be pretty bad already for there to be water all the way down here on the third deck.

The cabin had two beds either side of a window you couldn't open, and a cramped bathroom made of plastic that felt like being in a flimsy Portaloo. The floor flexed as you stepped inside, which made the walls shudder. Rachel stood in the doorway, bouncing up and down.

'It says here there's a cinema,' said her mother. 'Though I'm not sure you'll like these films.'

Rachel bounded back into the room and onto one of the beds. She stared out of the window, which was square, and not the brass-rimmed porthole she had expected. On the docks outside, huge containers were being hoisted off lorries by crane onto the back of a cargo ship, as if it were a giant pack animal being loaded up for its journey. A fat seagull looked on from a bollard. Looking at this chilled world from inside the cabin felt cosy.

'This is more like it!' her mother went on. '"The Captain's Table Canteen is located on the upper deck and will be serving a range of hot and cold meals well into your journey." I think we pair of pirates better get up there to the poop deck and install ourselves. What do you say?'

The Captain's Table Canteen smelt of school lunches. Red plastic chairs were bolted in sets of four to the tables. Pools of hot food simmered in down-lit metal vats.

'Maybe we should have gone to the "fine dining" restaurant instead,' said her mother, peering dubiously at the choices. 'You don't have to eat any of this if you don't want to. I've got muesli bars in the cabin.'

'This is fine,' said Rachel.

They sat by a rain-streaked window and ate: vegetarian lasagne for her mother, ravioli for Rachel. She concentrated on mashing up the individual parcels one by one with her fork, watching grey meat burst up through the prongs and intermingle with the vivid red sauce.

'Tell me again about the Merry Dancers,' Rachel said.

'It's only in the islands that they're actually called that,' said her mother. 'The rest of the world calls them the Northern Lights.'

'Merry Dancers is better.'

Her mother told her that the Merry Dancers were rare, and that she shouldn't be disappointed if they didn't see them.

A bright ping sounded over a loudspeaker.

Good evening, ladies and gentlemen, and welcome aboard The Maiden of the North. *We might run into some bumpy seas tonight, so please take all care when moving around. On behalf of the entire crew, may I wish you a pleasant...*

Rachel tuned out. 'Bumpy seas!' she repeated.

'Bumpy seas, oh dear,' said her mother.

Rachel looked up from her plate and saw that the docks were no longer outside, and that the windows were now black, and being pounded with water. They were under way and she hadn't even noticed.

As the ferry got further out to sea, Rachel's stomach lurched a couple of times, and their half-finished plates of food slid from side to side on the table, hitting ridged metal edges. Everything, it seemed, was stuck in its place, and when objects were permitted to move, they were kept as contained as possible. Rachel looked up to see if her mother had noticed that their dinner was moving, but she was working on her crossword again. Rachel watched the disturbances on the glossy surface of her ravioli, then sat swinging her legs from the chair. Two men on the next table were laughing, and drinking beer from long red cans with the picture of a Scotsman on them. Nobody was taking notice of the swaying of the ship, as though an unspoken competition were taking place to see who could ignore it the most. When they walked back to their cabin after the meal, the movement created invisible forces, like magnets pulling at Rachel's head. Again, those around them carried on as normal: whether playing video games with lit cigarettes, sitting at tables in groups or lying on seat cushions reading books, the people they passed were all bobbing in unison to the rhythms of the North Sea, as if it were a tune they were dancing to.

Her mother wanted to return to the cabin immediately, but Rachel paused at a window. She tried to raise herself high enough up to be able to look down the sides of the ship, as if over a steep cliff. The sea that flowed past outside was toothpaste white, putting Rachel in mind of the streams of foam that dribbled down her arm and between her fingers whenever she took the trouble to brush for the regulation ten minutes.

'Can't we go outside?' she asked.

'It would be like having buckets of water thrown over us,' said her mother, who hadn't said much since the vegetarian lasagne. 'Let's get back.'

Rachel knew what was going on: her mother wanted to start getting her good night's sleep to prove 'stupid old Dad' wrong.

In the stuffy cabin, the noise of all that water outside seemed to get louder. There were heart-stopping moments as the ferry was suspended high over giant waves, followed by slow, mighty crashes as it crossed them and landed on the other side. It didn't feel normal to hear big noises like that and not rush to the window to stare open-mouthed at what was making them.

Rachel's mother sat on her bed in the yellow light. She'd removed her cardigan, and changed into the long Tweetie Pie T-shirt that sometimes doubled as her nightie. Rachel watched her pop one, then a second, hexagonal orange pill from plastic, and swallow them both.

'What are those for? Are you seasick?' said Rachel.

'They're to help me sleep,' said her mother. 'You heard the captain: bumpy seas.'

'You said you wanted to feel us going north.'

'I will feel it. But we have to show Dad we're not landlubbers, don't we?'

Rachel brushed her teeth in the wobbly plastic bathroom for about five minutes (her father was the stickler for the full ten), then changed into her own nightdress and got into bed on the opposite side of the cabin from her mother, who turned out the light immediately.

Being in bed was funny: you could feel every rise and fall of the ship, and the crashes of water outside seemed even louder in the dark.

'Don't you want Benson?' her mother mumbled, face to the wall. Her voice sounded like it was coming through a wet towel.

'I know where he is. I'll get him if I need him.'

The cabin was heating up. Rachel wished she'd brought a glass of water to bed.

'Tell me about the islands,' she said, hoping to keep her mother awake.

'Well.' Her mother cleared her throat groggily, and turned to face Rachel. Her face had crazy shadows on it that made it look like a mask. 'The islands are a place like nowhere you've seen before. For one thing, there are no trees.'

'None at all?'

'Hardly any. They can't grow. The wind is so strong that it knocks them over.'

'So what do you see when you look out of the window?'

'You see horizontal lines in purple, blue and grey. And wisps of rain that hang like cobwebs from the sky.'

Rachel paused to imagine this, thinking of her father and his birdwatching books. 'Where do the birds live?' she asked. But her mother had fallen asleep.

Horizontal meant side to side. Here on the ship, everything was vertical. When she got on her knees to stare out at the black sea, she saw a distant light. It was thumping in and out of view like any normal lighthouse, but was itself also flying up and down in the window. It took her a second to realise that this was because of the rising and falling of the ferry, and not because the lighthouse itself was moving.

She lay back in silence until her mother's breathing had become regular and deep. Then she reached down between the two beds, into her mother's rucksack, grabbed the protruding freezer bag and pulled Benson out by his ears. A few dry lentils dropped onto the floor, with the noise of water spilling on canvas. She set Benson down on the bed and held the bag to the window to see how much of him had fallen out in transit. There was writing on it: THIS BAG IS NOT A TOY.

'Wouldn't be a very good toy if it was, would it, Benson?' she said. Holding him carefully by the back so nothing spilled out, she held Benson up to the glass to show him how foamy it was outside. Rachel couldn't understand why her mother wanted the night to go quickly. She wanted this to last as long as possible.

'Hey, Benson, look at Mum!' Rachel whispered, giggling.

Snoring, her mother was sliding up the bed as the ship rode the crest of each wave, then back again as it crashed down. Her head and her feet were hitting the ends of the bed with each slide.

She was like an unwrapped Barbie doll at Christmas, rattling up and down in her box.

Music filtered from upstairs. It wasn't fair, being cooped up down here. And Benson hadn't even seen the ship – he'd just been suffocating in his freezer bag. Listening carefully to make sure her mother hadn't woken, Rachel crept back into her clothes. Holding Benson close to her, she stepped out of the room, leaving the door ajar so that she'd know which was the right one when she came back.

Now the weather had got worse and they were properly out to sea, the ferry had turned into something from a fun fair, like the Mad House, or the Hall of Mirrors. Or maybe the corridor was a giant kaleidoscope being slowly rotated, with Rachel and Benson trapped in the coloured sand that patterned the inside. She walked slowly towards the end, grabbing a handrail to keep her balance, expecting to see a giant Gulliver-like eye peering in at her.

She reached the foot of the stairs. The music from above didn't seem so loud now: all she could hear was the low drone of the ship's engines and the steady churning wash of water outside. It sounded like the washing machine did at home when it had almost finished the clothes. On the stairs, her feet wouldn't step where she wanted them to, so she moved slowly.

The Captain's Table Canteen had closed for the night. The bar area beside it had thinned out but for a few men drinking cans of beer and laughing. Many dozed or read books, with their heads on bags and rucksacks. A big man sat with headphones on, smoking a cigarette, his huge beige boots wedged into a cushion, a magazine with pictures of oil rigs on it by his side. Next to him a woman spoke a strange language into her telephone. She wore a red raincoat and a woolly hat, with dirty blonde curls cascading from it like wood shavings from a carpenter's bench. Nobody seemed to have spotted Rachel, so she wandered out of the bar. As she did, she noticed that Benson had been losing lentils: the way back to the stairs was scattered with them.

'At least we'll know how to get home, eh Benson?' she said, trying to hold him by the back so that the hole there would be facing upwards and his insides wouldn't fall out any more. But there was more than one hole, and she knew he'd probably keep bleeding anyway. She imagined the voice of a posh doctor:

—*Nurse, we have to get this rabbit to surgery. Can't you see his lentils are falling out?*

—*Oh Doctor, I feel faint. That poor creature.*

—*This is no time for sentimentality. Somebody get me a nurse who doesn't faint at the sight of ingredients.*

—*I say, Doctor, maybe some fresh air will do the poor bunny some good?*

'Good idea, Nurse,' said Rachel, approaching the door that led outside. Water was being hurled at it, and the wind was making the spray go round in circles on the glass, like hosepipes when you turned the tap on but there was nobody holding on to the end. Standing on tiptoe to reach, she turned the handle and pushed the heavy door. There was just enough time to step out-side before it slammed shut again.

The wind knocked her sideways with all the force of a rugby tackle. A shock of cold spray slapped her face and part of her shoulder. The ship lurched horribly upwards (she thought she heard a distant shout from the bar) and Rachel was weightless, in the air. She fell hard onto the green floor of the deck, which was roughly textured to help you walk on it, and cut her hand on a NO ENTRY sign that hung from a chain across a staircase. Benson had been knocked away somewhere, but she couldn't see him; all she could make out were lifeboats, swinging massively overhead.

She clung to the chain. Her hand hurt. The nearest people to the door were the man with the big boots and the curly-haired woman, but he had music on and she was on the phone. Rachel flailed at the window a few times, but nobody inside noticed. Everyone was stuck in books and card games and drinks.

Through the railings, black water churned. The tops were being blown out of the waves; the spray that came off them looked like snow flurries on the peaks of mountains. She wanted to strike out and get back to the door, but didn't trust herself to get there, or to open it if she could. She feared that if she let go of the chain for one second, the ship would shrug her off its back, and send her tumbling down to the cliffs and shelves of water below.

She felt a large hand steady her from the back of the head.

'You okay?' said a voice with a thick, choppy accent she'd

never heard before, like Scottish but with more of a sing-song to it. It was the man with the boots. He must have seen her through the window.

'My rabbit blew away.'

Without letting go of Rachel, the man leant over her and picked Benson up from a place she couldn't see.

'Best come inside now,' he said.

He held open the heavy door for her and she stepped over the high step into the warm of the bar. Her heart thumped in her chest. She was soaked and freezing. But in here it was as if nothing had happened: the same violin music played softly in the background; the same people sat with their red beer cans and their glasses of whisky, talking in groups.

'See? Can't hear anything in here but the spray. You could be in all kind of trouble out there and folk wouldn't hear.'

'Benson's lost his stuffing,' she said, without thinking. It was true, though: somehow outside he'd got ripped open even more, and his body was limp and empty.

'I know someone who can fix that. Come with me and get warmed up.'

Rachel liked that he hadn't immediately thought to get her back to her mother.

She walked with him to the table where the curly-haired woman was sitting. The woman was off the phone now, and eating cheese and onion crisps.

'Told you there was someone out there,' said the man to

the woman. 'Found this peedie girl all on her own.' He turned to Rachel. 'Your folk in a cabin, are they? Should we make an announcement?' He laughed.

'I can find my own way back,' Rachel said quickly. 'Don't wake everyone up.'

'He's joking. We're not going to do that. What's your name?' said the woman, in English. Her voice sounded scratchy and alien, like the voices on old records.

'Rachel.'

'Mine is Malena.'

'I'm Davey. Malena can help you with your moppy before we get you home.'

'My what?' said Rachel. 'He's a rabbit.'

'Aye. A moppy. Put this on. You'll catch your death.'

The man Davey helped Rachel into a huge, oily sweater. It was heavy, like chain mail. He smiled at her, put his headphones on and leant back in his seat.

'I should get to bed,' said Rachel.

'It won't take long to fix your rabbit,' said Malena. 'May I?' She took Benson from Rachel's hands, her blonde curls tumbling forward. 'I always travel with a needle and thread.'

'But he's lost all his lentils.'

'So we find something else,' said Malena. She opened her rucksack, and took out a folded white handkerchief. 'This will do it.'

Malena crumpled up the handkerchief and then slowly

stuffed it into the gap at the back of Benson. Then, moving the crisp packet, an ashtray and her drink carefully to one side, she laid him face up on the table. She felt around in her bag again, and brought out a small black leather case, which she opened to reveal a sewing kit. She spoke softly to Rachel as she worked.

'Do you get scared easily, Rachel?'

Rachel shook her head.

'I didn't think so. Can you guess where I'm from?'

Rachel shook her head.

'I am from Norway. That means my ancestors were Vikings. Have you studied them at school?'

Rachel nodded.

Malena pulled a cigarette from the gold packet on the table, and lit it. 'Do you know what the Vikings used to do to their enemies?'

Rachel shook her head.

'You see Benson here? Just imagine for a moment that he's a real person. The Vikings would cut their victims open right here at the back, just where Benson is cut. Then they would pull out their ribs and spread the lungs out on a rock, like wings.'

Slowly, as if she were doing a magic trick, Malena pulled the handkerchief out from Benson once again, with the fingertips of both hands, until it was spread out behind him across the table on both sides.

'Then they would leave them to die in the sun. A horrible thing, isn't it?'

Rachel nodded.

'The ritual has a rather vivid name: "The Blood Eagle". It is written about in sagas. Ask your teacher.'

'It's disgusting,' said Rachel, thinking she hadn't said anything yet, and ought to reply somehow.

Malena laughed softly, exhaling smoke. 'Yes. It certainly is. I am sorry. I find these things interesting sometimes. I don't mean to frighten you.'

'You didn't,' said Rachel, realising that for the first time since being on the ferry, she wasn't thinking about the way it moved. She wondered whether that meant she had got her 'sea legs'.

'Is the handkerchief going to be enough, do you think?' said Malena, who had stuffed Benson's lungs back into his body. It was impossible not to think of the handkerchief as lungs now.

Rachel nodded.

Malena took a piece of thread and wet the end of it in her mouth to attach it to the needle. 'But if the handkerchief is his lungs, then don't we need to give him some other organs? What do you think? What about my cigarette carton? See, it says "Benson" on it. We could crush it up and make a heart, couldn't we? No? How about the crisp bag?'

Rachel shook her head, picturing Malena's lungs spread out on a rock, smoking in the sun. 'No, thank you. I think the handkerchief will be enough.'

'You're a very polite girl,' said Malena. 'Okay then.' Her hands were moving fast now, tightly sewing up the hole in Benson, and before long Malena was handing him back to her, fully repaired.

'Thank you,' Rachel said. 'I should go to sleep now.'

She waved goodbye to Davey with the headphones, gave him his jumper back and thanked Malena again. Then she set off, following the lentils on the floor to find her way.

As she followed the trail of Benson's stuffing down the stairs, she felt something that almost made her drop the newly repaired rabbit on the floor. It couldn't be the movement of the ship that was causing it, because she knew she had her sea legs now. She stopped walking for a moment to make sure, and felt it again. She was certain of it. Benson was moving in her hand. His chest was swelling and relaxing, at the point where Malena had stuffed him with her white handkerchief. He had been given a pair of lungs, and now he was breathing.

Rachel scuttled back along the corridor towards the cabin, following dead lentils along the floor, clutching the living Benson close to her chest. She had been preparing herself for the fact that sooner or later she would have to let him go, but now he had lungs, that would be difficult. The idea of putting him away for storage in an attic box with all the other toys Rachel had outgrown, wheezing in and out like an old squeezebox – it was unthinkable. And he could *never* again be transported in a freezer bag: he'd suffocate immediately (THIS BAG IS NOT A TOY).

The door to the cabin was still ajar. Her mother's snores seemed louder than ever, and her skull still knocked gently against the bedhead. At this rate she would have quite a headache when she woke up. Rachel changed back into her nightie and slid into bed. Only when she became aware of the moisture on either side of her face did she realise her hair was still soaked from the sea spray outside.

In the morning, the ship's engines made deep, juddering noises as it was backed into port. Rachel's mother leapt out of bed when the captain announced that *The Maiden of the North* would soon be pulling into her destination.

'Wasn't that fun?' she said, emerging from the plastic bathroom in a cloud of shampoo-scented steam, gripping a hairbrush. 'Come on. Let's go and find Dad, and tell him what he missed.'

Rachel sat up slowly to look outside. Her first sight of the islands was of a windsock struggling madly in cold blue light. She let her forehead thud onto the windowpane, feeling sick with exhaustion.

Her father had been quite right to predict a sleepless night on the ferry, but it was not illness or any other side effect of the ship's motion that had kept her awake: she hadn't slept because she was desperately concentrating on the rising and falling of Benson's chest against hers, terrified that it might stop, or be joined by a heartbeat.

The King's Daughter of Norroway

by Margaret Elphinstone

The only way to clear my name is to tell you exactly what happened on that voyage.

I loved that little girl. She should never… It was a wicked thing to do! She was delicate from the hour of her birth. There was never a sickness came near her father's court, either in Bergen or Trondheim, but that baby took it. Ask Signy – fetch her from Trondheim and ask her. Signy nursed Margaret from the day the wet nurse was sent away. Ask Signy about those long nights – those grey winter days – when Margaret tossed in her bed, all flushed and strange with fever, and day after day we feared she'd never see another sunset. She got through that. She picked up strength with her years, and as she left babyhood behind she grew like a weed. She liked to dance. She played ball, hide-and-seek and blind man's buff in the palace gardens with her maids. She asked questions. Oh, those never-ending questions! There never was such a child for questions! You could say she wanted to know more than a girl need ever trouble her head about, but it was different for her. Her fate hung over her from the day she was born, and after her grandfather Alexander died she quickly learned that she had to grow up and be a queen in a strange country. I don't know who told her it would be sooner rather than later. It wasn't me, and I forbade the maids to mention it. I thought, let her be a child while she can. Let her think the golden years stretch before her, and let this business of being Queen of Scots remain a dim dream, like the ending of a fairy tale. But as time passed it became clear that the days of her childhood were numbered. And she knew – oh yes, Margaret knew. She was as sharp a child as ever I dealt with. Her ears were as quick as a hare's.

I used to tease her: 'Is that you listening again, you wily bairn? I can see your ears flapping!'

Margaret would lay her hands over her ears and laugh. In fact her ears were as neatly curved as whelk shells.

King Eirik put off the voyage for as long as he could. He knew he'd have to part with Margaret sooner or later – but please God let it be later! Some men would have hated to look at the child, seeing she was the death of her own mother on the very day she was born. But our king wasn't like that – he loved her the more for her orphaned state. He loved her too much for her own good, but he couldn't stand up to those unruly Scots, let alone the King of England.

King Edward of England! I'd like to tell him to his face what he did. Of course, I'll never see him – I wouldn't dare speak if I did – but I dream about him. In my dream he plays chess on a great board that encompasses the whole north. He moves his knights, his castles, his bishops and his queen, and as they advance they scatter their opponents like so much chaff off the threshing floor. By force or by guile – it doesn't matter to Edward – Wales, Scotland, France… In my dream he sits at his chessboard in full armour, the helm down and his eyes glittering through the slits. He moves his pieces into the corners of the board, coming closer and closer as we cower away. All he sees are black and white squares, and the pieces moving across them. He doesn't see how the northern seas rage in winter; he doesn't feel the rain like icy needles with the north wind behind it. He doesn't feel the shuddering of the hull as the waves crash, or the white water sheeting over the gunwales. A power-hungry king in faraway London – what does he care for a seven-year-old girl playing in the brief sun of a Norse summer?

Many of you, including my husband Thore, thought it was to Margaret's advantage to marry Edward's son, that so-called Prince of Wales. But I say, what did you mean by 'advantage'? Did she ask to be Queen of Scots when she was three years old, just because her grandfather fell off his horse in a remote country, hurrying to the hot bed of his new French wife? No, of course she didn't! Margaret was a clever child even when she was three. The terrible cough that troubled her every winter meant she hardly left her bed for weeks on end. She'd lie against her pillows – such a little thing under the white bearskin – all flushed with fever, her dolls arranged in a row beside her. I see their wooden faces now, wrapped in odds and ends of wool to protect them from the draughts that whistled under the door. That's what Margaret cared about – *she* didn't ask to be Queen of Scots, and she didn't want to be Queen of England either (for everyone knew Edward's children were frail and like to die – she could have ended up queen of two great countries in her own right). But all Margaret wanted was a greyhound puppy – and that she got. Later I took her dog to our own estate; having been a princess's lapdog, it never learned that it was born to hunt. It outlived its mistress by six full years.

But now I must tell you about that voyage. It was the worst thing I did in my life. It was already too late in the year: Eirik kept his daughter with him for as long as he could, and when at last he gave in, the nights were already lengthening. There was a delay fitting out the ship, then we had to wait over a week for a fair wind. It was the feast of Saint Michael when we finally set sail – just about the season, in fact, when every sensible sailor is laying up his boat for the winter. You could say that Eirik's desire to protect his daughter was what destroyed her – but who knows?

At last the wind shifted north-east. It brought the smell of snow with it. One thing Eirik had insisted on – we were to sail to Orkney. The Scots messengers were to come north and meet their queen in Kirkwall. She'd leave from the haven of her father's lands, then she'd be established in person as Queen of Scots, before she was delivered into the hand of the English king. King Eirik pleaded for the shorter voyage on the grounds of Margaret's delicate health, but it was a politic thing to do. I was to look after the princess – queen, I should say, but here in Norway she was always our princess – until she was delivered to her Scottish ladies-in-waiting. Signy would stay with her. That was the only blessing I could give thanks for. Signy was terrified – of course she was!

'Scotland, Fru Ingebjorg!' Signy said to me. '*England!* Why, those places are right out of sight of land! My brothers say it takes days and days to get there!'

'But when you arrive you'll find land there too. Greener and warmer than here, what's more.'

'I don't like green and warm! And supposing we don't get there? The ship that brought us the princess's mother never got home at all. All the Scots lords were drowned in a terrible storm halfway over. As likely as not we'll all be drowned too!'

'Well, I'll be drowned as well then, because Thore and I are coming with you as far as Orkney. Signy, if you don't go with the princess, she'll be all alone except for a couple of foolish maids. She'll be surrounded by foreign ladies who won't know what to do for her. They won't even understand what she says.'

'What? You mean they won't understand what I say, either? Do they not speak good Norse?'

Poor Signy had thought it a great thing to move with the court from her native Trondheim down to Bergen. She'd never thought to have to learn a new language and strange ways. Well, of course it never came to that. But after I explained everything to her, Signy was prepared to go: in spite of her protests, she'd have done anything for her princess.

All seemed well when we left Bergen, although it was colder than I'd have liked. The king's ship was a fine craft – sixty feet long and beautifully equipped. Thore thought it was too heavily loaded. We were carrying luxuries for Margaret to take to Scotland – not that she needed them: it was all to impress her new courtiers. There were gifts for the six guardians of Scotland: the two bishops, the earls and the Steward of Scotland. There had to be presents for the Bruce and Comyn factions, who'd been excluded from the guardianship. We took bearskins, reindeer pelts, carved chests full of ivory and gold, tapestries, and barrels of wine and crayfish. Bishop Narve came with us; the king had appointed him to see that all agreements were kept before the princess was given into the charge of the Scots. Margaret was persuaded to leave her dog behind. She was a long time alone in her chamber saying goodbye to him. I gave orders to the maids to let her be. When she came down she was very pale, and said not a single word.

Margaret had always been an argumentative child. To be honest, she could be exhausting… 'Why is…?' Why does…?' All the time: Why? Why? Why? (Oh, what would I give to hear that shrill little voice at my ear again?) But now that the long-threatened voyage was actually going to happen, overnight she turned white and still. She asked no questions. I hated to see her so withdrawn. I didn't deceive myself that Margaret mightn't realise she was never coming home again. She was too clever for that. But she'd always been such a lively, loving child, even when plagued by those endless coughs and fevers. Although she was weak in body, she had a white-hot courage of her own. I think that's what kept her alive – she'd come through the woods, and I'm sure that if only… How could *anyone* think that I, of all people, could have harmed her? It's a wicked, bitter lie!

Choirs of monks were singing, swinging their censers so the east wind was laden with the smell of godliness as the royal procession passed through the town. When the king and his daughter, resplendent in red and gold, came through the city gate, the choirs fell silent. Then Eirik's court priest, a man called Haflidi from Iceland, sang 'Veni Creator' alone, in a voice so deep and strong it seemed to echo from the farther shore as if the land itself were singing farewell to its daughter. While Haflidi sang, Eirik hugged his daughter to his heart. She clung to him so hard that in the end Signy and her maids had to pull her away. Margaret did break down then – how could she not? She wept bitterly, and let her feet drag when they tried to make her walk across the quay. In the end Thore picked her up and carried her aboard. All through this Haflidi kept on singing, drowning the sobs of the princess. He sang until the ship cast off, and only when the thin stretch of water between us and the quay relentlessly widened, did the notes of 'Veni Creator' slowly fade away.

We'd thought that Eirik would take Margaret to Orkney himself. That's what he'd told King Edward's messengers, when they came in their great English ship to fetch the princess. They stayed twelve days, waiting to take her back to England, but Eirik hesitated and delayed, and in the end he said Margaret was too weak to travel. It was true she'd caught a cold, and at the time we were relieved she was allowed to stay with us a little longer. But when I look back…that English ship got safely to London in fair weather. If Margaret had left in May with the English strangers…but she didn't. Eirik told the English ambassadors he'd bring her across himself when she was better. I don't know why he changed his mind. All he said to me was:

'I trust you, Ingebjorg, more than anyone. You've known my little Margaret all her life. I know you love her. You'll see her safe to Orkney. Don't part with her until you've made sure there are kind women to look after her.'

'How will I insist on that, sire? I won't have any authority with the Scots lords. I don't even speak their language.'

'That's why I'm sending you to Orkney. You'll still be in my lands, and the Scots messengers will be our guests there. You can refuse to let her go with them until you're satisfied they'll care for her properly.'

'They can promise me anything, sire, but once Margaret is out of my sight, how can I be sure what will happen?'

'That's a risk we have to take, Ingebjorg. It's in their best interests to look after her. We have to hold on to that.'

As we sailed through the straits south of Holsnoy all seemed well. We were running before the wind so we didn't feel the force of it. When Margaret stopped crying I took off her ceremonial robes and dressed her in a thick woollen gown and fur cloak, and an oiled woollen sea cloak on top of that. I persuaded her to crawl out from under the awning they'd rigged for us in the bows. It was cold: I pulled her cloak tightly round her, and tied the strings of her hood. Margaret was always curious; in spite of her troubles, she couldn't help looking about. The smooth sea was awash with sunlight, and as we passed between the islands we smelt juniper on the earth-warmed breezes. Our red and white sail flapped gently in the fluky winds. The master kept the oarsmen in their places to keep us on course.

Margaret slipped her cold hand into mine. 'Fru Ingebjorg, is the sea going to stay flat all the way?'

'I hope so, sweetheart.'

'I don't. I want to see big waves!'

I crossed myself. 'Don't, Margaret! You don't know what you're saying!'

Bishop Narve saw me cross myself. He came over and asked if all was well. 'Very well, my lord,' I said, 'if only the weather keeps this way.'

'Please God this fair wind holds!'

Around midday we reached the open sea and hit the swell. I clung to the gunwale with one hand and gripped Margaret with the other. Sunlight twinkled over broken water like fallen stars.

The wind pierced our cloaks and furs; we might have been standing in our linen shifts. The leather curtain of our awning blew inwards like a sail: there was no shelter there. I helped Margaret into the lee of the bales amidships. Grey clouds raced us westward. I clung to a rope with one hand and held Margaret tight. Each wave lifted the stern before we saw it, rose under the bow, then dropped us so suddenly our stomachs clenched, before vanishing onward. The oarsman to starboard – a grey-haired man as gnarled as an old root: how had he lived so long at this trade? – flung me his blanket. I didn't care how verminous it might be; I gratefully tucked it round Margaret. I could feel her shaking with cold.

A rogue wave caught us on the beam and drenched us.

'Margaret!' I put my mouth to her ear. 'We must get under cover!'

'No!'

'We'll be soaked!'

'I hate under cover!'

'Why? We've made it all cosy with furs, and you're freezing.'

'It's *not* cosy.' She shouted against my ear. 'It's worse than hell!'

'Margaret!' I crossed myself rapidly, then laid my hand across her lips. 'Nothing is worse than hell! You mustn't say that!'

She muttered something, and I put my ear close, to catch it as she repeated it. 'Cold and wet is worse! Everything jumping about in the dark is worse!'

We stayed where we were. I felt Margaret shuddering under the seaman's blanket. She grew paler, a tinge of blue under her eyes. I caught her as she lurched forward, and grabbed the leather bucket I'd been holding under my cloak.

The poor child was sick till her stomach was empty. When I thought she could be sick no more she started retching again. I tried to get her under the awning, but she screamed and held tight to the rope. 'No! No! No!'

'We have to get you warm, sweetheart!'

'No! No! Not into the dark! No!'

But the dark was coming to us. Blackening clouds overtook the sun and swallowed it. With the dark came squalls of hail. I pulled the blanket over our heads as the ice drummed down. The waves grew white crests that gleamed like silver in the fading light. The master roared from the helm, 'Fru Ingebjorg! Get the princess under cover!'

As we stumbled forward the ship broached. A wave broke over us. Freezing water ran down my skin inside my shift. We got the full blast of the wind. The waves tossed every way at once. Margaret screamed. I seized her with one hand and clung to a cross-stay with the other. Seawater sloshed around our hands and knees.

'Get that child forward!'

I dragged her under the awning as the next wave hit. 'Signy!' I could hardly hear my own shout. Under the awning it was all noise. The thin curve of the bow was all that lay between us and the tumultuous sea. 'Signy!' It was too dark to see. 'Signy, the princess needs you!'

I held Margaret down while my eyes adjusted. The maids were lying prone among the furs. They didn't raise their heads. Signy lay with her hands pressed to her eyes. 'Oh, Fru Ingebjorg, I—' She had the wit to lean away from the piled-up furs before she was sick.

Not one of those women was in any fit state to look after herself, let alone the princess. Thanks be to God I'm never sick. I wrapped Margaret in a bearskin, and held her close to keep her warm. When I bent close to hear what she said, her teeth were chattering like pebbles in a brook. The furs that had looked luxurious enough for a king's bedchamber when we were lying in harbour might have been so many soaking rags. I made her drink some water. She couldn't eat. I couldn't move her. Even lying down I had to hold on to stop us being flung across the ship. The bow anchor clanked behind our heads as it shifted in its socket. The ship rose with each wave, hung like a held breath, then skidded downhill like a runaway sledge. Margaret lay silent in my arms. I dreaded the moment when she'd need to relieve herself. I couldn't see how I'd manage the pot myself, let alone help her. But when she did pull my cloak to get my attention it wasn't that.

I held my ear close to her mouth.

'Fru Ingebjorg!'

'What is it, sweetheart?'

'My loose tooth has come out!'

'Your loose… Where is it?'

'Here.' I groped for her hand. It was tightly clenched, but when she felt my hand she pushed something very small and hard into my palm.

'Fru Ingebjorg!'

I held my ear close to her mouth again.

'Will the elves come for it now we're not in Norway any more?'

I found her ear and shouted into it over the roaring of the sea. 'The elves don't come to sea. But there'll be elves in Orkney you can give it to.'

Her mouth was against my ear again. 'Will you keep it safe till then?'

With difficulty I knotted the tooth into my handkerchief. I have it still.

After that she slept. When dawn came I made Signy lie with her while I went out. As soon as I moved I realised our furs were sopping wet. No wonder we were chilled to the bone. I crawled under the useless curtain that hung over the awning, and pulled myself to my feet.

It was daylight. I was startled to see the sail down, collapsed across the boat amidships. The white-tipped waves were short and choppy, sometimes riding under us, sometimes taking us unawares on the beam. The sea had that grey sheen a gale gives to it. As I clung to the roof of the awning, Thore crawled forward under the sail, holding tight to the ropes that lashed down the cargo.

The wind whipped away his words, and he had to shout in my ear. 'We weren't expecting this! The princess? Is she all right?'

'Of course she isn't! But she's sleeping now.'

'She's what?'

'SLEEPING!'

I think he muttered, 'God keep her that way!' but I couldn't be sure.

At least now I could see what was happening. They'd raise the sail just enough to catch the wind, then lower it to stop us sliding forward too fast. Each time the sail came down I saw the master crouched under the helm as he steered. When they raised the sail I felt the familiar lift of the hull, and the horrible skid, as if we were taking to the air like a gull. The waves were so short that twice we sagged amidships, held up at either end. I gripped Thore's shoulder. He put his mouth to my ear. 'We're all right… running before the wind…daren't go any faster…at least it'll be a quick passage.'

I was torn between fear for Margaret and reluctance to crawl into that wet, sick-smelling space under the gunwale. I lost count of how often I crept back to take my place beside her, so Signy could stretch herself and have a drink. I couldn't get Margaret or Signy to eat. I was the only one who chewed on the dried fish they'd given us – bread and cheese were too difficult to manage. If we foundered, nothing seemed worse than to die under that wretched awning, suffocated in wet fur and cloth, with never a last look at the light. Whenever I stood in the open, clinging to Thore, it seemed impossible to move, let alone get back to Margaret. And yet the child must be kept warm. If I could do nothing else, I must at least try to keep her warm.

The long hours of the following night aren't clear in my mind. I think Signy slept. Margaret woke suddenly in an agony of retching. I gave her water, but it didn't stay down. All I could do was hold her, and say stupid things into her ear to try to comfort her. Whether she heard me or not I don't know. Over the shriek of wind I heard seawater thumping on the cloth above our heads. When I held up my hand the roof had sagged much lower. God send we got to Orkney! We were moving fast enough, surely to God, but for all I knew – for all anyone knew – the wind had changed and we could be going anywhere. I didn't see how the best shipmaster in the world could know where he was in a night like this.

Margaret was so sick I feared she'd die of thirst. Whether I got any water into her I don't know. I don't know when the night passed or the day came. I don't know what the men did to keep us on course. I drank water. Signy drank some too. Margaret still clung to my hand, but her grip was growing feebler. If she spoke I couldn't hear. I don't think she spoke. I hope she slept. Pray God she slept. I don't know. Have I made you understand how dark it was? I couldn't see Margaret. I couldn't hear her. Even when the day came it was still dark. Bishop Narve was with us sometimes.

He prayed – I know he prayed. I remember the Latin words coming out of the dark and the turmoil, and although I didn't know what they meant, I found comfort in them. I hoped Margaret might hear. I think she was asleep. I hope she was asleep. We were chilled through. The sea had come in. She must have wet herself. How could she not? She hadn't moved for more than a day and a night. She'd always been a very particular little girl – but how could she not? I felt the shudder of her sobs once or twice, which was how I knew she was crying. But even her sobs were growing weaker.

The worst thing as we lay there was that she ceased to be the little girl I'd known. She was turning into something else – something smaller, more animal. I tried remembering the Margaret I knew. I thought about her as she had been. I conjured up sunny days in the garden – evenings beside the fire in winter when I'd tell her stories. Now her own story was falling to pieces, as if she wasn't a real person any more, only a little animal hunted to death, or merely a princess – a pawn in someone else's game. But even before the end she'd stopped being my Margaret. If I betrayed her at all, which I don't believe I ever did, it was only in that. Although I could never have harmed her – whatever you're accusing me of now – perhaps I have a sorrow of my own, that even while I still held her in my arms I ceased to remember who she was.

I must have fallen asleep, because the next thing I knew the swell had eased. I didn't have to hold on any more. The anchor wasn't crashing against the stem. Margaret lay limp in my arms. She was barely warm, but when I laid my hand against her heart I felt it faintly beating. I roused Signy, who took my place, and crawled outside.

Fog lay thick around us. Everything on the ship dripped water. The seas had flattened. The sail was spread full. I found I could stand upright, clutching the gunwale. I peered into the mist.

The fog lifted. I saw rocky shores on both sides. We were sailing fast. The master shouted an order. The crew reefed the sail. The fog came back, enclosing us in a bubble of cloud and water. Thore ducked under the sail to join me.

'Orkney!' he said. 'How's the princess?'

'Bad.' I heard my own voice tremble. 'Thore, we have to get her ashore as soon as possible.'

He looked concerned. 'It won't be long. It's hard to tell – the mist keeps rising and falling. We passed an island just now, and that's in the sailing directions. The island to the north'll be Shapinsay. And we're coming in on the ebb – the sailing directions warned us about that. Nothing's what you expect in these islands. That's why she's sailing so fast. The tide'll carry us through the straits. Then we watch for the next voe to the south – so they say – and that'll be Kirkwall.'

'So it won't be long, Thore? It won't be too long?'

'Not long at all. She'll be in her father's house before the morning's out.'

He was wrong. The island was there, and the straits, and sure enough, the ebb tide swept us westward where we wanted to go. But the straits were very narrow, and that puzzled the master, and the coast beyond was confused in the mists. We turned south and beached in a small voe, but it was a poor landing. Peering through the fog, there was no cathedral, no town, most certainly no palace.

But I wasn't watching. I was back under the awning, trying to rouse the princess. I threw back the leather curtain so we could see. Signy and I chafed her hands and feet. We rubbed her cold chest, and breathed our warm breath against her back. In vain I held the flask to her lips. Margaret never stirred. She was unconscious before ever we got to land.

How can you say – how can any of you even suggest – that I would have betrayed her? It was only twelve years ago. There's never been any secret about what happened. The bishop was there, for God's sake! Bishop Narve himself carried her ashore through the breaking waves. If we'd made Kirkwall there'd have been clouds of witnesses. We'd have been lodged in the palace – everyone would have seen us.

As it was, we took Margaret into a fisherman's hovel – that's all the shelter there was. But the woman was kind, and we soon got a good fire going. I wanted to send to Kirkwall immediately, but the woman said we were on a different island. She said it was St Ronald's Island, and as I set about making do with what we had, I breathed a quick prayer to the saint to spare my little girl. Even as I shook the lice out of the fisherwoman's sheepskins and ragged blanket – at least they were dry – and wrapped up the princess, I kept on praying. I stripped off my wet clothes and held Margaret skin to skin. It was like holding an icicle to my breast. My own heart melted, but I couldn't get her warm. She chilled me through, then Signy took my place. The maids too. We tried to give her our warmth, but she was cold, cold… The blue smudges under her closed eyes were like great bruises in her pinched face. She never spoke again. We broke up the carved treasure chests – there was no other wood to be got – and piled wood on the fire till the bare room was like an ironmaster's furnace. We never got her warm. The storm had spent itself; the fog had burned away. Outside the sun broke the bright sea into a mass of starry lights. But for all the warmth we had, we couldn't kindle a single spark in the princess.

Bishop Narve said the last prayers, and anointed my Margaret while she still breathed. It wasn't just the women who wept. Bishop Narve stayed until the end. She died between his hands.

Signy and I made a winding sheet from a length of the fine linen that was to have gone to the Scots lords. We didn't need much. It doesn't take a lot of cloth to wrap a seven-year-old, and Margaret was a skinny little thing, though long for her age – long and thin – you could tell she'd have grown tall. Her hair was sticky with seawater when we plaited it.

Margaret came to Kirkwall in her coffin. The Bishop of Orkney wanted to keep her. Alive or dead – that's what the Bishop of Orkney said – alive or dead, the Scots messengers must see her.

He expected them any day. The Scots would see her buried in his cathedral. She was the King's daughter of Norway – that's what he said – and a Queen of Scots who might have been Queen of England too. That's all he cared about – the sea had taken the Scots' queen, and Edward of England had lost his game.

Bishop Narve said Margaret was going home to her father. Thanks be to God, our bishop had the last word.

We sailed with her coffin lashed down amidships. The sun shone, the wind and sea carried us kindly all the way. That made me bitter beyond tears – why couldn't it have been like that on the way out? But there's no point asking why. Yet Margaret asked 'why' all the time. She got more 'whys' into seven years than most of us fit into a lifetime. I can't believe she was wrong to question everything. As I get older I question things more than I ever did before.

And now this woman comes, twelve years after that dreadful voyage, and says she is my own Margaret, and that I sold her to a German merchant in Orkney. Just to make a couple of crowns I'm to have sold my princess as a slave! You know that isn't true! You know no one recognises this impostor! Why, she's too old! My Margaret would be a beautiful young woman, just nineteen years old. Everyone knows that when we brought Margaret back to Bergen, King Eirik opened her coffin and looked at her face for a long time. Who would know her better than her own father? He loved her: of course he recognised her! You've heard my story. You know I'd never have done what I'm accused of. Ask the shipmaster! Ask Thore! Bring Signy back from Trondheim, and ask her! Ask Queen Isabel's maid – she was one of the maids on that voyage. Ask the crew – some of them are still in King Haakon's employ. Ask the Bishop of Bergen himself – ask Bishop Narve. For my Margaret died between his hands, and he knows everything. He knows what happened. He's a man of God – perhaps he even knows why.

Omar's Island

by Robert Minhinnick

Increasingly I seek out Omar because he knows things. In fact Omar seems to understand most things that happen on the island. Because the city is an island. I've proved that to myself in my increasingly ambitious expeditions. But Omar also understands what has already happened, and I'm sure that's the key. That's the secret to this place. And that's the secret that interests me. Because the past will explain the gods. The gods of this island.

One day I join the party of Germans he is leading around the ramparts. I have my photograph taken beside a cannon with two blonde fraus in leather and mimosa. The barrel points out to sea, the cannonballs are piled in a pyramid at our feet. Black seed, I think. The iron hearts of the papaya fruit. There's a cat, one of the island's orange cats, curled on the cannonballs. All the cats here, so my scouting tells me, belong to one clan: the skinny, manky, orange clan. And how they love the sun. Even this scabby tom is sleek in its beam.

After thanking their guide, the party drifts away. I join Omar at a table in Café Leone and we talk about the weather. How unseasonably warm it is. I want to ask Omar about the gods, but he seems determined that I should learn about the island's ships and the captains of those ships.

Yes, says Omar. Our fortune is built on such men. So God help us. First there's Oscar, who lives in a hovel on Mediterranean Street. Oscar's family have been sailors since the beginning. But Oscar likes the Marsovin too much. He owns a paint-bleached barkazza and a broken gondola, and he sails out of an evening, looking for octopus.

Then there's Georgiou of St Ursula Street, who steals lobsters from the pots under the western ramparts. That used to be a capital offence, I've seen men keelhauled for such. But of course, a sailor is a man and a man must live.

Have you met Manoel from Eagle Street? Ah, Manoel, he braves seas so rough in that old ketch of his, you think he's never coming back. Force 9 is a child's breath to Manoel. But as I say, fisherman must live and Manoel casts nets for brisling and white pilchard.

And you must have seen the African from the warren in the walls? He's made a boat from the planks of other boats, bits of driftwood and floats. He sets off in that raft with his five-tanged fork searching for angel shark. Maybe he was a great captain in his own country, which is Sierra Leone, a kingdom of cruelties where most of the murderers are children. Or so I'm told. And yes, there are scars on his back, healed violet. And burns on his wrists and ankles. But sometimes I look at him and see a stateliness in his eye.

Then there's Hilario of South Street, who puts to sea in a gharbiel, the water coming through the joints, a real sieve, hardly a bucket, more like a night-soil barrel, yes a pisspot with a crack in it, that's Hilario's galleon, mad old Hilario who couldn't catch himself but one morning came back with a mermaid, and friend I tell you, Hilario married this mermaid and she lived with him on South Street. Well, that's the story. Dispute it with Hilario when he's sober. He comes out with us sometimes when we go after flapper skate. Bloody old Hilario, he's fathomless to me, bobbing out there like a cork, an old man astride his mustardiera, the wind taking the sail of his trousers. Old Hilario, blown along by his farts.

Of course, you can't forget Marcello, coming across the harbour in his scow. That's Marcello of St Elmo Street, where there are more boats than headlice and the nets hang like spiderwebs.

Now Michelangelo, he lives on Old Theatre Street and works on the dredger *Sapphire* in the grand harbour. He borrows his brother's gondola and rows to the islet where the soft-bodied crabs live in the rock pools. Sometimes he brings us a coffee-sackful, the whole bag wriggling and the crabs wheezing like tiny bellows. That's a peculiar music to hear at dawn.

Don't forget McCale, the nostronomu. He doesn't usually come on our voyages. But he offers us stories. Once, marooned on the Black Isle, he milked a cowfish. That's how he survived. The milk, he said, tasted as diamonds might taste. The milk was sweet as caviar. Yes, yes, McCale, we say, go back to your cactus juice and Neptune save the ships you steer towards port. Why not sleep it all off in St Pawlu Street with your fat wife?

Then there's Aurelio, a good boy from the poorest barrakka on the western side, who will dive from the side of any boat and bring back cowries. Once he came up with an oyster filled with a rainwater-coloured pearlseed that somehow Hilario swallowed when he was sniffing it. May it grow to choke that imbecile. Or maybe I think, maybe Hilario is not as stupid as he pretends. That gumboil of his.

Of course, there's the Macedonian too. He cannot swim nor sail and once went round all night under the moon. We found him the next morning in the same place, that Macedonian moonstruck, babbling away in his abominable Greek. We gave him espressos in the QE2 bar, and the next day he brought us aubergines from his garden, and sweet peppers he had grown in a window box. Stay home, we told him, and water your seeds, or we will be lighting a candle in a red glass for you down at the shipwreck church. The fool had seen meteors all night and had thought them portents of his own death. Ah, we laughed there in the tavern, you must be a great man for heaven to fill with fire for you. Look, we'll take you to the fishmonger in the suq so you can learn why we sail out. Why we do what we do. But no more ragtime with ragworm for you.

Maybe you've seen Azzopardi, who weights his line with a spark plug and casts for flounder from the stern of the pilot boat when there's no traffic in the bay. You never know what's there in all that oil and plastic, he says, in all the shit from the Russian billionaire's yacht and all the cruise liners with the captains in gold braid and the retired bank managers in their white tuxedos looking down at the greasy dock. I spit on them.

Hey Azzo, we say, watch they don't spit on you. You'll never see it coming.

But who knows what lives in the port? A child brought a sea horse once, nodding in a pickled onion jar. And once there was a harbour dolphin laughing as if it had heard the greatest joke in the world. Old Azzo lives in the apartments on St Giuseppi Street, but his salmon is John West and then only on Friday. Hey presto, Azzo, we shout, are you coming? And he comes.

Sometimes we have Ahmed too, from East Street, who will light a candle at Our Lady of Damascus before every voyage, because, my friend, even our pleasant excursions are voyages. For those in peril on the sea? Please don't smile. We are seafarers too.

But Ahmed, we say, you have no place in a good Catholic church. Go and bow your head and wiggle your arse under your broken moon. And Ahmed calls us ignorant fools for not knowing our history, and I agree with that. And he helps with the ketch and off they go, looking for lampuka, though I remember he and Oscar coming home once with an old grandfather octopus.

The beast had a beak like an eagle, that old green grandad from the wrecks, grumbling and waving its arms, and we said no, take the monster back. It lay there and looked at us with disdain. A grumpy old patriarch with the sea hissing in his flesh. It will be tough as a tyre, we said, your axe couldn't cut it. And anyway, it's bad luck. This one's old enough to have met the Emperor Napoleon himself. And it has survived those Sicilian pirates in their speedboats. Think of the life it has led. When that beast dies maybe the last memory of Lord Nelson will be lost to the world. And Ahmed looked at us then with octopus eyes.

But Masso? He lives with his mother behind Our Lady of the Victories. It's a cellar like some whisky-dive but it's their home when he's not taking passengers around French Creek in his water taxi. Masso brings that djhasja across the bay sometimes, and sometimes I go with him, or Oscar, or the African, even the Macedonian, if he promises to sit tight, and we have a good time with our rods in the summer evenings, the ocean flat and the air still warm, and flocks of songbirds crossing the bay, blackcaps and those little warblers no bigger than olive leaves, always heading away, away from us and the snarers' nets. And maybe we play a flawt or guitar but nothing to scare the fish. It's bream we go for, slippery bream for our baskets, and sometimes we're lucky, but then Masso gets worried about his mother.

What if she's fallen over? How will a bream help that? he asks.

She'll only fall over if she has another suck of that duty-free she keeps under the floorboards, Oscar will say, but all too quickly it's ended and our taxi man is taking the boat backwards, edging towards the walls, and soon we're under the ramparts' shadow, where the air is cool and purple.

Ciao, Masso, we say, and he putters and phutters back round to his mum, the lady of the victories all right, her shrine where his balls should be, the bottom of his boat full of torn-up tickets.

Then there is David, who lives on the ramparts above the yacht club in a room that once was a gun emplacement. Snug and dark. That's the best that can be said for it. At night he will look out at the stations of the stars all the way to Tunis. David spends his money at the tattooist in Strait Street, that little entry between the Smiling Prince tavern and the Consulate of the Grand Duchy of Luxembourg. A story is unfolding upon his back and shoulders and it concerns his greatest dream. To catch a devilfish. David has heard many stories about them, but none of us, apart from our kingly African, will ever accompany him. Why? Because he sails out for days in an old motorboat with an oil drum of drinking water and hardly a tarpaulin to hide from the sun. David, bless him, has read the great books and his hero is Odysseus.

David, I say, beware the tales. The poets are never to be trusted. They are an eelish tribe. But that young man has decided he has a quest. We need such things, he says. A great work. A challenge and a life's undertaking. And I nod and smile and say no more. Too soon David will sleep the iron sleep.

Ciangura? His home is an attic behind the Palazzo Carafa, opposite the Societa Dante Alighieri. You must have seen it? Near the amateur football HQ. Ciangura is determined to catch cerna to sell to the restaurants. His cousin is a chef and looks out for our catch. Well, this Ciangura, he lives with a dumb woman, her hair is greasy as sump oil. A skinny cat, not bad-looking. Or so I'm told. And jumpy as a hare. That's a poor corner now, though much of the district has become offices for notaries and advocates. You know the type. Well, this woman plays the zither and that's what you'll hear if you ever climb to Ciangura's apartment, someone's transistor in the middle flat, then this slithery zithery thing at the very top, zinging and zanging, not an atrocious sound. Not an insult to the ear, I have to say. And the sky blue in the roof.

Scibberas's idea is always to go for ceppulazza, which doesn't excite many of the others, though they sometimes agree. We always think he has an interesting life because next to him on St Christopher Street is a Moroccan trading company that claims to import furniture and musical instruments. But the door is covered in dust and there's few have seen it open.

Hey, Skibbo, we say. What goes on?

Then he will shrug and say 'search me' and pull his boat down the steps on a set of pram wheels. But we are suspicious of that smile. It is a dolphin's smile. Because when the dolphin smiles it is thinking about something else. Well, we've heard that Scibberas and Aurelio and Ciangura sometimes help the Moroccans, lugging rugs out of vans. A bit of muscle. And as payment they are each given a pinch of haschich.

Skibbo, we say, any fool can smell that sweet smoke. The air about you is like a dolceria. And your eyelids, Skibbo, are heavy as a goshawk's, and there's a dreamy look upon your face and no edge to you, man, these days. No zip in your zobb.

But Skibbo will pull the boat along on its wheels and laugh and stumble and tell us of his dreams and his girlfriend's dreams, because they dream the same dream. And we always groan at that and shake our heads. We are experienced men. You must understand that. Men of the world. That kind of talk is bread dipped in tea. The same dream? Sop, we call it here. Bloody sop.

If Omar is not telling tourists about the island's past, standing on the steps of a palazzo or in a cobbled yard where blue bees crawl through hibiscus, I ask for an hour, or an afternoon, of his time. Often, he agrees, and I feel honoured. But so far he has said nothing about the gods. Yes, he tells me of the baroque churches. Of the Renaissance art. But that's not what interests me. I'm not that kind of scholar.

Today he takes me to a place I must have passed a score of times, yet never noticed. Under the western ramparts the walls are a maze of tunnels used by fishermen and lovers and the klandestins. Down a flight of steps we stop in shadow. There is a string of washing hung against an entrance, and above this door are two eyes painted blue and white, and the word *Caccarun* in flaking paint.

Omar leads the way past the shirts and vests on the line and beckons me inside. It is a small room, perhaps a kitchen. There is a table and two chairs and shelves of jars and bottles. The room is dark, so dark I cannot see that around the wall this space continues. Omar leads on. The room becomes a tunnel. Ahead a candle is burning. There are two diesel drums with a piece of driftwood between them. In the gloom, I think, someone might be sitting at this board.

Wine? asks Omar, and he himself lifts a bottle and two dusty glasses from a shelf.

Where are we? I ask.

Under the bastion, says my guide. It's time you met the Phoenician. Hey Nannu, your health.

Omar is toasting the shadow in the corner. I look closer. There is a man there with hair the colour of a spiderweb. An empty glass waits before him. Omar offers to pour him wine, Omar already the host, Omar the leader. But the figure places a palm over his cup. This man is very frail. In the candlelight his skin is yellow.

No hurry at all, smiles Omar. Nannu has waited a long time. He will wait longer. But you, sir, you should learn more.

Of course, I say. I'm here to learn. But...

Then listen, says Omar. We're in the warren here. These tunnels run a long way. Above us is a palace of many rooms and in its history it has been many things. Now, it's a kind of hotel. Fifteen women live there, not as many as before. But if you would know the island, you must know them.

It's less the present, I say, than the past. The ancient days. And the...

But Omar holds up his hand.

First, the lovely Rusatia. Ask her, and she will dress as a priest for you. Or the Emperor himself. As a gladiator if such is your taste. No, she is never without callers.

Callidrome is a little older. She keeps a goat in her suite and feeds it radishes. It is tied to her bed with a toga cord and Callidrome rouges its white cheeks and puts lipstick on its nanny-goat lips. Yes, Callidrome's goat is a beautiful creature, its eyes like dates. Once she gave it cocaine and she swore it spoke monk's Latin.

Fortunata is inseparable from her mother. They are, I suppose, a team. Once mummy put a love potion in the communion wine, then they waited in their room. The first to knock was the Bishop of the Blue Lagoon, and soon a schoolteacher with his class dinner money. Yes, powerful medicine.

Now Fabia, she has style. She drinks ouzo from Milos and listens to Cole Porter songs. Ah, she whispers, I was his muse. In love with the night mysterious? Of course. He came here, you know. To this island. Ah Mr Porter, sang Fabia. What shall I do? Night and day, you are the one. I get no kick from champagne? That's Fabia's best line, I think. Of course, it didn't last. Poor Porter with his limp and his money? The hotel was no place for him and Fabia such a demanding child. But they got along. They were artists, you see. He could no more stop writing his music than Fabia turn down one million Turkish lire for a tick of her eyebrow pencil. People like that can never switch off. Because you should never retire. Ask old Nannu here. Still keeping a bar. So Fabia stays working. What should she be doing? Watching the island's TV? As she will say, I am a witness, as are all artists.

Nica is always in demand because she owns the strongest mosquito spray. Pif Pif, I think it is called. Yes, a powerful poison that gives those swamp flies no chance. But as to losing blood, doesn't little Nica have that all her own way? How sweet, Nica will say, after her pearly whites have done their job. Advocates taste of palm oil, she tells the other girls. And MPs of mothballs. Her favourites, of course, are the orchestra from the theatre. Apparently, violinists are salty as the Ligurian deeps. Oh, what blood, little Nica will say. I can taste the music in it.

Felicia drinks like no other. Her tipple is anis, which has deranged many a fine mind. Men often challenge her to a bulb of wine. Always Felicia wins. How? Because she doesn't swallow. The wine simply disappears into her gullet, though sometimes, of course, I can hear it sloshing about when I place my ear to her belly, a belly golden as a communion plate. Yes, little Felicia, outdrinking the Lascars, the *Ark Royal* stokers tattooed like Scythians, the trireme oarsmen still in their chains. How often have I seen her hands in their pockets or lifting a greasy tarboosh while they slept it off? Often, brother. Oh yes.

Cressa and Drauca work together for safety's sake. They come from Siricusa and know all the wiles of the dockside trash who want to try their luck. But one day they were duped. Some old fool offered an IOU. He swore that the next day, or the next, he'd have the brass. Together they tipped him upside down and found only grape seeds in his suit. So they christened him with the chamber pot. No credit notes, no plastic, no Albanian squindarkas are their rules of business. Couldn't he read?

Mula is from the island. Her father makes brandy from prickly pears, and delivers a cask of it to the hotel every month. So the girls look after Mula, who cannot read, but is kind and plump and sunburnt. A friendly girl. And the brandy? Rotgut. But cut it with luminata and they can stay sober for at least an hour.

Now Helpis's speciality is haschich. On her door and her website is the sign of the snake that swallows its own tail. Her shift is the blue of michaelmas daisies, and Helpis is suitably melancholy. As to Ianuaria, she speaks some dialect that no one understands. Maybe she comes from Durazzo or Izmir, tough cities. Yes, the girls are a United Nations all by themselves. But those opaque vowels are no matter when she begins her love talk. Then she is the oriole the snarers crave. Yes, with her words, Ianuaria can make anyone disgorge their soul. Her tongue is a goldsmith's anvil, all right. Where did that woman learn to speak such a language? Such whispering behind her boudoir door.

Faustilla? Dear Fausty's tongue is pierced with a ball bearing. It serves as a clapper for the bells that God cannot ring. So who better to serenade the priest, who has brought wine with honey and whose biretta is crushed under his fat arse?

And I know Palindrome as well as any. She is white as gesso and looks like a ghost. In her cupboard once I found the following: a charioteer's whip, sea holly, a barbed-wire torc, a packet of angel dust, Valium, blindfolds, scarabs, a map of the port of Alexandria, a stone jug of raki, pale green as I recall, and a letter from the Caliph. Oh yes, she is known in high places is our Palindrome.

Restituta wears a veil. A gorgeous hoodwinker she. Who do you favour, sir? she will ask her regulars. Am I your Dominican today? Or your grateful poor Clare? Such admirable humility. You see, Restituta has truly been a nun. But it was a roofless convent with cactus in the garden. The well had collapsed. She came here, to the island of lightning, from Kriti, where she had already learned much of her science.

And Philomena? A Nubian princess they say. Experiencing interesting times. She keeps a panther, and this beast has a shrivelled leg. As a deterrent to intruders, it lives on the roof, shitting in an old roasting tin filled with torn-up *Gazzetta dello Sport*.

Yes, smiles Omar. They live above us. It's one of my jobs to help them out with the money. And to learn their stories, of course, because all the girls are great raconteurs. What can I do with these? Nica might ask. That Moroccan in the Hugo Boss suit paid in dirhams. So I take them, as I take the dinars and the kroons and the leks and the forints and the tolars and the dollars Canadian, and turn them into money the girls can understand.

A lovely family, I hope you agree. My fireflies, I call them. How they glow.

One day I arrange to meet Omar at Nannu's place. When I arrive there is no one but Nannu present. I wait in a darkness lit by one red candle on the board. Outside, the light is shattering and the sea wild, a curdled milk. Inside, it is midnight.

As usual the Caccarun is silent and I pour my own drink. I wonder whether it is his laundry that hangs over the entrance. The Caccarun must have better things to think about than personal hygiene, and I too must look unkempt, a week's bristles, and sour wine in my armpits, appropriate for the tavern of the two eyes. If I need a pexpex, there's a slop pot. But no lavaman that I've seen. My research is not going well.

At last Omar arrives.

Has the catastropher been talking to you? he asks.

Nannu?

Wars and invasions, Nannu knows when. And why. Ask him, man. He'll tell you when the rains are due. The new rains. He understands how hot it will become. Nannu has predicted how far the tide will creep up the ramparts. And yes, Nannu has even counted how many people are moving towards us, across the desert, over the waves. Towards us now, at this moment. He can see them all. Or rather...

Omar takes a shell from a shelf and gives it to the old man.

What do you hear, Nannu?

The old man remains silent.

Does he hear the sea? I ask.

I'll tell you what Nannu hears, says Omar. Ships' bells. So much louder than church bells. And so many more of them. Many men with many oars. That's what Nannu hears in the shell. The sound of oars. The galleys coming this way, the galleons with bells in their rigging, the gondolas, the gharbiels, the lazzarettos, the cruise liners. And the king astride his driftwood shaking that five-pointed fork.

But does he hear the gods? I whisper. Maybe Omar doesn't hear.

Occasionally on my travels I pass a derelict barrakka on the west side. The blocks in the wall have shrunk and the building is unsafe. So there are plenty of places to stow away, to squat, to put a bedroll in the dust. I suppose that's where I see most of the illegals, in the holes in the walls, holes such as the fishermen use. The ramparts are a honeycomb, entrances and dead ends, and who knows how deep a labyrinth it all is? And there they are, rats in the rock, or in and out like flying foxes, because I've seen the bats too in the dusk on their own journeys, sharing their chambers now with these unfortunates.

Many's the time I've seen klandestins go in one hole and come out another. I've looked in too and seen dried palm leaves covering blankets, old clothes, yoghurt pots with rainwater, stale bread from the wheelies and bags of olives. Because that's what these people do. Pick up olives. They sit under the olive trees and fill a bag, green going black, medicinal-tasting olives, most of the crop already soft and trodden to oil under the benches.

Who's going to buy? I always wonder. There are more olives than cockroaches on the island. More olives than children and there are children everywhere, hanging from tenement windows, bobbing still in the sea before me, the coal-coloured sea with clouds massing in the north. The coral is black now and the fishes invisible. So slight in the sun, the slim fishes that silver the eye as light stuns time. Those fishes have vanished. But who will buy when they can pick the olives themselves? There are olives everywhere.

Yet that's what the klandestins do. They pick olives and look at olives as if they have never seen olives before. Maybe they haven't. Perhaps olives are a strange fruit to these people.

Takes all sorts, I suppose. Perhaps they don't know the olives need to be soaked in brine. Soaked for weeks and even then they're not ready. They'll have to learn the hard way.

Who are they, these visitors? I ask Omar. A troupe of outcasts from the desert?

Everyone comes to the island of lightning, he says. Eventually. The Greeks in their gold breeks, Palestinian farmers whose peach trees are full of cluster bombs. They all find themselves adrift, and the currents bring them here.

We go to the highest rampart and look out. The sky is dark and there are lanterns lit.

The rafts will come ashore in the night, says Omar. They don't have long to wait. You can imagine the passengers. Pregnant women who had never seen the sea before their journey, teachers, students, the brave, the mad. Think of them now out on the ocean, their skins indigo in this light. Behind one another one, and behind him yet more. What if a wave takes a child from the stern? Who would know? When the snake steals the chick does the mother remember? Swallowed whole, it was never there.

Why do the superintendents let them in? I ask.

The island's grown old, he says. It's full of old men. And women. Old men are like cicadas, telling all they know. Children are the same. We are talkers now, not doers. Not warriors. We're cicadas on a tree. And ugly as cicadas. No one listens, so we sing louder. Who can tell when one of us falls, because the racket is the same? But if we could learn from cicadas we would have already done so. You wish to contact the ancients? You wish for the gods? Oh yes, I know what you wish. Those voices in our heads? Maybe those are the gods' voices. Certainly they are the cicadas. Dream sounds. The dreams of old people with the sheets up to their chins and their teeth chattering. We should honour the cicadas.

But the gods, I say.

The gods? Yes, it is always the gods with you.

I thought I was a scholar, I whisper to Omar. Until I met you. Sir, you understand everything on the island. Surely you can show me the gods. It's the gods I came for. Not the sailors. Not the fireflies. My research grant is spent.

Omar smiles. I was at the bakery this morning, he says. Down the passageway I stepped and into that chancery, a man carrying the hot trays, his mother counting the cents out on the table, flour in her eyes and apron. And the loaf she handed me? As big as an ox-cart wheel. That's what I thought this morning. And I remembered wheels I once heard go rattling through the prickly pear. You will come with me.

And so the next evening I go to see the Venuses. Omar directs me to the bus, but warns I will have to make my own way home.

It is the far side of the island. Wind blows, the stone dust flies. But the Venuses are not hard to find. They sit together on a hillside looking east. The rain has worn their brows like temple steps. Loaflike they squat, and I think of Omar's loaf, his great wheel. For the Venuses are loaf upon loaf. Their bellies are bread and their faces swollen dough, globular in the dusk and gilded with the last sun upon them. Sowlike, I suppose, these beady-eyed matriarchs, with clefts in their bellies and shadows conglomerating in those gourds. A race of lumpen stone, these Venuses, looking where they have always looked, for ever out to sea.

I sit down. I sit amongst the Aphrodites in their ancient easiness.

How venerable, these Venuses. Their breasts and buttocks so cool under my fingers, these women who wait for time to stop, heads crushed into their shoulders' yoke, seven thousand years patient in this limestone sorority, their faces hidden, expressions concealed, knowing what they know and grown fat on the wind's salt, resting here on their millstones.

In the dark the gods are carboys of greenish wine. I gaze with them out to sea. The moon is coming up but is no whiter than their shepherd-polished thighs. These are the gods. These are the goddesses. They have survived so long that their religion is dead. And I think of the women I passed on the track out of town, grandmothers come from market with halva and grapes, the last bus late.

Fresh Water

by Chris Cleave

Danny Zeichner sat at the back of my navigation class, staring at a pair of nautical dividers. He opened up the brass arms to the span of his upturned right hand, placing one steel point on the ball of his thumb and the other on the pad of his little finger. The alignment, the equivalence – it seemed to please him. On his desk – on all of the desks – lay the Admiralty chart of the approaches to Le Touquet.

Our classroom was half of a community centre. It was windowless; a former store room, strip-lit and squeezed in beside the exercise hall. Through the wall you could hear a woman shouting over high-energy music. And one and two and *hips and tummy* and five and six and *work those thighs*. I liked the woman. Her name was Annabel. At 9 p.m. her class would have lost weight and mine would have lost their bearings, and then we were going for a drink.

The bass line from next door rattled the pens in the tray of my whiteboard. Some of my class were struggling to concentrate. Not Danny Zeichner. He was staring at his dividers as if they spanned some greater truth.

I drew the class's attention to the vast flats of sand that stretched out to sea from the Baie d'Étaples, denying entry to Le Touquet. The only hope was the thin and convoluted channel scoured out by the winding Étaples river, but at most states of the tide even that channel would just be dry sand. So to get into Le Touquet, one would have to be patient. One would have to wait for high water.

Danny looked up from his dividers.

'I should be so leisurely,' he said.

The rest of the class twisted their heads to look back at him.

'What?' said Danny Zeichner. 'And you people have never been in a hurry?'

He raised his eyes and his palms to heaven, as if he alone saw through the polystyrene ceiling tiles of the community centre.

The class turned back and faced front. It was a good bunch, nine students, with the usual mix of ages between twenty and sixty. Quite bright enough for basic chart work. I reckoned I'd get all of them through their theory exam, even if I had to write the odd mnemonic on their shirt cuffs for them.

The students gripped their biros and watched me. The youngsters wore T-shirts and trainers, the seniors favoured corduroys and cardigans. If the tone was informal, then Danny Zeichner struck a descant note. In the back row he sat upright in a sober lounge suit, with his thick black beard groomed and shining. Fifty-five or sixty, slim, with a squash racket protruding from the sports bag beside his feet. Half-moon spectacles perfectly aping the semilunar bags beneath his eyes. Gazing into infinity between the points of his dividers.

I stepped up to the whiteboard and ran the class through the tidal height calculation for Le Touquet. *Yvonne, how much does our yacht draw? That's right, two metres. Okay, good. So we need at least two metres' depth of water to keep our boat afloat. Now, Mark, what is the shallowest part of the channel into Le Touquet? 6.2 metres above the line? Yes, that's right, it's a drying height. That means it's just dry sand there at low water. So, Phillip, what is the minimum height of tide we need for our yacht to float over that shallowest point in the channel? Exactly. Well done. Two metres of keel plus 6.2 metres of sand gives a minimum tidal height of 8.2 metres. Let's imagine it's our own yacht and say 8.5 metres, to be on the safe side. So, Danny, will you look at the tidal curve and tell me how many hours before high water we can expect a tidal height of 8.5 metres. Danny?*

Danny Zeichner lifted his eyes from the dividers.

'Mmm?'

'When will we have eight and a half metres of tide on our side, Danny?'

'Why do you ask me that?'

'Excuse me. So you can sail your yacht safely into Le Touquet, without going aground.'

Danny shrugged.

'Why would I want to sail my yacht into Le Touquet?' he said.

'I don't know, Danny. The fine wines, perhaps? The air of faded elegance? They say it's quite a pleasant resort.'

Danny sighed.

'I don't drink wine and I have never visited a resort in my life,' he said. 'And this Le Touquet, it's in France, isn't it? I'm suspicious of the French. You know, the Dreyfus affair, Vichy, and so forth.'

Some of the others were muttering. This was a subsidised evening class, but it was still costing everyone seven pounds an hour. Danny ignored the comments. He stroked his beard and looked down at the chart on his desk. Thoughtfully, he stabbed one point of the dividers into downtown Le Touquet, and slowly described a circle on the chart – a circle with the radius set by the span of his hand – as if he was establishing a minimum safe distance. Just at a glance, I couldn't help noting that if he was planning to stay that far offshore, he would be untroubled at any state of the tide.

'It's just a hypothetical exercise, Danny,' I said.

'You say that now,' said Danny, 'but some of the most dangerous ideas in this life start out hypothetical. One morning scientists start measuring hands and noses, and that very same evening it's *Kristallnacht*.'

Danny looked calmly at the faces turned towards him. No one

spoke in the classroom. Next door, the exercise class seemed to get louder. And one and two and *change the subject* and five and six and *let's move on*. I ran a hand though my hair.

'Okay,' I said. 'Sally. Maybe you can pilot our hypothetical yacht into this nominal French haven.'

Sally was game, and she read the tidal curve correctly, and we established that one might safely enter Le Touquet on the rising tide one hour before high water, assuming of course that one was motivated to do so. I told the class I'd see them next week, and watched them shuffle out. I tidied the classroom and left it ready for flower arranging, or Reiki healing, or whatever the suburbs were mastering next.

Outside in the corridor, Danny Zeichner was waiting for me.

'I'm really sorry,' he said.

'Yeah,' I said, 'what was all that about?'

'I just got a little bored, I think. Sometimes I like to provoke.'

'Well, you did that.'

'I'm sorry.'

'No harm done.'

Danny smiled.

'Well,' he said. 'You are actually okay.'

A phalanx of overweight women burst into the corridor. Pink from exercise, they chattered as they pulled coats on over their jade, puce and leopard-print leotards. They giggled towards the car park, past a noticeboard labelled 'COMMUNITY'. Among the notices, there was a library that needed saving. A three-legged cat that was missing. A Phil Collins CD for sale.

Danny put his hand on my shoulder. I saw a flash of white shirt cuff, and the gleam of the fluorescent lights on his thin gold watch.

'You really can do navigation, can't you, sonny?'

'Yes, I really can.'

'You truly can find your way from anywhere to anywhere? Even when the satellite navigation breaks? Even in storms and crazy tides?'

'Of course, Danny. I can navigate coastal, ocean, astro. I can go anywhere.'

'Then don't you want to get out of *here*?'

Danny looked up and down the corridor, pulled me down to his level, and whispered the words in my ear. Looking over the top of his spectacles, he held my eyes for a moment, then turned and walked off. I stood there and thought about what he had said. I scuffed my toes on the grey linoleum floor until Annabel came out of the exercise room.

'Hi!' said Annabel.

She was holding a bulky portable stereo in one hand, and fifteen hula hoops in the crook of her other arm. I got the door for her.

'Good class?' I said.

Annabel slumped against the wall and blew a strand of hair out of her eyes. The hula hoops rattled.

'Some days,' she said, 'I look at them and I think, *It's nice you ladies are making an effort.* Other days I just think, *God, you fat bitches.*'

'Bad day then?'

'Futile, really. You?'

'Weird. I think one of my class is a mental case.'

'There's one aboard every ship, sailor.'

'I suppose so. What say I navigate us to a bar where we can drown all our troubles in rum?'

'God,' she said. 'Is that your answer to everything, you old sea dog?'

'Well,' I said. 'Old habits, you know.'

Annabel smiled.

'You can take the sailor from the sea...' she said.

'I know, I know...'

Later, as we lay on my bed, I listened to the drone of the traffic on the A3. I couldn't sleep. I got up and stepped onto my tiny balcony. There was some unopened mail out there – it always seemed like a good place to stow it. I toed the stack of envelopes. Something black from the council. Something red from the bank. Something silver from MasterCard – apparently I had been pre-approved.

I lit one of Annabel's cigarettes and leaned on the balcony rail. Through the orange haze of the Greater London sky, no stars at all were visible. I felt a warm hand on the back of my neck.

'What's wrong?' said Annabel. 'Can't sleep?'

'Yeah,' I said. 'Can't stop thinking.'

'Anything in particular?'

'Just something someone said to me today.'

'The nutter?'

'Well, I'm wondering, now, whether he's so crazy after all.'

Annabel ruffled my hair and sighed.

'Maybe you'd be happier if you moved in with me,' she said.

'Maybe.'

'I mean, look at the way you live here. You've got no TV, no pictures on the walls, hardly any furniture. We always dial out for dinner, and when it comes you don't even have two plates that match. It's like you live here but your heart's not really in it, you know?'

I said mmm, and looked down from the balcony to where the endless cars were turning off the A3 onto the slip road. Their wipers worked against the thin drizzle. The exit was signposted New Malden, Kingston and Raynes Park. Everything was signposted round here.

'Hypothetically,' whispered Danny Zeichner, 'what if?'

I blinked. I looked around. My other students were bent over the exercise I'd set them. *Plan a passage from Portsmouth to Poole. The spring tide sets west at 0500, the wind is forecast southerly four to five rising six to gale eight by 1700, and one of your crew tends to get seasick.* Beneath the booming of the stereo from the exercise class next door, the only sound was pencils being chewed and lines being scratched on charts. I leaned down towards Danny, alone in the back row of desks.

'What if *what*?' I said.

'What if I bought a boat?' said Danny. 'A yacht? A pretty little yacht with two sails? Say blue. Say thirty feet long. Would that be about right?'

'For what?'

'For a long trip.'

'I don't know, Danny,' I said. 'Hypothetically speaking, that would be a short boat for a long trip.'

Danny nodded slowly. Fingered his beard. Looked up again.

'*Blue*,' he said.

He fixed me over the top of his spectacles, and waited.

'Blue is good,' I said.

'So let's imagine I'd already bought her,' said Danny. 'This morning on the internet. Let's imagine she was only ten years old. Let's suppose she was ready right now, in the marina in Marseilles. Let's say the only thing holding her back from the open ocean was two short pieces of rope. Hypothetically speaking, would an old man just have done a foolish thing?'

I shook my head.

'I can't tell you that, Danny,' I said. 'I can teach you how to navigate between any two points on this globe that are connected by at least two metres' depth of water. I can't tell you whether you *should*.'

Danny nodded.

'Actually I wasn't thinking *I* should,' he said.

'No?'

'No. I was thinking *we* should.'

'Should what?'

'Should go on a boat trip. From Marseilles to, you know, Tel Aviv.'

'*Uh?*'

'Hey, don't look at me like I'm crazy,' said Danny. 'There is two metres' depth of water all the way. I checked. It's called the Mediterranean Sea.'

I stood. From next door, the stereo boomed. And one and two and *oh my god* and five and six and *I just might*. I leaned back down to Danny.

'Why me?' I said.

'Because you are a sailor, sonny. You are the only sailor I know. Why do you suppose I come to this class?'

'So I can teach *you* to be a sailor.'

Danny chuckled.

'What, you think I have time to learn all this? All this tidal vector and juju eyeball and I-don't-know-what? I'm an old man! All these memories I have in my head, you think I have space for your fancy mathematics? Are you nuts?'

I smiled.

'Listen,' I said. 'I'm flattered you asked. But I can't come on a long trip with you. I have two of these classes a week. I have a, you know, a sort of a girlfriend.'

'I'll pay you, of course,' said Danny. 'Cash per diem, more than you make here, plus your flight into Marseilles and your flight back from Tel Aviv.'

'It's not the money,' I said. 'And it's nothing personal. I don't do that sort of trip any more. I can't just take off, these days. I'm trying to settle down. On land, I mean.'

Danny's head drooped. He stared down at the chart of the Western Solent that we were using for the passage-planning exercise. I couldn't help noticing that the stubborn pencil line he'd drawn for his course would drive him straight onto the breaking sands of the Bramble Bank. In his groomed beard and lounge suit. In the driving rain of a rising southerly gale. Danny looked back up at me and made a small, sad gesture at the flat, clean chart.

'Is this all the sea is to you now then?' he said. 'Just a paper sheet to draw lines on?'

I sighed.

Thirty-six hours later we were walking along a marina pontoon in the dazzling white sunshine of Marseilles. Danny skipped ahead, intoxicated with joy, wildly excited. He seemed dressed for golf as much as for sailing. Lime green canvas shorts, black and white checked shirt, gold watch and a brand new pair of red leather deck shoes. He jumped over cleats and leapfrogged bollards. I followed more carefully, pushing our kitbags in a big wheeled caddy. It was late spring and the mistral was blowing, screaming in the rigging of the yachts in the marina, sending halyards clanking against five thousand masts, whipping up a fine spray over the pontoon deck.

It was hard work pushing the caddy – one of the tyres was flat, and the thing was overloaded with Danny's seafaring essentials. I thought his bottles of Scotch were a good idea. I was less keen on the antique brass telescopes he'd found on Portobello Road. The caddy's flat tyre groaned, and I looked forward to the moment when Danny would stop and show me his boat. When he finally did, and I saw what he'd stopped next to, I wished he'd carried on.

Danny's yacht was a twenty-eight-foot fibreglass sloop. The hull was royal blue under the bow and transom where the overhang had offered it some protection. Everywhere else, the boat was bleached by the sun to a streaky azure. Barnacles clung along the length of the waterline. I watched a school of fat grey mullet cruising through the clear green water between the fronds of weed that trailed from the hull. Above deck, three of the saloon windows were crazed and cracked, and the fourth was boarded over. The standing rigging was rusted, the deck was streaked with seagull shit, and the steering compass had been removed from the binnacle and replaced with a drinks holder. In the well of the cockpit there were empty beer cans and cigarette packets, a desiccated seabird, and an open tin of antifouling paint over which a thick crust had formed. The tiller was cracked, and reinforced with a child's beach cricket bat. The bat was lashed to the tiller with orange nylon fishing line. On the boat's bow was the name *Allegro*. The letters were formed in the block style from black electrical tape. The sailing vessel *Allegro*, as we found it, was listing on its mooring at an angle of maybe fifteen degrees. It leaned like an old man's dream, ironically italicised.

Danny spread his hands and beamed.

'Isn't she a beauty?' he said.

I removed my sunglasses and looked the boat over from the waterline to the masthead while Danny hopped from foot to foot and watched my face.

'What do you think?' he said.

I looked down at our kitbags.

'I think we won't be needing these just yet,' I said.

We checked into the Mercure Grand on rue Beauvau. We stayed there while the mistral blew itself out and Danny blew six thousand euros. I had his boat lifted and high-pressure hosed to get rid of the barnacles and the weed. I painted the hull with a new coat of antifouling. It took one whole afternoon, applying the new blue paint over the grey undercoat. With each stroke of the roller, I felt the weather improving. Close to the end of the job, I looked up past the blue hull into the ultramarine sky streaked with jets of white cirrus, and I breathed in the smell of fresh paint and salt air, and somewhere off in the boatyard a radio played Georges Brassens, and I realised I was humming along.

I had the boat's engine thoroughly overhauled. I hired three tanned marseillais in blue overalls to replace all the standing rigging, and I fitted new running rigging myself. I removed everything soft from below decks, and burned it. I persuaded a sign writer to remove the electrical tape and paint 'Allegro' on the bow in cursive, in exchange for a bottle of Scotch. I sent Danny off to buy a compass, and I sent him back again when he returned the first time with an instrument for drawing circles.

Early one calm morning, with dew on the deck, I unfurled the genoa. The sailcloth was grey and ragged, and there was a hole in the centre of the sail through which I could see the Baie de Marseille, stretching in indigo flatness from the Iles de Frioul to Méjean. For a whole minute I stood transfixed. Then I measured up the boat for new sails, sat in a café in the vieux port to drink an espresso in the warm morning sun, and realised I was happy. A text came from Annabel: SEE YOU TONIGHT? I realised I had told no one I was leaving.

We returned the boat to the water, and it no longer floated at an angle. New sails came, and we screwed up our eyes against their perfect whiteness. I set Danny to loading the stores, distributing the weight of the tinned food and the dried rice evenly between the lockers, while I filled the boat's drinking-water tanks. I was there for half an hour while the hose ran on and on. That boat had a voracious thirst for fresh water.

Danny stood there, frowning at the hosepipe and the scrubbed deck and the glittering metal rails.

'Look,' I said. 'Aren't you enjoying yourself? Is all this preparation getting you down? Because for me this is all part of it. For me this feels like a fresh start already.'

Danny shook his head.

'Maybe I'm suspicious of fresh starts,' he said. 'You know, I went up to the top of the Basilica this morning and looked south. It is a big ocean, sonny, wouldn't you say? One little coat of antifouling is not going to subdue it. One little New Testament does not cancel out, you know, Leviticus.'

'But isn't that what this trip's all about for you?' I said. 'A new start in the promised land?'

Danny sighed.

'This is what I thought,' he said, 'but now I'm not so sure. I'm getting a bad feeling about this trip. Jews on boats? See, I don't know. Usually when God wants us to cross a sea he fixes it so we can walk.'

'Right. Look, are you anxious about setting off?'

Danny pushed his spectacles up to the bridge of his nose, and looked straight at me with no expression on his face.

'Anxious?' he said. 'Sure. Aren't you?'

'I'm scared of *not* setting off,' I said. 'I feel like if I stay here too long, my life will find me – it will find some reason to call me back – and then I'll never get away. Don't you get that feeling too?'

Danny shrugged.

'Sure,' he said. 'Who doesn't?'

'So what do you want us to do? You're the client. It's your boat.'

A quick squall of breeze whipped through the marina, darkening the face of the water.

'Let's get ready, *as if* we were going,' said Danny Zeichner. 'I really can't decide yet.'

We loaded gas tanks, diesel oil, batteries, engine spares, distress flares. We loaded our own kit last. We sweated through the hot part of the day while the group on the next-door yacht sat under their cockpit awning, drinking pastis, smoking and watching us over their playing cards.

When the day cooled I showed Danny how to strip down the deck winches. He was good at it. He eased the winch drums off their spindles, carefully removed all the gears and bearings, cleaned off the old grease in a biscuit tin of mineral oil, and reassembled each winch with a care and precision I hadn't guessed he possessed.

'Danny,' I said, 'what do you do for a living?'

'I'm retired,' he said.

'Since when?'

'Since ten days ago.'

'So what did you do, before you retired?'

Danny sniffed.

'Nice sunset,' he said.

The sky was carmine shot through with gold. Starlings boiled over the rooftops of the vieux port. I started the boat's engine, to hear how it sounded, and we lay back in the cockpit and opened beers. Little wavelets slapped against the hull.

'So how do you like retirement?' I said.

Danny shrugged.

'Maybe I'll like it better when we're moving.'

The sun blazed scarlet on the lenses of his half-moon spectacles. I stood and looked out over the brooding roofs of Marseilles. Aloft in the higher darkness, the first stars were unfurling. I turned back to Danny.

'Now would be a good time,' I said.

'What?' said Danny.

'You can cast off the mooring lines, if you like. You can just untie them and bring them on board.'

Danny stepped down onto the pontoon and held the stern line in his hand.

'Now?' he said. 'Really? Just like that?'

'Yes,' I said. 'You do still want to go to Israel, don't you?'

Danny looked down at the rope in his hands and then he looked back up at me.

'What kind of a question is that, to ask a Jew?'

'A navigational one,' I said. 'Yes or no?'

'It's a very complex issue,' said Danny.

'It's a very simple rope.'

Danny's hands on the rope shone white in the gathering

darkness, and I listened to his breathing, fast and nervous, for a full two minutes. Then I watched the way his hands shook as he cast off the lines.

We slipped between the harbour walls, and set about coiling the ropes and stowing the fenders. It kept us so busy that when we finally looked back, the lights of Marseilles were already small and sinking behind us. When we had enough sea room to clear the Iles de Frioul, I pointed the bow south-east, and the deck beneath our feet began to move with the swell. The engine note lifted and fell with each wave, and the sea received us into its vastness.

I cut the engine and we got up some sail – half of the genoa and the mainsail with a reef in it. I thought we should just take it easy till Danny got the feel of things. I gave Danny the boat and laughed at the way he gripped the tiller and stared forward into the blackness, with eyes as huge and wide as a squid's. I opened him a beer.

'Relax,' I said, 'you'll get used to it.'

It would have seemed elemental and fearsome to him, that first night on black salt water. The hiss and surge as we lifted to the waves. The boat suddenly lying to an unheralded gust, then coming up again. The beams of unseen lights sweeping the cloud base to the north, the lighthouses themselves long sunk beneath our horizon. The dipping white of fishermen's working lights. The red, white and green navigation lights of container ships, seeming motionless at first and then looming past with silent and frightening velocity. Sometimes a spray of salt across the deck.

Sometimes an inexplicable scent of land: turnips, or sewage, or pine trees. A crackling from the hull. Below deck, the red light glowing above the chart table, preserving our night vision. The pair of us moving through dim crimson and drinking more beer and laughing when we clung to the backstay and pissed in the ocean and a bright outrage of phosphorescence rose from the deep to meet the hot stream.

Danny wore a yellow fisherman's oilskin top with the hood pulled tight around his spectacles and beard. He crawled along the windward rail to the bow, hung on to the forestay and looked forward into the blackness as the foredeck lifted and fell. He turned, and laughed, and shouted.

'This is the life, eh sonny?' yelled Danny.

'This is the life,' I shouted back.

Exhausted by wonders, Danny fell asleep in his oilskins in the well of the cockpit. I smiled down at him, and reckoned the hours till dawn.

It occurred to me that I should call Annabel and explain things, but when I looked at my phone there was no signal. I set the auto-helm to steer the boat for a few minutes while I went below deck to look at the chart. According to my reading of it, there was going to be no signal for the next two thousand nautical miles, give or take. It occurred to me that I should have got things straight with Annabel before we left Marseilles. I had a long night to think about it.

The sun rose out of the sea on our port bow. The wind was

coming from the north, a nice breeze, maybe fifteen knots. I shook the reef out of the mainsail and unfurled the rest of the genoa. The boat picked up speed. Danny woke up, stood and scanned the horizon through 360 degrees. Then he shaded his eyes with his hand, and tried again. Finally, he said, 'Okay, where is it?'

'Where's what?'

'The land, sonny.'

'Back there over the horizon. Next land we see will be the north of Corsica, in a couple of days if this wind keeps up. Then we'll turn right, down the coast of Italy.'

Danny nodded, stood with his legs wide apart and gave a nonchalant shrug.

'Sure,' he said. 'Turn right after Corsica. No problemo.'

I watched the empty horizon dance over the glass of his spectacles. Then I held the spectacles for him while he vomited, again and again, over the leeward rail.

When Danny was recovered, I slept through the morning while he took the watch. I told him to wake me if there was anything he wasn't sure about. He woke me once for a cloud he said was funny-looking, and once to ask me if I believed in God.

The wind stayed in the north. We fell into a routine: four hours on and four hours off. We sneaked between Corsica and Elba under a huge saffron moon that gilded the wave tops and bronzed our white sails. Then the wind died and we took a week just ghosting down the Italian coast. We used the thermal winds, hugging the coastline, using the land breeze at nights and the sea breeze in the afternoons. Some nights we went in so close you could hear the kids screaming down the promenades on their Vespas. Through the long windless mornings we drifted in the hot blue sea, flat and oily as ice, and watched green-fringed jellyfish going about their silent purposes.

'We're sailing through our history here, you know that?'

Danny stood on the rail in his Y-fronts and peered into the water, watching the golden ropes of sunlight coiling into the cobalt deep.

'Just look at it,' he said. 'This is the same Mediterranean the Romans rowed their galleys through. The same one Odysseus got lost in. It's like we could close our eyes and open them again and there would be Jason and the Argonauts, right in front of our eyes, because they are in their time and we are in our time, but there is always two metres' depth of water to navigate between us. Did you ever think about that?'

'No I hadn't, Danny. I like it.'

Danny beamed.

'So! Finally, sonny, the old man is teaching *you* something!'

At dusk the wind blew up from the west. We bowled down the coast with the spray sluicing across the deck and the sheets twanging like guitar strings. The boat was heeled down to its rails. We did seventy miles in the night, and when the dawn broke the deck was strewn with crash-landed flying fish and there was an ugly crack in the mast. We reefed the sails right down, fried the flying fish for breakfast and put in to Salerno for repairs.

After a fortnight at sea, Italy was pungent and brash. When we stepped up onto the concrete dockside, it rose and fell beneath our feet. To get out of the noise and heat of the city we took a bus to the ruins at Pompeii. The regular streets, the ashen greyness, the careful signage – it all reminded me of the suburbs. I pulled out my phone. I was getting a good signal. There was a text from Annabel. TAKE ALL TIME YOU NEED, it said. LOVE YOU. HERE FOR YOU WHEN YOU GET BACK. I read the message and then I read it again, and then I stood for a long time looking at a pair of calcified figures, entwined in the ash. I tried to think what to text back.

With the mast repaired, we refilled the fresh-water tanks, paid our marina fees and cast off at dusk. The wind was in the north, unsteady, sending little growling squalls that slammed into us, surged us forward, then left us in near calm. A big fish took the lure we trawled behind the boat, but it broke the line before we could haul it aboard. And that was thick, orange fishing line you could have held the weight of the anchor on. We saw one huge, gut-churning flash of moonlight on silver skin, but the monster never broke the surface. All night we watched a column of dull red sparks rising out of the sea far ahead, and as dawn broke the sparks dimmed and a colossal plume of smoke took their place, boiling up into an angry black anvil of cloud that reached into the stratosphere. As we drew closer later that day, the purple cone of Stromboli rose above the horizon to claim the base of the smoke.

Danny never once took his eyes off the volcano until it sank into our wake that night, in a sullen ruby glow of flame that lit up the underside of the low black rain clouds amassing on the horizon.

'So,' he said finally. 'This was a thing you might go through your life imagining was not in our world.'

At night, with no moon, emerging out of the boiling currents and sluicing whirlpools of the Straits of Messina, we hit a fishing net. It snagged the rudder and the boat stalled in the water. The drag of the net held the stern up into the strengthening wind. The waves thudded against the transom, the tiller swung unstoppably from side to side, and the rudder post squealed as it ground against the hull fitting. I had to go into the water and cut the net away, immediately, before it ripped the rudder out of the boat.

I tied a line around my chest, under my arms, and gave the other end to Danny. I said I needed him to hold on tight. I told him this had finished being hypothetical. I watched his knuckles whitening around the rope as I slid off the stern ladder into the black water.

I felt with my feet for the net. The boat's stern slammed up and down in the rising waves. I lost my grip on the stern ladder. I felt the mesh of the net on my leg, and I grabbed it and pulled myself along on it, under the water to the rudder. While the boat bucked and crashed down on me, I cut away the net with a bread knife. It fell away from the boat, but I was clumsy and a part of the net got wrapped around my leg. The net took me down with it. I saw a flash of torchlight on Danny's petrified face, and then there was salt and darkness. I saw myself drowning. I saw the faces of the Italian fishermen as they hauled my swollen green body aboard. As they dumped me out in the catch amidst the iridescent fury of sardines. I saw their interested faces, taking in my Reebok swimming shorts and my cropped blond hair: *Inglese?*

Then the line came tight around my chest. Danny Zeichner hauled me back into life. I stared at him for a long time, after he had pulled me back on board. Somehow, in the open sea, and terrified, the old man had worked out how to get my lifeline around a winch.

'I feel like Jonah,' I said.

'Actually I think Jonah was better-looking,' said Danny.

We drank Scotch.

The wind rose. I took three reefs in on the main, furled the genoa and ran up a storm jib. The boat lifted to waves as high as a bus, then sank sickeningly into each trough. The rudder post hammered against the hull fitting, and I worried it had been damaged. The wind screamed in the rigging. I took down all sail. I put on a survival suit and sent Danny down below deck to be safe. I put the boards over the companionway hatch, to keep out the spray and the breaking seas. I clipped my harness lines to both rails and tried by feeling alone to keep the boat afloat as each monstrous wave rolled onto us in the darkness.

The pale sun rose over a sea that was driven to a pure white fury. The spray came horizontal. I could see nothing. I held on, half frozen. Night came again. I dozed, exhausted, dehydrated. I hallucinated pop songs in the noise of the wind in the rigging. I thought the bucking deck was a flight simulator, and then a rollercoaster. I kept asking if the ride was nearly finished. In the darkness, I heard Annabel laughing.

By dawn, the wind had died to nothing. I woke to a ragged sky, circling seabirds and a long, confused swell that the boat was lying side-on to. I unclipped my harness, checked the boat topsides for damage, then went below. Danny sat on the saloon bunk, ashen, covered with bruises from the canned stores that had burst out of their lockers in the storm and now lay in dented chaos on the floor.

'Is it over?' said Danny.

'Yes,' I said. 'Are you all right?'

Danny stared blindly towards the light that came from the companionway hatch. His spectacles were lost or smashed.

'I thought God had decided to finish me,' he said.

I waited, but he said nothing more.

'Why would God do that?' I said.

'You asked me what I did before I retired. I was ashamed to tell you. I haven't lived a good life.'

'Well,' I said. 'It looks like God is giving you another chance.'

Danny smiled then, and I smiled too. I was thinking of land. Of places where fresh water sparkled in glasses, quietly on tables.

Of calm suburban evenings where the sea was a sheet to draw lines on. Of Annabel, bedecked with hula hoops. It seemed incredible that I had never seen the beauty of it all until now. The sea smelled clean and new, and the sun streaming down through the ragged clouds was the warm golden colour of honey, and the tea we made was hot and sweet and good. I closed my eyes and reckoned the days till our landfall.

It was Danny who noticed the water rising around our feet. Quickly it rose above our ankles, sluicing from side to side in the swell. It lifted the floorboards and rose so quickly – as high as our calves now – that it was obvious nothing could be done about it. No pump, no relay of buckets could get water out of that boat as fast as it was coming in.

Danny gripped the edge of the chart table and rocked back and forward, moaning. I made him put on a life jacket and I grabbed one too. I cast my mind around in panic to all of the places water can get into a yacht. I splashed through the rising flood to check all the stopcocks, and ripped out the companionway stairs to check the engine's water intake. Nothing. Then, with dread, I understood where the water was coming from. The rudder post, weakened by the fishing net, must have cracked in the storm and broken off in this swell. The jagged end had burst through the hull fitting, and now the sea was raging in through the rent. We were two hundred miles offshore, the hull must have a hole in it the size of a football, and we were sinking fast. The life raft had broken loose in the storm. We didn't even have bunk cushions to use as floats. I'd burned them in the dockyard in Marseilles.

Danny stopped moaning. He stared at the rising water while I explained the situation to him. His face was expressionless. He stood there blinking while I took the radio handset and made a hopeless Mayday call into the howling ocean static.

Then, standing in the cabin with water up to our knees, Danny nodded, and patted me on the shoulder, and said it was time to pray.

I had no words but I knelt with him in that rising water, feeling ourselves sinking into history. Two metres' depth of history, and under that, plenty of spare.

I realised I was weeping. Danny was cupping the flooding water in his hands, letting it run through his fingers. He nodded. He seemed to accept it. He even raised his cupped palm to his mouth, and tasted the approach of silence.

I watched his eyes go wide in surprise. Then he tasted the water again. For a long moment, he looked desperately confused. Then he smiled. The smile broke over his face like sunrise, and he began to laugh. I realised he had cracked. I felt the terror of madness entering into the place of our death.

'What?' I said. 'What is it?'

'The water!' said Danny. 'Taste it! It's sweet!'

I felt an overwhelming pity for the man.

'That's impossible, Danny,' I said quietly. 'This is the middle of the Mediterranean. It's all salt water here.'

'Taste it!' said Danny.

And I did. And the water was sweet.

When I realised what had happened, I began laughing too. I lay back in the cool, fresh water and let it wash all around me. I jumped up, and Danny stood too, and we kicked the fresh water up at one another and laughed and shouted and screamed for joy into each other's faces until our voices were gone and the world was changed and the future rose back into sight and breathed hugely, like a whale surfacing after sounding very deep.

The boat's drinking-water tanks, weakened by the storm, had shattered. The fresh water had flooded the boat, but once the tanks were empty, the water stopped rising. We collected as much of it as we could in bottles and jerrycans, and pumped the rest overboard. We saved enough fresh water to last us nearly until Crete, but by the time we sailed into Heraklion, bearded and wild, we were frankly down to Scotch.

It speaks its own language, the sea. It fades like a dream, and much of the sense of it is forgotten when your feet touch land. I sometimes try to explain to Annabel what I understood, that morning after the storm, as we hoisted the mainsail and unfurled the genoa and set out into the blue east with the quicksilver wake bubbling up behind us. I have tried, and Danny has tried, but both of us agree that a part of it is forgotten out there.

I remember that we laughed a lot, that morning. I remember we felt in awe of a world that was new and unfamiliar. With absolute certainty we knew that our position was 34 degrees and

47 minutes North, 17 degrees and 38 minutes East, but that no longer seemed sufficient to describe how far we had come.

From the rack beside the chart table, Danny Zeichner took the pair of brass nautical dividers. He opened them up to the span of his hand, and looked lovingly down at them, and smiled.

Bathyspheres

by Niall Griffiths

Fish markets in coastal towns and cities, wherever in the world, are fascinating, appalling places. I have been drawn to them from an early age. In west Wales, I've seen tubs of gutted flatfish, still thrashing emptily; de-clawed crabs blindly butting against palings, as if the theft of their weaponry has also robbed them of sight. In the Arctic Circle I witnessed the flensing of a minke whale, slabs of silvery corrugated skin slobbering away from the bone, the maroon jelly attached shimmering in the low and never-sinking sun. In the same place I saw thickets of narwhal tusks, arranged upright like bamboo. I saw an Inuit set up a stall on a street corner, his only wares a shot seal, which disappeared to the skeleton with each stroll past, until those bones too became sellable items, for soup or dogs, or delicately carved into *tupilak* – tiny statues of animals or sea demons – or holed and threaded onto seal-hide strips, to wear as adornment. I have seen beings made of foam, of seeming stone; beings that appear to be all mouth and stomach, fanged and red, lives measured only in gulps. Summations of both the predacious and the vulnerable, fish markets are; the thickly armoured and the terribly fragile, things that break under the mere weight of air. I can spend hours at such places, sniffing the air, accepting the colours. Wondering at the jumping whiskery things I share a world with, not all of whose eyes are dead; a kind of intelligence, unknowable but there, pleads from slabs and creels and nets. And the god that lives in my skin has a residence in these spotted scales and gaping mouths too, on this antenna, on this carapace. Fish markets are antidotes to solipsism, enabling us to gaze on a part of the planet that repels yet sustains us. Great cities we have built on the fins of fish. You can see, in the exhaust from chimneys, the echo of the plume from the blowhole of a cetacean. And there is a taunt in the ribs of ships, or in the deep green slime that carpets dockside buildings, concerning a world that you will never know; a mockery of a hunger that will never be assuaged. What else is down there, you think, as you stand agog amongst the cries of vendors and flash of scale and click of claw and dull gleam of landed shell. What else is down there.

I pointed to the crevettes and the lady behind the stall held up a wriggling handful of them and raised her eyebrows and said something to me in a language I didn't understand. The shellfish's scrabbling became more frantic as they were reanimated by the warmth from her skin. They pinched her fingertips with their claws. It looked painful. She didn't seem to mind. I held up five fingers, an open palm, and she shook her fist above a pot of boiling water, dislodging five into the hissing steam. The moment they touched the water they curled up like ferns, spade-tails to whiskers, and began to change hue, from their grey-blue black-laced quick colouring to their pink death shade. As they boiled I pointed at the slatey mound of oysters and again held up the open palm; the lady shucked them with impressive deftness and laid them on an open sheet of paper. She sliced a lemon in half and chucked that on top of them, then lifted the crevettes out of the water with a slotted spoon and tipped them on top of the oysters, then wrapped it all up and held up some fingers to indicate cost. I counted the unfamiliar coins into her hand. Thanked her and took my parcel down onto the beach, at the foot of a slipway whose mat of barnacles popped and spat like Rice Krispies in the pounding sun.

I sat in the shade of a beached boat and ate. The oysters flinched when I squeezed the lemon on them, and flinched again as they went down my throat. Their taste was astonishing: iceberg-clean, iceberg-cool, but strongly of the surroundings – the black sand, the scrubby bushes, the horizon's islands and the heated sea so blue that if you dipped a foot in there it'd come out coloured as if dyed. Each crevette I squeezed at the base of the head until I felt a crunch and then I pulled the head and guts away and, after tweaking the pincers off, flung them to the skinny and feral cats that gathered in an alert-eared and big-eyed group a safe distance away. I positioned my thumbs either side of the seam on the belly shell of the crevettes and applied pressure in opposing directions until the shells split and butterflied away and I could get at the dense, white, salty meat. I bit the pincers gently until they gave and I was able to suck the strings of flesh out of them. Then I sucked the empty shells. Then I licked my fingers. I lay back in the shade and dozed for a while, then got up and left the beach. The thin, small cats darted in on my leavings and when I looked back at them from the top of the slipway, they'd all found something to chew on and were happily doing so, the bones on their backs knobbling the fur. Scrawny little lions everywhere.

A drink was needed to both wash away and enhance the taste of the ocean that was filling my mouth. A beer at one of the beachfront bars would, I knew, taste so good that I'd stay in that bar until it was full night and I was helplessly drunk, so I bought a bottle of water and drank from it as I walked back up into the town, through the narrow alleys of near-white stone and across marble paving and into sudden and surprisingly big squares dominated by bell towers and ringed by cafés and bars. A sea town, this. So present was the sea here that my eyes began to ache from the perpetual squinting, even behind the sunglasses, against the glare of the sun rebounding off the water, no matter where in the town I went. When I licked my lips, I tasted brine. The stone floors beneath my feet were thick and solid and millennia old, yet seemed to rock and sway in imitation of a wave. Looking across a square, the floor in heat shimmer, and warped as it was by time and sun, appeared to roll and swell, roll and swell. Seasickness on dry land.

Never been earth creatures, us, not really. Gills we lack, but we're as at home on the water as off it, like gulls, if not quite seals or amphibians, because such grace we do not possess amongst the waving weed and bright and darting shoals. But see how our cities erupt from sand. How we plant flags on the tideline. The people in that town, their eyes were blue, and the plosives and sibilants of their speech would lap then crash then hiss on both rock and sand. The men moved in quick, busy flickers; the women, with a slow and swaying elegance. Even the lizards that scampered up and down the trunks of the palm trees on the seafront looked waterborne, as did the cats and dogs with their ribs visible through their fur, as if the older form beneath sought to break through, as if scales were trying to reclaim the limb and flank. As if all life on the land was simply killing time before, as one and as if at a prearranged signal, it would drop its tools and food and leap for the water again, even if what new forms awaited down there were incomprehensible and terrifying to those grown accustomed to a floor that stays still. No wonder the slabbed fish in the market died in mid-howl. Such hunger.

I wandered. I saw statuary and cathedral. Bought a bandanna in the clothes market which, within a few minutes of being wrapped around my head, was drenched in sweat. All roamings took me seawards. In the early afternoon I ate again, more sea-food, this time a thin sheet of white and flaky fish flash-fried and slipped into a soft bread roll, which I ate on a bench in a breeze off the ocean, offering some crumbs to pigeons which made the same noises there as they do anywhere else in the world. I wandered around the back of the town to skirt it on its mountainous side, but all roamings took me back seawards.

The sun suddenly seemed to be heating my knees instead of the top of my skull and I felt that I must drink. A sensation at my jaw and at my elbows. At the far end of the promenade I could see lights coming on at the harbour bars, so I aimed myself there. A large trawler was heading that way too and as I walked I watched it dock and saw its boom swing out over the harbour-side and lower a net containing a square object that looked like a large safe onto the concrete. A crowd gathered. The boat's crew leapt ashore and the net fell away from the object. The crowd circled it but didn't touch and I could feel, even from afar, that the distance they kept was a frightened one. Only one crew member touched the box, running his hands over its sides as if looking for a way in. I walked faster. I forgot about beer and joined the crowd and regarded the object, which still looked like a large safe, except stippled with barnacles and draped with weed and reeking of ancient mud. The sinking sun bounced back off something reflective on the object's side: glass. It had a window.

—English?

An old man at my shoulder. Tangled white beard and bald,

sunburnt head and faded blue eyes and scarlet starbursts of broken veins on his cheeks enriching the tanned-leather skin.

—Well, I told him. I speak the language.

He smiled with his gums, just three rotted teeth like the strut-stumps of an old pier the tide might reveal as it recedes from a shore.

He nodded at the object. A man was now pointing a long metal bar at it; scaffolding pole or something.

—Know what that is?

I shook my head.

—It's a bathysphere, he said. Old one by the looks of it. Maybe prewar. Must've broken off; they used to do that sometimes, in those days. Hauled it up in their nets. I really don't think they should open it. Be a big mistake, that would, to open it.

The man with the bar jabbed at the box and a clang resounded and a crust of barnacles fell off in a slab. The crowd was jabbering, excited, but when the man made another stab and the bar seemed to sink into the object, all voices were silenced. The bar was levered back and forth and a rectangular outline appeared on the bathysphere's side: a door. More levering warped the sodden metal and air escaped and brown water gushed and stagnant gurry sluiced across the dockside and another man joined in in pushing the bar and the door opened further and I caught a whiff of something that no one should ever smell, of something utterly alien and vile and hostile to human life, from a world of sucking slime and no light whatsoever and complete airlessness and suffocating wetness, home to gulping mouths to which a human body was a morsel and nothing but that. Sodden blackness, wet hell.

Rusted metal groaned and the door gave further. Rank air hissed out into the crowd and some vomiting went on and the crowd stepped back as one and some turned and fled. I felt a terror come into me. I didn't want to see what was inside that box. Terror crawled on my skin, wrapped me, prickling like a cobweb. Some gloop spilled from the door. More stench. Black gloop. Foul. Blindly groping its way across the dockside as if alive. Someone screamed. In that stinking black gloop, what looked like a large shell began to emerge. A large shell with teeth and eye sockets. Someone screamed.

—Aw bloody hell, said the old man. What did they think was going to be in there? Knew it'd be a mistake. You okay?

Stuck down there. In that metal box. In the wet blackness, all alone and confined, sinking further. How long would it take to die?

I managed a nod. The old man said:

—No, you're not. We need a drink.

His grip was strong on my arm as he led me away from that dockside and down an alleyway and into a small bar. He was greeted in the local language and I found a seat and the old man ordered drinks and sat by me and the drinks arrived; two beers, two brandies. I drank them quickly. To stop the shaking and to take away the vile taste from my mouth and to stop that rank air hissing in my ears and to arrest the gloop that crawled in my head. To swamp the thoughts of that box down there in the blackness and the panic and the terror inside it. To help me to sleep, although at that moment sleep felt as distant as my homeland.

—You okay? the old man asked again.

I nodded, and we spoke. He was very old; an ex-seaman. Been living in that coastal town for nearly four decades. He told me about his wives and his children and grandchildren. Told me that the sea hates human life. Told me that we should leave it alone because it doesn't want us down there and that in fact the sea past a certain depth contains all that we will ever need to know of horror and of hell. Bathyspheres, he said. Pure hubris. Complete stupidity. Why the need to look into the eyes of the devil? To descend that far? He had first-hand experience of it, he said. He'd been down in a bathysphere, many years ago. And he told me what he saw.

It was only a few years after the war. I'd missed the fighting by just a few weeks and my ship was patrolling the waters off the coast here. Course, many ships had gone down and were lying on the seabed. Subs and divers were exploring them for salvage and for anything that could be used as information about how to improve armaments and protection, searching for weak spots, that kind of thing. There was also some people that said that some men could still be alive down there, but I didn't believe

them. It had been too long. And just say if there *were* some survivors, if they'd somehow managed to find an airlock with food
in it or something like that, would they be worth rescuing? What
would've happened to their minds, down there? Smashed, they
would've been. Completely shattered. Best to leave them down
there until they just wasted away, that was my thinking. Callous?
Christ no. There'd been a world war on. The whole planet was
torn to shreds.

Anyway, a destroyer had gone down in deep water. Hundreds
of souls lost. U-boat torpedo. It had come to rest in a trench too
narrow for a sub and too deep for a diver but just right for a
bathysphere. There was a shortage of trained men. They needed
to know where the ship had been holed so they could make engineering alterations and strengthen certain areas, if needs be. Or
at least that's what they said. I've thought about this and come to
believe that their motives were different, but Christ knows what
they were. Testing the effects of underwater confinement on the
human mind, maybe. Something like that. Never trust those bastards. They wanted someone to volunteer for the job. No training,
nothing. Just straight in that bloody bathysphere and splash.
Down ye go. I put my name forward right away. I was young.
Wanted to explore the world. Wanted new experiences. And I'd
just missed the war and I was trying to work out why I was here,
on the earth. What, if anything, I'd been put here to do.

Wasn't much bigger than a fridge freezer, really. Just room
to lie on your side with your knees drawn up and your face by

the window. Claustrophobia didn't bother me, never has. Still would've volunteered anyway. Crammed myself in there with a pad and a pen and a torch and some food. Learned in minutes to use the valves on the oxygen tanks and how to operate the light and that was it. Thought it was snug. They winched me over the side. In my little box. Down into the sea.

It was blue at first, beautiful, with the rays of the sun slanting down. Then it went darker blue. Then it went green. Then darker green. I wasn't panicking then, no, there was no fear, I was excited to be entering an unknown world and at the thought of doing something worthwhile, y'know, helping humanity, doing something to justify my life on the planet. Not many men had gone where I was going. I was joining an elite group. Gradually it got black outside the window. Blacker and blacker. They'd told me not to use the light until I'd stopped descending, so I didn't. I just lay there as all light went. Until I could see absolutely nothing. Until the blackness was total. Until it was like I was in a box stuffed full of soot.

I went down for a very long time. I just sank and sank and sank. Thought to myself that no ocean trench could be this deep, that I was sinking to the very centre of the earth, that I'd appear out of the ocean off a shore in New Zealand or somewhere. The fall seemed never-ending. Surely there wasn't enough cable to drop me this far. I thought I'd never stop sinking. Had an image of myself, a tiny dot in a blackness so big that it couldn't be measured. Like one star in space. I prayed then. In my mind

I pictured myself in a bright green field, a sunny field. I prayed more. Cried, probably. Then the fall stopped and the box jerked and started to sway slightly from side to side and I knew that I wasn't resting on the seabed but that the chain had either run out or I'd reached the required depth, one or the other. I waited for the descent to begin again but it didn't. I don't know for how long I waited because the time had gone with the sunlight. I can't describe to you how black it was. I reached out and felt the glass in the porthole, then felt above that for the switch that would trip the spotlight. I flicked it.

They'd done a good job, those wreck-finding fellows. Knew exactly where to stop my descent. Because there, not twenty feet in front of me, was the downed destroyer. She'd landed on her hull and tipped a bit to the side so her portholes were tilted back. I could see the hole beneath her propeller where the torpedo had gone in. The light was dim but was bright enough. Things floated past my window, between me and the wreck, things like worms, flat like ribbons, without faces, wriggling. I couldn't breathe. The oxygen supply was working fine, it seemed, but still I couldn't breathe. I was deep under the ocean. Looking at a holed destroyer. I took up my pad and began to sketch and make notes, but my fingers weren't working very well. I was freezing cold. The side I was lying on was aching. There was a booming in my head. I reached for the lever that would move the spotlight and turned it so that the beam illuminated the vessel's portholes.

There was faces at them. At each porthole there was a face,

sometimes more than one, with eyeholes and mouths gaping. At me. As if those empty sockets could still see and those mouths still cry out for help. The skin was white and the hair was green like a weed and waving like one too. I pissed myself. I'll never forget the sudden heat of it under me and how it turned ice-cold in an instant. The faces went away from the windows and then, from the jagged hole underneath the propeller, I saw them come, not swimming as you'd expect, but crawling, dragging themselves through the slime of the seabed. I saw a dog move like that once, after its back legs had been smashed by a truck. Coming for me, they were. Their mouths and eye sockets wailed and I could hear those wails even through the metal of the bathysphere. Ever closer they dragged themselves. The mouth on the lead one was opening and closing like a fish and he was just a skull with skin on. I realised I was screaming. I turned the light off and lay there screaming in the blackness, and then a few minutes later I felt the box rock as they reached it. Side to side it rocked. They thumped on it with mushy fists. A face appeared pressed up against the window and I closed my eyes and screamed until I was deafened by the echoes and I just lay there in the blackness screaming until the box had stopped rocking and banging.

Time had gone away. I don't know how long I lay there, alone in that box in the deep. Hours it may have been. Maybe I thought I'd passed out and dreamed it all, because for some reason I turned the light on again. Found the strength from somewhere. Or even the curiosity still. There was the holed destroyer. There were the men, or what had once been men, dragging their way through the slime back towards the sunken ship, and there was a colourless fish the size of a bus going from man to crawling man and sucking each up into its mouth. Just hoovering them up, one by one. It had no eyes and its body was transparent and I could see its internal workings and I could see the screaming faces of the men it had swallowed, inside it, beating their fists against its sides.

When they winched me up they told me that the mechanism had jammed and I'd been down there for too long and had suffered a temporary psychosis brought on by lack of oxygen. Lucky I wasn't brain-damaged, they said, or worse. The mission had been worthless. My hallucinations were of no use whatsoever.

I've never been on the sea since; the last boat I went on was the one that brought me to shore, off that bloody ship. I've lived here decades and I will never set foot on a boat again. But maybe there's a kind of life down there that comes into land animals when they drown. We're aquatic in the womb; we're descended from sea creatures. All life comes from the sea and maybe it goes back to it, too, only in a form we'll never know. It's life like nothing we could ever imagine up here, breathing air, but a kind of life it is still, if life is just a yearning and a reaching. Or maybe it's just hell. Just hell.

They'll cremate me when I go, which won't be long now. And they'll spread my ashes on an inland mountain, into the wind. Fire, earth, air. Never water, no more. Even in my death.

The Greenlandic Inuit say that the sea is heaven; that, when they die, their souls are released into the place that has fed their bodies, that has allowed their earth lives, that has offered them bounty when in their fleshy forms. I wonder what that old man would say to that. I wonder too if he's still alive, or whether he's a drifting grey cloud whirled by the wind on a mountain top, baked by its proximity to the sun. Whether he's found rest in that dry death.

The sea is a discoverable realm like any other. Enter it and you push at a confinement. I'm still fascinated by fish markets.

In Time:
A Correspondence

by Erica Wagner

– for M.

They had stopped in the bandstand; he rested his bike, a mountain bike, against a bench. This was their third meeting, and the April day was generous to them, spreading clear light on the tufty grass like a blanket. Later she would remember this day like something held in a glass sphere; it would seem apart from everything else, as if it should be preserved, a marker of something, a beginning or an end. But then an end is always a beginning and a beginning is always an end; two for the price of one. Anyway, they had stopped in the bandstand.

Later she would consider how strange it was that everyone (by which, she wondered, one meant exactly whom?) wrote about love, or what was called love, when love was not mysterious at all. Love was simple, or at least the form of love that one most often found in stories was simple. This was usually, in fact, desire, but *love* has a better ring to it. Love is a bullet from a gun or a thrust from the hilt of a sword: love has a clear trajectory, an arc from point A (*he feels his heart move*) to point B (*she feels her heart break*). Nothing to it.

This was not that.

And so she began to tell him a story. An old story, here at the beginning of the 21st century. It didn't come out of nowhere, this story, it arose from the juncture in their conversation when she realised how much of what they said was somehow aligned, although they had, she would have said, not very much in common (only one peculiar thing, the thing they never talked about). She began to tell a story about a boy who walked through the cold to find the woman he'd met in his dreams, a woman black as coal, red as blood, white as snow. He left his home, his mother, his life; he carried nothing with him except five gold coins left to him by his father, a father who died long ago. She'd never told it before, but it came easily from her mouth, and he listened to this story of a journey, a story of ice, of death and hope. It was what she had to give him, though it did not belong to her.

Early afternoon, late afternoon; her phone peeped and she ignored it. The green dome of the Observatory on the hill had become a rising moon.

—Are you cold? she asked.

—Maybe, he said. Maybe it's getting cold.

—Well, she said, we could get something to eat.

—Okay, he said. That sounds like a good idea.

There was something in the story that had made them both hungry. There are certain kinds of stories that do this. They usually are stories which travel, stories with cold, stories where you're waiting for a hut and a fire and bowl of stew. As the spring wind began to pick up it was easy to imagine, on this tidy heath, how lonely it might be out in some northerly place with only five gold coins to keep you warm.

They walked down the hill – he was rolling his bike – passing the neat brass line that marked the two halves of the world. The gate that guarded the line was shut now, so they couldn't play the game of skipping from one half to the other, or holding hands across East and West. And yet, as they walked (now, just now, in silence) she understood that the two of them could be standing on opposite sides of the world and yet still be near, each hear the voice of the other, even if they never spoke of the peculiar thing that had led to their meeting.

The third time they had met. Luke, Sylvia; Sylvia, Luke. No romance. Something better. *This was not that.* And so they walked, in step, side by side, down the hill to where the street lights dropped their yellow eyes to the pavement, where the river slid on to the sea.

—Are you cold, Miss Cruikshank? he asked.

—They were standing by the rail. She was wearing only a light coat, and although she had a scarf, she had neither hat nor gloves. He had not expected that, to see her auburn hair, just like that, lifted away from her broad brow by the ocean's wind.

—I'm all right, Mr Norman, she said. She smiled at him, and the tip of her nose was red. Her knuckles were white.

—We should go inside, he said. He did not say, *Please, Alice, call me Robert*; that would not have been correct. He wished to be correct.

—Not yet.

The first time he had seen her he had noticed how she walked. The sea had been calm, flat calm, you would have said, like glass, and yet there was always motion, the great ship's engines roaring her along, the pull and push of the waves which rippled so lightly along the liner's prow but still somehow showed the water's cold green strength. So that when you walked even in a calm sea (not that he had ever been on any kind of sea before) you had to hold the movement within yourself, allow for it, somehow, and the ones who had to clutch at the rails or deckchairs, the ones who stumbled or didn't like the stairs or hesitated, were the ones who had not absorbed the motion into themselves. He had discovered that he liked the feel of the sea in his legs, in his hips, and when he saw her he thought that she must, too. She had walked to a settee carrying a book under one arm and a cup of something hot – he could see a curl of steam, a miniature of the steam that rose from the ship's funnels – in the other. She had sat; opened her book; begun to read, begun to sip. He had not said anything to her, that first day.

Of course there had been girls, back home. But this was different; not that he could have said how. Perhaps it was because his new life was beginning: what had been was no more, he could be whatever he would now. Back home he had done what had been expected of him, whether that was to keep his distance, or allow himself to be teased, or accept an invitation for tea where his back ached within five minutes from sitting up so very straight and the cup rattled on the saucer when he put it down and the girl was, all of a sudden and in the presence of her mother, no one he could recognise. Never mind the presence of his own mother, perched there always in the back of his skull. It was not on this ship, but on the train down from Glasgow, perhaps, that he'd begun to feel an expansion inside him, the seed of his own life waiting there and ready to sprout. A suitcase, a trunk, the skill in his hands, Canada. What was not possible now? It was the 20th century, after all.

So it was possible, the second time he saw her, to notice the tiny diamond set into a ring she wore on the third finger of her left hand and not feel disappointed, or afraid. It was the late afternoon, before dinner, and for something to do he had seated himself at the piano – how fine, that there was a piano – in the dining room, and played a little, some Bach, as well as he could. Strange, the way one makes one's own life; how he had hated his piano lessons! He had sworn that when he was grown he would never play. But here he was, on the ocean, at the piano, playing, and she had walked by, again with her book, and she had smiled at him, a small smile, and he had seen the light from the chandelier catch the stone on her hand. A glitter and she was gone, just like that. But he kept on playing, and wondered if the sound would carry out to her as she passed into the corridors of the ship.

The stone still flickered on her hand as she held the rail.

—Not yet, she said. Don't let's go inside, not yet.

Sylvia and Luke found a restaurant by the river that had white cloths on its wooden tables and a piano at the back. She found herself wondering if he played; there was something about his hands that made her believe he might. They ate the bowl of bitter black olives that had come to the table with their basket of bread; he ordered a bottle of red wine in the manner of someone who knew what he was talking about but didn't quite like to show it. She asked for a steak, very rare, and so did he; there were green beans too, cooked with soft slivers of garlic. She was hungry.

The waiter had brought their steaks and walked away; out of the corner of her eye she saw him talking to the maître d'; then the maître d' came over to the table.

—Excuse me, sir, he said, I think perhaps you dropped this?

Luke put down his steak knife and looked at the folded napkin the man was holding, and which he now unfolded before them. She sat up straighter in her chair to see, without wanting to seem to peer; the maître d' held whatever was in his hand as if it might be a secret.

—Why, yes, Luke said, sounding startled. That is mine. I had no idea… He reached down, as if to his belt, and frowned. The chain seems to have broken, he said.

It was a watch in the napkin, a gold pocket watch. She was surprised. With his wraparound sunglasses and bright white trainers, she would not have expected this, an antique, which it certainly was. The gold had that look of softness that comes with age, fine scratches laid over other fine scratches, the surface dulled with years of use, of being drawn against cloth, held against skin countless hundreds or thousands of times, even the bulb of the winding knob seeming worn by friction, by time itself.

The maître d' laid the napkin on the table, smiled and retreated. For a moment they sat in silence.

—Guess we leave a good tip, she said, and that made him laugh. It's a beautiful watch.

—Yes, he said. It was my grandfather's. I didn't know… He unhooked the little chain he must have had at his waist and pulled it up and into the light. One of the delicate links had stretched, and then snapped; she could see the jagged edge of the metal and then, when he put it in her hand (their fingers did not touch), feel its rough edge against her thumb.

—Lucky, she said. She sliced off some steak and put it in her mouth, chewed and swallowed. Suddenly, she felt extremely happy; as if Luke's good luck, his grandfather's watch, the steak, beans, red wine and bread were something she could keep, its textures, sights, flavours perfectly preserved for her like an object in a museum, even the maître d's grin and the little bow he had made before leaving them to their dinner.

—Can I see? she asked. She wanted to hold the watch, because it belonged to him, because it had belonged to his grandfather, because she had been there when it was lost and then found.

—Of course.

She set the chain on the table, and he passed her the watch. Again, he held it so they did not touch.

She took a sip of wine. Candlelight slipped over the glass face of the watch; behind the glass were narrow Roman numerals and, where the 'VI' would have been, a circle, inset, the second-hand dial, which ticked sturdily along. The hour hand and the minute hand were almost the same length, but the hour hand had, to distinguish it, a flourish at its end, nearly the shape of a slender spade from a deck of cards. She could feel the movement of the watch in her palm, tick tick tick, the wheels and cogs and springs busily turning within the casing, the golden house. She watched one full revolution of the second hand, and knew the minute hand would have moved. She sensed the machine's energy in herself, its pulse: as if she were sealed within its body, under its crystal dome. Contentment was not usually in her possession; and she wondered if it were much in his. Both of them seeking something not easily found, something rare. Across from her, he was eating his steak, drinking his wine, taking up a forkful of green beans. Time passed and did not pass, as if this moment would always exist.

She set the watch on the table between them and they continued their conversation as if they had not been interrupted, and as if their conversation had been going on for years. But then, when he had finished his steak, he wiped his mouth and looked at her, an expression on his face she could not quite read. Something contained or withheld.

—Let me show you something, he said.

Alice Cruikshank was travelling unchaperoned; just before the ship had sailed, Mrs Quinn (she had told him), who was due to accompany her, had been taken ill: appendicitis, she said. But her fiancé was waiting for her in New York and she did not wish to delay her trip. She would have the cabin that had been reserved for herself and Mrs Quinn; she would be (she had assured Mrs Quinn, as she was assuring him now) quite all right. Quite safe.

All this was said over dinner; the night after they had stood together on the deck, the third night of the crossing, he had invited her to dine. She had accepted. She viewed him, he had decided, as an older brother, let us say, and that was all right with him. Their table was set with good china and heavy cutlery, and the food was quite delicious, much better, he thought, than anything he had eaten before. He told her so, and although she agreed with him he wondered whether she was being polite. It seemed she might have been used to eating finer food than he all her life, but perhaps that was just her manner, her way, along with the graceful angle of her neck and the elegant curve of her wrist. He told her what a marvel it was that there were electric lights in the cabins of the ship; and began, before he could stop himself, to explain how the generators worked.

She laughed, but not unkindly.

—How do you know such things? she asked.

Blushing (he was sure), he explained himself. How queer that he took their acquaintance, as it were, as read! That was his work, he said: electricity, the making of it, the conducting of it, the use of it for illumination and power. Everything was changing, he told her. This was a new world. Gas lamps, oil lamps, the grease and weight of coal; all these would become things of the past. Of course, this great ship was powered by coal, but coal could make not only steam but electricity too. Electric light, steady and unchangeable as the sun. Electricity was the future.

He had made a speech. He had not meant to. He took a bite of his beef. It was very tender.

—You look, she said after a moment, as if you have an electric spark in your eyes when you speak of all this. She smiled, her gaze direct and unflinching. How bold she was, and yet how serene. The diamond shone on her hand, a spark in itself. He hardly knew what to say.

—I am a lucky man, he said. I believe in my work. In what I do.

—And you will bring your belief to the new world. That is good. I am happy for you. Then she paused. I am happy, she said.

Happy altogether. How strange to notice! One doesn't, normally, does one?

—No, he answered. I suppose one doesn't. And I am happy too. He was. Usually one was too busy to be happy; there was always movement forwards, towards some goal. Now he wondered if, because this great ship was doing all the movement for him, for them both, cutting north through the freezing sea, he could, for the first time, allow himself to feel content. Content in friendship. There could be something as simple, as precious, as that.

Neither of them had noticed the waiter who had stepped silently over to their table.

—Excuse me, the waiter said.

They both looked up and the waiter held out his hand, unfolding as he did a cloth napkin wrapped around an object: a gold pocket watch.

—Is this yours? I was told you might have dropped it. The waiter kept his voice low, as if losing a gold watch was a species of faux pas.

—My life. Why yes, he said. Why yes, it's mine. His hand moved to his ribs, where his watch chain was; and sure enough, the broken link was rough against his thumb. It would have slipped from its pocket – he knew not how – but no matter, here it was. His father's watch, given to him as he set out on this journey. Both the voyage and the watch marked his arrival in the world, he felt.

—I can't thank you enough, he said to the waiter. In his pocket there was cash, and he made to reach for it, but the waiter waved his hand.

—It is my pleasure, the waiter said. Please. He bowed and stepped away.

Across from him his companion took a delicate bite of halibut.

—You are a lucky man, she said.

—You don't have a watch? Luke asked. They'd ordered espressos, and outside on the street a siren skirled by, carrying someone else's distress or fear. In here there was safety, content.

She did – although, like him, she didn't wear it on her wrist. Her watch had a clip, not a chain, and she kept it hooked on her jeans. It was a blunt, modern thing, no delicate heirloom. She took it off, handed it to him, and he played with it for a moment, feeling its weight in his palm. Unlike his own watch, it was simply useful rather than useful and beautiful. He set them side by side on the tablecloth.

—What time is it? he asked her, although they were both looking at the two watches, the old and the new.

—Ten past eight, she answered.

—Exactly, I mean, he said.

She looked again. Eight-twelve, she said. And – some seconds.

Eight-twelve on both watches, but the seconds are different. Yours is a little faster.

—Right, he said. Good. Good.

He began to talk to her then. Listening, she worried that she had done too much talking in the course of their unexpected evening. It was a fear she always had: that she was for some reason afraid of silence and would fill any aural vacancy with noise, her own noise. She noticed, as he began to speak, that he had a coin in his hand, a fifty-pence piece. She had not seen him take it from anywhere – it was just there, as if he had made it appear out of thin air – and as he spoke he rolled it over his fingers, the fingers of his left hand, the fingers of his right. He did not look down; his movement worked of its own accord, patterned in him. Then the coin was gone, and his hands were empty. What, exactly, had he been speaking of? She laughed, and looked at him. *Trick* was not the right word for this. A trick was a swindle, a theft. *This was not that.*

You never know who you might meet, she thought. What they might be. Where you might find this, this particular moment, or sensation, or point of contact: she did not know what to call it. Here with her friend, in a place she did not expect to be, somehow away from the world – and yet this was the world. What if she did not have to leave this world? That was a fantasy, a dream.

—Thank you, she said. Thanks. I liked that.

—Good, he said. The thing is, he continued, I'm glad to be here, Sylvia. Are you?

—Yes, she said. Yes. Of course.

—We'll have to go back out, he said. To whatever else is there. You know. Life. All the other stuff. I don't know much about your stuff and you don't know much about mine, he said, shrugging his shoulders.

—No, she said. I suppose not. I don't care.

—Neither do I, he said. And I like it here. I like it here. I like right now. Do you like right now?

—Of course, she answered. I like right now. Right now is – perfect.

—So then, he said.

He passed his hands, quickly, over the two watches. He did nothing else. He did not touch them, or pick them up. And as she watched, the second hand of each one jerked, just at first, jerked, halted – and then: stopped. Stopped completely. Stopped dead, she would have said, and she was so taken aback she was surprised still to feel her own heart beating. Was that the noise and bustle of the restaurant, or was that simply the blood rushing through her body as he – her new friend – ground it all to a halt as a gift to her so she could hold it here, still? His hands open over both watches, steady, as if between his palms there was some force of energy, whatever it was that was stopping time. She bent down closer. Stopped. She looked up at him. He had seen what she wanted. Only this. One moment. Only this.

—Perfect, he said.

Pocket Watch of *Titanic* victim,
Robert Douglas Norman.

Unknown maker, *c.* 1880

Robert Douglas Norman perished in the *Titanic* disaster on the morning of 15 April 1912. He was one of more than 300 second-class passengers aboard the vessel heading for New York. Norman worked for an engineering company in Glasgow but had resigned his appointment with the intention of visiting his brother in Vancouver before completing his world tour. This gold-cased watch was found among his clothing when his body was recovered. The rusted watch hands still show the time the watch was reading when he entered the water: 3.07 a.m. Clocks and watches on board the *Titanic* would have been set daily to account for the ship's new local time but at the time the ship sank, approximately 2.20 a.m., it seems Norman had not had the opportunity to reset his watch from the previous day's local time.

ZBA0004/D8137

[From *Treasures of the National Maritime Museum*, edited by Gloria Clifton and Nigel Rigby, National Maritime Museum, London, 2004, p. 212]

Something Rich and Strange

by Charles Lambert

Pushing aside the Joyce lecture he has been working on since breakfast, Andrew Clough takes from his jacket pocket a small green book. The cover is stained and warped, brown cardboard exposed at one corner where the cloth has frayed. He plays with it for a moment, turning the book over in his hand, then flicks through the first few crinkled pages, fine as rice paper, almost transparent. Comments, now faded, have been written in the margins, but he ignores these, pausing only when he comes to a page on which parts of a passage have been underlined more than once. He reads:

> And if there were some way of contriving that an army be made up of lovers, they would overcome the world. For what lover would not choose rather to be seen by all mankind than by his beloved when abandoning his post or throwing away his arms? Or who would desert his beloved or fail him in the hour of danger?

Sliding the book into his pocket, he stands up and crosses to the window, looking down into the car park and then, when his vision has cleared, across the city's rooftops to the distant hills. He was offered an office larger than this and facing the sea, in recognition of his years of service, but turned it down.

Andrew has always hated the sea. Long before the war began, as a child, when his parents used to take him to his aunt and uncle's in Aberystwyth and dress him in trunks his mother had knitted him that sagged as soon as they were wet; he hated the cold dark sucking of it against his skin, the boundlessness of it. That's Ireland over there, his father said, pointing towards the horizon, but Andrew didn't believe him. Andrew imagined an edge over which the sea poured endlessly.

Even now, his most lasting memory of holidays is of the day a boy his age was drowned, not far from the beach. He'd watched him being brought up out of the water by two men, the dead eyes staring out, the skin like milk-soaked bread. The sea can be very treacherous, he heard an old woman say in a café that afternoon. Later he asked his mother what 'treacherous' meant. It's when someone lets you down, she said, because she hadn't heard. But it was odd to think of the sea as someone.

Andrew spent the first months of the war building defences and undergoing basic training near Birmingham. When he could, he would leave the barracks and walk along the canals of the city, reciting poems under his breath or scribbling lines of verse in a notebook he carried with him. He didn't think about the sea at all, didn't consider that as soon as the training was over he would be forced to travel to the fighting inside a ship. Then, after four months in the camp, they were posted abroad.

Davies, one of the other lads from the training camp, must have seen the colour drain from Andrew's face as they climbed down steep metal stairs, their boot nails rattling on the rivets, no space to turn. We'll be snug as two bugs in a rug down here, he said, slapping Andrew's back, and Andrew swallowed and nodded, unable to speak. He had never been in a space with walls that curved and stifled. I can't swim, he said in the end, because he had to say something, and Davies, an apprentice butcher from Peterborough who had latched on to Andrew since the first few days of training, when no one else had wanted him, laughed. Swimming won't be much use if you're stuck down here, he said, in his sneering way. You'll be dead before the water gets to you.

The crossing was rough, but Andrew's stomach, to his surprise, held out. He envied those men who were sick; even vomiting seemed an occupation of a sort. When the others slept, he read, with the light from a torch, the book his mother had given him.

It was Shakespeare's collected plays printed on India paper; it just fitted into his pocket. That's what you're fighting for, she'd said, pressing it into his hand. If you have any doubts about defending England you just read Shakespeare and remember that.

He opened the book and read: *Now would I give a thousand furlongs of sea for an acre of barren ground, long heath, brown furze, any thing.* Closing his eyes, he thought of the open land behind his parents' house, where the tinkers kept their horses and he had learnt to ride his first bicycle. He thought of the way the grass broke his fall when he tumbled, the way the earth held him up. Beneath his breath, he said the words *long heath, brown furze.*

After an hour or so, when the roll of the ship had abated, he went to the mess deck and up the narrow stairs until he stood beside an unmanned gun turret. Sinking down on his haunches to avoid the wind, he lit a cigarette, took his Shakespeare out of his pocket again. There was just enough light from a porthole above his head for him to see the page.

'What are you reading?'

Andrew, startled, looked up. It was hard to see who had spoken.

'*The Tempest,*' he said.

'Isn't that rather tempting fate?' the man said, crouching down beside Andrew so that his face and officer's uniform were visible. His leg was almost touching Andrew's. Andrew was about to stand up and salute, but the man caught his arm. 'At ease, soldier,' he said, with a smile. 'I imagine we're neither of us supposed to be here, so let's ignore protocol, shall we?' He glanced down at the book. 'How far have you read?'

'Prospero's just telling Miranda how his brother betrayed him.'

The man nodded. 'Ah yes. That bit about trust. Have you reached it yet?'

Andrew nodded.

'Well, be a good chap and read it out, will you? I don't suppose you've got another fag, by any chance?'

Andrew gave the man a cigarette, found the passage and read it aloud, his voice at first hesitant and then more confident, until the last but one word, before which he paused:

> and my trust,
> Like a good parent, did beget of him
> A falsehood in its contrary as great
> As my trust was; which had indeed no limit,
> A confidence sans bound.

'That's the way trust ought to be, isn't it?' said the man in a slow dreamy voice, as though to himself, drawing on his cigarette, his long face hollowed out, his eyes half closed so that Andrew could examine him for a moment. He couldn't have been more than a year or two older than Andrew, his hair the same light brown, a razor burn on his neck. They might have been brothers.

'Sans bound.' Like Andrew, he pronounced the word 'sans' in the English way, to rhyme with 'cans'. 'Nicely read, old chap.'

'Do you know where we're going?' said Andrew, flicking his cigarette away from him, into the sea. He felt grateful, he wasn't sure why. He had never been praised for reading aloud before, except by his mother. He had learnt to listen to the words in his mind. The man shook his head before turning to smile, an unexpected smile that startled Andrew.

'They don't tell us officers any more than they tell you lot half the time,' he said, and the smile disappeared. 'It's a bloody foul business, that's all I know.'

He stood up, shaking the creases out of his trousers. To Andrew's surprise, he put out his hand to help Andrew up. He didn't let go immediately, but held Andrew's hand for a moment, staring into his eyes with a quizzical expression, and then, as if the idea had only just occurred to him, began to shake it. He was taller than Andrew by a couple of inches, and thinner, slightly stooped at the shoulders. His uniform looked too big for him.

'Toby Spender,' he said, bowing his head a little. 'How do you do?'

'Andrew Clough.' Andrew paused, then added: 'Spender? Like the poet.'

Spender smiled. 'Well, that's true for both of us, isn't it? Good old Arthur Hugh Clough. *Amours de Voyage.*' Another pause. 'No relation, I don't suppose?'

Andrew shook his head, amused. Behind Spender's back, like

fireflies, were the flickering lights of a distant ship. Andrew had the sense of the sea beneath the hull of his own ship, so large, so fragile; a depth he could hardly imagine.

'You've read him? Spender? Stephen, that is.'

Andrew nodded. The other man's hand was warm and dry in his, the pressure constant. He felt uncomfortable, as though they were being watched, and was about to take his hand away. At that moment, as if he had understood, Spender let him go and turned to leave.

'Well, Andrew Clough. See you on dry land,' he said. 'And I'd get back to your berth if I were you.' He grinned, an eyebrow raised. 'Before an officer catches you.'

Andrew himself had almost drowned, the summer before the war began, during a cycling holiday in Cornwall with a colleague from the bank. They had taken the train to Exeter, and then a local train, sitting side by side on the wooden seat as it travelled along the coast, not talking, unread books in their hands. After the third day's cycling, they stopped at a pub near Helston. Neither of them was used to alcohol; the local ale loosened their tongues. They began to laugh at how silent they had been. Outside, in the cold air, Greaves suggested they cycle to Kynance Cove.

Greaves stripped off and ran down the sand, his white back luminous in the moonlight, his high-pitched cry like a tear in cotton as he cartwheeled into the water. Soon he was nothing but a head and beckoning arm. Andrew, sobered by the ride, would have watched him from the beach, but Greaves called to him to come and it would have broken every bond they had made if Andrew had refused.

He took off his clothes and walked into the water. It was colder than he had imagined, and heavy; it held him and settled around him. It suckered to his skin. He stared out into the emptiness, where no line indicated the edge of the sea, the edge of the sky, as though the world were one dark element. Greaves was nowhere to be seen.

Andrew called out his friend's name, aiming at high-spiritedness at first. Greaves, he shouted. Then, with a sense of barely earned intimacy: Richard. When there was no reply, his voice changed tone, he couldn't help it. He turned to the beach, but the sea wouldn't let him leave. It seized him by the chest and waist, threw supple, unbreakable bands around his thighs. He raised his arms, then plunged his hands back down into the water to push against the tide, if that was what it was, fighting against the strength of it, *this thing*. He had no idea of time.

Greaves was waiting on the beach, towelling his hair with his shirt. You're white as a sheet, he said. I can't swim, Andrew spluttered, and began to laugh, bent over naked, hands on knees, his heart pounding frantically against his ribs. I thought I'd never get out alive. Greaves rubbed his back with the wet shirt until the skin began to burn.

They disembarked at Cherbourg. Andrew didn't see Spender again for over a month. After a night march across country, through fields of turnips and disgruntled sheep, his platoon had been billeted in farms outside a village whose name no one knew. Andrew was in a barn with Davies, who would not be put off, and six others from the platoon, asleep on rudely made beds of straw-stuffed sacks. Exhausted, he couldn't sleep. He knew they would soon be woken and moved on, or expected to form a team for football, because they had to be occupied at all costs. Anything rather than think. Yet not a day went by that he didn't think about Spender and wonder where he was.

He left the barn and walked along the road from the farm, keeping it in his sight, until he found a fence he could sit on. The thing he loved most, he now knew, was to be alone. He had never understood this before, it came as a shock to him. To be left alone, with a cigarette and a book. Patting the Shakespeare in his pocket, he thought of Greaves, who had signed up for the Navy shortly after their holiday and not kept in touch. His ship had been sent up to Norway after the Germans invaded; he might easily be dead. What was it Spender had said? This bloody foul business. Some miles from where they were now, Andrew had seen a burnt-out truck with the driver hanging out of the hole where the door had been, his left arm, crimson and black, burst open like a sausage. *Of his bones are coral made; Those are pearls that were his eyes.* Even that would be better than drowning, he thought. To lie full fathom five.

Two men and a young girl in a coat too big for her passed with suitcases, looking away from him as though ashamed of themselves, or for him, he wasn't sure, and then some boys leading a donkey and a cow. He closed his eyes, saw Greaves staring at him that last evening, like someone condemned to death. I won't come back, he'd said.

When he opened his eyes a moment later Spender was watching him. He was standing on a high bank on the other side of the road, his expression patient, his hands in his pockets, as though waiting for a bus. Andrew wanted to see what he would do, throat dry, his breathing interrupted.

Spender began to smile, a slow smile that transformed his face, then took one hand, his right hand, from his pocket and gave a little wave, low at the waist. Andrew, in his turn, held out his cigarettes as if to entice a child or nervous animal. Spender leapt over a ditch and darted across the road as it filled with people on the move, stumbled against a woman with a crate of hens on a makeshift trolley drawn by string. Andrew moved to salute him with his free hand but Spender, glancing round, caught his arm as he had done the first time, shaking his head. *We don't need that.*

'How goes *The Tempest*, Andrew Clough?' he said. Andrew grinned, flattered to have his name remembered.

'Blown over,' he said. 'Where have you been billeted?' Spender jerked his head down the road, in the opposite direction from the barn.

'In the notary public's house.' He twirled his hand in mock obeisance. 'With his wife and three lovely daughters.'

Andrew didn't answer, wasn't sure what should be said. He glanced up the road. 'I'm in that barn,' he said. 'At least it's dry.'

'You won't be there much longer,' said Spender. 'We're on the run, old chap. Leaving the whole sorry cock-up to the French.' He scowled. 'But I expect you knew that, didn't you?'

Andrew nodded.

'I didn't expect the hot gates,' Spender said, 'but there's something rather squalid about turning tail quite this keenly.'

'The hot gates?'

Spender smiled again. 'Thermopylae. Where three hundred Spartans fought to the death in their bid to hold off the mighty Persian army.' His tone was playful, histrionic. Andrew had never been spoken to like this by any man before. 'Five million soldiers strong, according to Herodotus. Which presumably makes us the Spartans. Or would do if we decided to stay.'

Andrew nodded again. 'T. S. Eliot,' he said. He started to recite, his voice excited:

I was neither at the hot gates
Nor fought in the warm rain
Nor knee deep in the salt marsh, heaving a something,
Something something, fought.

'I didn't know what the hot gates were when I read it,' he said, shaking his head as if at his own stupidity. 'I'd wondered. I didn't know who to ask.'

'The benefit of a classical education,' said Spender, one eyebrow raised. His eyes were brown; they gave him a foreign look, thought Andrew. 'Perhaps the only benefit.' He reached into his pocket. 'You should read this,' he said.

Andrew took the book from him. Opened it. On the left-hand page was Greek, on the right English.

'It's Plato's *Symposium*,' Spender said. 'I'm afraid I've scribbled in it a bit, but you can read round my nonsense, I'm sure.' When Andrew tried to give it back, he shook his head.

'No, no,' he said. 'I'd like you to keep it.'

'Thank you,' said Andrew, sliding the book into his pocket. And then there was an unembarrassed silence, the two men looking curiously at each other, expectantly, it seemed to Andrew; a silence that was only interrupted when two red admirals lifted from the hedgerow behind them, bright flickers of scarlet and black, and danced for a moment around their heads in what struck Andrew as a sort of blessing. He watched Spender's eyes follow the butterflies, return to him, questioning, unhurried, as though there were no retreat, no war.

'And what do you do?' Spender said. 'When you aren't defending France against the Persian hordes.'

'I work in a bank.'

'Like Mr Eliot himself.'

'Yes,' said Andrew, who surprised himself by adding: 'In the warm rain of the Worcester branch of Lloyd's,' then revelled in Spender's amusement. Because now it was Andrew's turn to speak in a way he had never used with anyone before, to speak about books, about himself, as though these things could be shared. It felt, more than anything, like confession. 'I think I was more use there than I am here.'

Spender reached over and brushed Andrew's fringe off his face, then rested his hand on the side of Andrew's head, over his ear, his fingers curled round towards the neck in a sort of cradle. Andrew pushed his head harder against the man's hand, the way a dog butts into its owner's palm. When Spender removed his hand, Andrew's skin felt hot.

'We never know where we might be useful,' Spender said.

Back at the barn, the others were shaking straw out of sacks, shaving with cold water from a bucket. They looked up when Andrew walked in, but left him alone. We're off, Davies said, hurrying into the barn from outside. Andrew wondered where he had been. Davies came over, spoke to him in a low, offended voice. I was looking for you, he said. Sergeant's been in, in a right old paddy. Effing and blinding, he was. Says we're being evacuated sharpish. You'd better look lively, Dopey; he'll have your guts for garters if he sees you mooning round.

As they left the barn, Davies sidled up again. Chumming up

with the brass then, are we, Dopey? he said in his thick voice, teeth too big for his mouth. Andrew felt sick. Had Davies been watching? I don't know what you mean, he said. I think you do, said Davies. He took a few mincing steps, turned back. I think you know just what I mean.

Thirty-six hours later they came to a forced halt a dozen miles from the sea, the road to the beaches clogged by soldiers and civilians. Ambulances were parked at the side of the road some distance from where they were standing. The column had been strafed twenty minutes ago, someone said, by a lone Stuka. They'd be held up until the dead were cleared away, the wounded attended to. Andrew walked over to the ditch to piss. Beneath him, surrounded by broken cow parsley and bramble, was a dead boy in a white shirt, no more than fifteen, his legs blown away but his face untouched, his lips in a half-smile. Andrew remembered the face of the drowned boy he had seen as a child, bloated and bleached by the sea. The dead hair plastered to his head. He buttoned his trousers up and moved away. Brown furze, he thought. *Long heath, brown furze.*

Soon after, he reached into his pocket and pulled out the book Spender had given him, the first chance he'd had to look at it, although he'd thought about nothing else; he opened it at the first page and found 'Toby Spender' written there and, beside the name, a date. February 1933. Andrew held his breath, felt his eyes smart. Toby, he whispered. And again. Toby. There was nothing he could do about it. He felt as though his life, his heart and head, had been handed over, without condition, to Toby Spender, who must have had this book at school, seven years before, and had saved it for him, had carried it with him until the moment had finally come and he had given it to Andrew.

Later, when he read the parable of the perfect spheres, how each of us is half a sphere in search of its other half, he thought, of course, how could I not have known at once. This was what Miranda had meant when she said to Ferdinand:

> I would not wish
> Any companion in the world but you;
> Nor can imagination form a shape,
> Besides yourself, to like of.

The port had been bombed earlier that day. They were told to head to the beaches east of the town. Shattered glass crackled beneath their feet as they trooped along empty streets until they reached the dunes, where the glass gave way to sand. It was like being on holiday again, thought Andrew wildly, weak with fatigue, that mixture of expectation and fear as the sea approached. But between him and the water stretched ten thousand, a hundred thousand men, each lost to the rest as though the world had disintegrated into chaos.

He looked beyond the men towards the sea, expecting ships. But there was only the blank expanse of water. It was almost dark, the Channel looked glass-like, grey. We're here again, he thought.

They've fucking ditched us, said a voice at his side. He turned and saw Davies. They've been and gone, the bastards, they've fucking let us down, Davies said and looked at Andrew with contempt, but also need, as though Andrew might know something, or have something that might be useful. All Andrew wanted was to get rid of Davies and track down Toby, because surely Toby would be there as well.

He strode towards the promenade, followed by Davies. They're going to leave us here to fucking die, Davies said. They came to a row of corpses laid out on the path in front of them, heads pointing towards the town, feet out to sea. Skirting the bodies, they walked to the beach. They'll never get ships in here, said Davies, it's too fucking shallow. We'll have to fucking paddle back to Blighty. Andrew began to laugh. If only that were true, he thought.

It was two days before any ships arrived, the sky criss-crossed by Stukas. Andrew couldn't shake Davies off. When he snatched a few hours' sleep, Davies would be there beside him as he woke, boots off and tied together by their laces, doleful eyes fixed on Andrew, with food he had scavenged while Andrew was sleeping.

Bread, some rinds of cheese, a rabbit carcase they ripped apart with their hands, washed down by flat warm beer, gritty with sand. Behind them, thick smoke rose from the town front into the blackness of the sky. Davies had heard that boats were coming and was cheerful now. They'll get us back, he said, rubbing his grease-smeared hands on his backside. You and me together, he said, we'll be all right.

Andrew ignored Davies most of the time, his eyes on the men around him as they came and went. Once he thought he had spotted Toby, but he was mistaken. Another time, convinced, he broke into a run, with Davies hobbling behind him, whining about his blisters. On the beaches, engineer units were building jetties out of abandoned lorries so that the troops could clamber along them to the boats. It struck Andrew that Toby might be among them, and he struggled through the milling soldiers to see, but had no luck. Men gathered round the empty jetties, ready to embark.

Early on the second day, exhausted, Andrew sat in a shallow hole dug in the sand and read the book that Toby had given him, with Davies at his side, grumbling under his breath, trying not to sleep in case Andrew took his chance and wandered off. In the half-light, protected by a lorry bonnet he and Davies had dragged from the road, Andrew read what the book had to say about love and found his vision blur with tears of gratitude. He felt as though each word gave him form and substance. He felt like someone lost at sea who'd woken to find himself on land. When Davies finally succumbed to sleep, Andrew left him to search for Toby.

And then the evacuation began. Andrew filed with the rest of the men towards the piers made earlier that day. He stood on the rough planks secured to lorries, with soldiers pushing him from behind and on every side, his head turned back towards the beach. Small boats of all kinds, half visible in the fading light, shuttled between the piers and the ships waiting further out. Perilously close to the edge of the rocking planks, Andrew tried not to look at the sea, black-shallow and slicked with oil. I'll wait for him, he thought, I'll find him somehow.

When a rowing boat filled with soldiers swayed close to the pier, no more than feet away, someone pushed up beside him and grabbed Andrew's arm. There's room in that one, Davies said, as if they had never been apart, and, to Andrew's horror, dragged him over the pier edge and down, into the water. They were trapped between the pier and the tall side of the rocking boat.

Grab fucking hold of it, screamed Davies into his ear, it won't be for long. Andrew, choking, felt hands reach down for him to clutch at his tunic, lifting him by the scruff of it from the water. He had put the *Symposium* in the breast pocket of his shirt, next to his Shakespeare, where it was best protected. Oh God, please keep it dry. His kicking feet touched bottom, which gave him the strength he needed to struggle up into the boat, falling across the men already there, who cursed him as they moved to make room. Davies, gasping, slapped him on the back.

I'm not going to lose you now, he muttered, as though Andrew had become some sort of charm. The words struck Andrew as irrevocably as if he had said them himself to Toby. Not now, he thought. Not now. He stared back inland, towards the beach, straining his eyes in the dark to see the single face that counted.

He heard Toby calling before he saw him. He heard his own name being called from the water. The boat he stood in was no more than a dozen yards away. He could see Toby's face quite clearly, strained and white, as he swam.

Andrew held out his arms, shouted to the rowing men to stop. He was about to jump back into the water, careless of its depth, when Davies pulled him back by his jacket. You leave him be, he said, he'll be all right; and then, to the rest of the men in the boat, We don't want any nancy boys in here now, do we, lads? Andrew faltered, too shocked and ashamed to move. For a moment, he seemed to lose his sight, his speech. He spun round to Davies, whose face was inches from his, sour breath in his nostrils, and pushed him away with a howl. But Davies grabbed Andrew's arms and began to jig about while the other men laughed. Andrew struggled to get free as Davies pulled him in hard to his chest and hugged him, pushing his cheek against Andrew's, blowing a kiss into his ear. Tiptoe through the tulips, Davies sang. He might have carried on if the sea behind them hadn't been strafed by a Junkers. We're under fucking fire, said one of the men.

By the time Andrew flung Davies off, Toby Spender had disappeared.

Often, Andrew dreams that he is standing on the deck of a boat. The sea around him is flat and still, with a hard metallic sheen. He watches the surface pucker like water in a pan about to boil, then erupt into bubbles that rise and swell and become men's heads. The men nearest the boat lift up their arms as one, and hold them out towards him, and call his name.

He has never slept beyond this. He lies among the tangled sheets of the bed until his heart stops pounding, then goes into the bathroom and turns on the light. Looking at himself in the mirror above the basin, each time with surprise, he sees that his face is wet. His throat aches and feels empty, as if he has been shouting.

Forgive me, Toby, he says.

The Island

by Roger Hubank

In the end she went home, in spite of herself. She decided to go by coach in the hope the long, slow journey might give her time to think. Yet when it came to it she sat there passively, her mind a blank. There was even something soothing, sedative, in letting herself be carried along. Yielding to familiarity. Knowing what was coming next.

The miles went by. Prosperous farms slid past. Green hedgerows filled with flowers.

Then the hillocky country. A country of many small lakes, the hillocks emerging above the water as tiny round-backed islands. Winding lanes. Now and then, in a sheltering cluster of oaks or sycamores, a low, whitewashed farmhouse with black-tarred plinth. Outhouse doors brightly painted. Potatoes and oats to the verge of the bog.

Further west the land fell into its familiar desolation. A wilderness of bog and heather. Raw wet trenches where the turf had been cut. Tumbled walls and roofs proclaiming the harsh history of a district that offered little now beside the fish farm and the road gang. The stony land and the sea.

At Drumbeg, changing to the local bus, Caitlín O'Malley wondered again why she was always drawn back. For days it had been hanging over her. It was something she'd always done. Every year the same, though with increasing resentment as she'd grown older. And she couldn't explain to herself why she gave in to it. This venerating the dead. Where she came from, a man got off his bicycle, took off his cap and stood in the road as a funeral passed. Was it the deceased to whom they paid their respects? Or was it something deeper, something bred in the bone? Hugh James, her grandfather, used to say it wasn't by chance a man was born on Inishmor rather than the mainland. He said that the cruel and remorseless old foe that had given shape to the island shaped the destiny of every man and woman born there, even to their children's children. He shared the fatalism of all that generation.

No, no, it's my life, she used to tell herself. *To do with as I please.* Because otherwise she was nothing.

Yet her life was also a story which began inside another, older story, and around all the stories circled the imprisoning sea.

Westward, though, the skies were steadily brightening. At Delaney's, at the head of the glen, lambing was in full swing. Mickey Delaney grinning, raising a hand as she waved to him from the window.

The big barn must be full of lambs, she thought. For the

holding pens were full of frantic ewes milling about. The air filled with their urgent baaing.

Now the bus was rounding the head of the lough. And now, with a shifting of gears, engine racing, it started on the twisty climb over the mountain. Up there, under a thin skither of snow, with the winter sun low in the sky, an eye that knew what it was looking for could trace the lines of ancient fields and walls. Habitations that went back a thousand years. Forts, stone tombs and burial mounds of a culture that was old before Christ was crucified.

Then, as the coach bustled through a rocky cutting, the first glimpse of the islands. Inishmor. Inishbeg. Chunks of malachite in a sea of shimmering pearl. Never quite real.

The coach pulled into the side of the road and drew up with a hiss of brakes. The unofficial stop for visitors. Today there were no more than three or four. Off they trooped, Willie Roche jumping down from the cab and going round to greet them. She watched him pointing, gesticulating, spinning them the tale as they trained their binoculars, gazing out at the islands. Usually they were disappointed. There was rarely anything to see.

At last they set off again, descending the mountain. Below, a chequerboard of little fields. White houses scattered this way and that, battered by Atlantic winds. Now, familiar things were looming up to greet her at the roadside. An old phone box invaded by a tree. A derelict shelter. In a field a cart dumping dung. A man walking after, forking it up, flinging it about.

In a place where nothing changes, it struck her suddenly, past and present are the same.

She had herself experienced more change in a year than her father had known in a lifetime.

At first she was terribly homesick. She grieved for a whole term. She grieved for a pattern of tiny fields. Dry stone walls. Bogland marching away to distant mountains. She grieved for the swell and fall of sea wrack. The creamy swirl of the tide over the stone flats. She found she could visualise every stone and tree around her home. Even the people waving as she passed them on the bus. Not like the city. She found it a place of volatile emotions. Its people disputatious. Sharp-witted and sharp-tongued. Oh, and bold. A country girl from an old-fashioned place, she could never quite get used to the naked stares of workmen whistling after her. The lorry drivers hooting at her in the streets.

Yet if Kate O'Malley was not conscious of her looks, others were. P. J. Byrne, the schoolmaster and language scholar, remembered little Cáit Ní Mháille as a child blessed with the beauty praised by the poets of old. Black hair. Black brows. Cheeks the colour of foxgloves. Martin Lavery, seeing her working behind the bar of Quinlan's singing lounge, fancied her dark curls hung down like grapes. Clusters of grapes, on each side of her face.

Her father never looked at her but saw with a pang the sweet face of his dead wife.

It was Martin who showed her the city. One autumn afternoon they wandered along the embankment. On Merchants' Quay, beside the Monument, they came across a mad old man. A familiar figure in the city, Martin told her. Searching the litter bins. Sometimes dogged by taunting children.

That day he was addressing the gulls. Scattering crusts, all the while chanting in the high bardic manner.

It was a blustery day. A salt wind gusting off the river that pummelled her cheeks, and brought the tang of home.

Martin took her hand as they listened to the old man's singsong, buffeted by the wind. The startled gulls blown backwards.

He seemed fascinated by the old man's chanting.

'I wonder what he's saying.'

'He's telling them that he's the poet Mac Grianna. He had a love. She left him for another. Many sons he had. Where are they now?'

She was conscious of his gaze.

'You're a native speaker, then?'

'Until I was five years old I spoke nothing else.'

Her first earnings she put towards a double bed. It came up Steep Street in a van, together with a half-length mirror bought from a junk shop in Little Bolton Street in the West Wall. It was a decorative mirror with a transfer printed on the back. A peasant girl peeping out from a shawl, one slim hand gathering its swamping folds about her. Though Caitlín O'Malley would have been embarrassed had anyone suggested it might reflect the image she cherished of herself.

The two men she'd hired to carry her purchases up the passage from Mercer's Court had to make three journeys.

'Hope he's worth it,' one of them grunted, as they humped the mattress up the stairs.

She had never known passion before. All she'd known was her father's life-long passion for his long-dead love, the mother of whom she had no memory. So she was quite surprised to find how hungry it made her. She discovered, too, the companionable character of a bed when there were two of you. What before had been a narrow cell for solitary dreams become suddenly a grassy bank. A glade. A picnic spot. Venue for delightful meals and playful conversations, where you could eat, sleep, make love, eat some more, and talk of all things under the sun.

Sometimes Martin would get her to tell him stories. Tales from a world long vanished from the world as he knew it, in which nature tolerated marvels unthinkable elsewhere. Ships that sailed in the air, and kingdoms under the western wave, fish with gold teeth, and islands where no corpse would decompose. Tales of irascible saints and lovelorn girls, and battles fought in a magic fog, and epic duels with giants.

'Ach, the men that is now,' she teased, 'couldn't lift the boulders those heroes hurled at one another.'

So saying, she turned on her side, burrowing back into the bed.

Her home was in Irrul, to give its ancient name. A remote peninsula, beyond the paps of Bresna in the far north-west. The old road used to make for a long weary trail right round Lough Suibhne, then in and out along the coast. Now a fine new road swings round the head of the lough, then climbs directly over the mountain, and down into the glen. Going up this way, you see below you, as you breast the hill, the little townland of Skerryvore, open to the eye of heaven. As like as not, a spitting wind from the west. Clouds sullen with rain. Then the wind suddenly ripping apart the sky, sunlight sliding over a patchwork of little fields, whitewashing houses, shadowing hollows, setting free the leaping hills. Out beyond the point, like nuggets of green ore in the Atlantic, the islands of Inishbeg and Inishmor. Deserted now. No one has lived on Inishmor for more than half a century. Not since the great storm that overwhelmed the fishing fleet many years ago.

The islanders were rehomed on the mainland, Caitlín's father among them. He was only a little boy then. Yet he still had a terrible hunger for the old holdings. All of the older generation spoke with longing of the island. Nowhere in the world, he used to say, were there greener seas, or silkier sands, or milk more yellow than that given by the cows of Inishmor. No place the dew fell on could be more beautiful. Yet none but the very oldest had any real memories of living there. What they had was a kind of folk memory that told of the great storms of autumn. Huge seas dashing against the cliffs of Borra Head, rocking the island to its foundations. And the ceaseless racket of the shingle, rolled everlastingly by the Atlantic breakers. They told of otters rippling over the strand and down into the surf. Of flights of geese leaving for the Arctic every April, taking with them their great noise. And the silence they left behind, that made a space for the song of little birds.

Her uncle, Tadhg O'Donnell, still ran a few sheep on Inishmor. Of the village little remained but ruined walls and gables, and the old burial ground where wrens hunted for spiders among the stones. Tomás O'Malley's dearest wish was to be buried there beside his wife.

When her body was recovered, he'd had her laid to rest among the ancient graves of the O'Malleys. Each spring on the anniversary of her death, when the big seas abated and it was possible to make a landing, he went out with fresh flowers to tend her grave.

Since Caitlín was a little girl he'd taken her with him on his annual pilgrimage. She'd thought it a melancholy task. Yet he seemed almost happy, his cracked tenor mingling with the larks and pippets as he swung his scythe.

She had no memory of her mother, drowned in the whirlpools of the tidal race that separated Inishmor from Inishbeg.

That loss shrouded a mystery she was never able to penetrate. It alarmed her sometimes to think how much of her own deeper history remained a blank, her earliest childhood little more than a ghostly 'I' flitting through empty rooms. She had no memories before the age of three or four. Mammy, she knew, had been taken, and she was frightened Daddy would leave her too. Absence had left a space imagination filled with dread.

Like all the children of Skerryvore, she had grown up with the story of *An Cailleach* rising out of the sea to fall in fury on anything that strayed into her waters. Whoever was swallowed up by *An Cailleach* was sucked down the whirling circles of the sea, down, down, a hundred fathoms down, to the bottom of the deep pit under the rock where the creature had her lair.

Caitlín had never seen *An Cailleach*. But sometimes, with a spring tide sweeping westward and a westerly gale driving against it, clear across six miles of water came a screeching and a howling that was like the hounds of hell.

As she'd grown older, leaving her father to his task, she'd taken to wandering off on her own, sometimes climbing to the top of Borra Head, looking across the Sound towards Inishbeg, gazing at the incoming tide clashing with opposing waters, and the overfalls dissipating into whorls and whirling surges, and the turbulent white horses sweeping west.

A mile of stormy water separates Inishmor from Inishbeg. The tidal streams set through the Sound, east on the ebb, west on the flood, at speeds of 8 knots or more, the deep water in the fairway boiling and fermenting with increasing turbulence as the stream gathers strength. Deep below the surface a chaotic seabed of banks and hollows and irregular rock formations gives rise to numerous torrents and overfalls. The most dramatic of these underwater features is a deep abyss descending far below the surrounding seabed. The sea sweeps into this chasm then surges up and out the far side, effecting a multitude of upthrusts and back-eddies, forming and dissipating, contending with the main stream.

The Sound is at its most dangerous when a strong westerly wind sets against a spring tide. Downstream of the abyss a great, submerged stack presents its face to the main stream, bringing about a violent upthrust of water, erupting from the surface in pulses swept away westward by the tidal flow, dissolving into numerous water streams merging into one another, forming the whirlpools for which the Sound is so notorious. Just west of the stack wells up the most violent of these whirlpools. In a westerly gale this can swell to a standing wall of seething white water rising to a height of several metres. And this the men of Inishmor knew as *An Cailleach*.

There were no braver seamen than the islanders. In their bones, their sinews, they carried centuries of experience. Yet they feared *An Cailleach*, and avoided her at all times.

If they attempted the passage of the Sound to get to or from their fishing grounds, it was only in slack water, with a neap tide. And never without anxiety, for the sense of danger was ever-present, the interval of safety brief, and a miscalculation, if only of minutes, they might pay for with their lives. And they never fished the Sound.

By Tomás O'Malley's time the old wood-framed boats, dressed in animal skins or tarred canvas, had given place to modern wooden currachs, with an outboard engine to take them out for the crab and lobster which were so plentiful among the rich inshore reefs. But the old taboo still held. The men of Skerryvore wouldn't fish the Sound.

Next day Caitlín found herself in the stern of her father's currach heading out across the bay. It was a brilliant morning. Sun dancing on the water. The light dazzling. Sitting amid a roar and churning of water, the screaming of gulls, cheeks stung with the salt tang, she succumbed to the thrill of an old excitement. Never was death so peripheral, so out of place. The air thrumming with vast currents of energy flowing, driving everywhere, animating sea and sky. Parties of feeding guillemot, see-sawing up and down on the swell, dived as they whipped past. Once, a sleek grey head broke the surface to stare astonished. At Caitlín O'Malley. Lilting an old homecoming song of the islands. The exile's song she used to sing for Martin:

Light as a swan on the water,

Sorrow a stranger,

Spirit leaping the height of joy.

Then her father cut the engine. They coasted in to the landing amid a piping of oystercatchers.

Not wishing to be drawn into his dark communing, she left him at the grave. Wandered off along a narrow path that followed an old drainage ditch through sedge and rushes. A path remembered from childhood. Little more now than an animal run. Overgrown. Squidgy underfoot. The stream flowing strongly. Grasses, rushes, lush beside the burn. Margins filled with a sweet profusion of wild flowers. Ragged robin, campion, meadowsweet, spikes of vivid montbretia. The air soft. Moist.

Gradually, as she went, the scents and sounds of summers long ago stole up on her. She was a child again, lying in bed, listening for the corncrake. Like a cork, her father used to say. A stiff cork drawn from a bottle of stout. Though you never saw it. When first she went away, sick for home, it was the memory of that mysterious voice that brought home closest.

She went on, tunnelling through head-high reeds, rushes. Memory pressing down hard on childhood places. Images coming up sharp, distinct, as if freshly printed. A handkerchief field of lush green grass. A crumbling sea stack. The two merging. Then, in her mind's eye, she saw it whole. Entire. The great stack teetering on its rocky platform, thrusting aloft its green sloping summit. The leaping, snapping waves. A fearful place. A place, her father told her, never to go near.

Her cousins were afraid of nothing. They took her there. She saw them now across the gap of years. Liam. Francie. Cut-down jeans, wellies. The ragged farmhouse haircuts. Done by Mammy outside the kitchen door.

The tide was on the ebb. Rocky flats laid bare. They led the way across the slopping pavement to a shoulder of rock, cut off from the main stack by a shallow channel through which, whenever a wave crashed against the stack, the sea raced foaming, sending up great clouds of spray. They said it was *An Cailleach*. They leapt across the channel, and dared her to follow. Then, sick with terror, with Liam and Francie shrieking encouragement, she ran blindly – leapt, just ahead of the wave. She was drenched with spray.

Linked hand to hand, they'd crept by ledgy flats, with the sea licking, sucking, a foot or two below, round to the seaward side. The rock there so deeply scored, grooved, it was possible to scramble up to a hollowed-out basin under the main wall of the stack itself.

While her cousins shrieked and clambered about way above her head, she'd cowered in a rocky scoop, too terrified to move, mesmerised by the ceaseless motion of waves breaking, washing this way and that where a heel of rock broke the surface of the sea. In the end Liam had to fetch her Uncle Tadhg. He'd carried her clinging to his back, her face buried against the nape of his neck, leaping through the spray.

In front of her a sudden soft *plop*. Some small animal slipping into the stream. The current was picking up, sliding through dark peaty pools, now issuing between banks of boulders, down to a tiny cove.

A strong wind off the sea was driving big breakers up onto the strand. Caitlín slithered in her borrowed boots over the stones. Here at last was the beach of coal-black sand. Another wonder. The black sand. The wet black stones.

Instantly the wind began to batter at her, knifing through her thin coat, spattering her cheeks.

She picked her way along a melancholy line of jetsam. Broken boxes. Fragments of rope. Plastic floats. Containers. Stalks of kelp and leathery wrack. Timbers tunnelled by sea worm.

The stack was all but cut off already. The tide racing over the flats. The devouring sea dashing in great clouds of spray against a caving wall.

There it was. A stark finger of rotten rock teetering on its platform. Its jewelled summit accessible only in a child's imaginings.

A hundred yards in front of her the line of cliffs began its climb to Borra Head. Here the black strand ended in crags. Black basalt, dripping everlastingly. A few rock roses. Tushes of grass, green on black, bent before the wind. On tiny sloping terraces, far above the boulders of the beach, her uncle Tadhg O'Donnell's sheep placidly cropping the turf. At the top of the strand a washed-up seal lay stinking.

She turned back, away from the strand, and struck up the

bank, cutting across the old tillage land towards the ruined houses, strung out over the hillside. Over it all there hung an air of desolation. As of a place where life had failed. Timbers rotted. Roofs fallen in. Sand sifting over the empty floors. Echoes of ancient grief clinging still to the stark gables, the tumbled stones.

Twenty currachs had set out that night. Her grandfather Hugh James and his brother Dessy among them. The barometer had swung to low, but they went out all the same. *And why wouldn't we go?* he used to say. *It had been a soft day. No wind. A calm sea.* After a single boarding of mackerel Hugh James turned back. Some instinct, he always said, had warned him. He shouted for the others to do the same. Midway from the fishing grounds the storm came at them out of the night. On Inishmor they were lighting bonfires to guide them back. Dessy lost his oars, so Hugh James had to row for both of them. He brought them safely home. They were among the few to get back alive.

She wandered on past empty doorways, thinking of winters here when all contact with the outside world was cut off, when the sick were denied a doctor, the dying a priest, when nothing that might be needful could be fetched from the mainland without risking life itself. And encompassing it all, the vast indifference of the sea.

She thought of the old songs and stories, forever stirring the bones of something that could never be left to rest because the sea never changed. For centuries the men of Inishmor braved their doom upon the *fág*. Or went to their watery grave. Or were washed ashore. Were laid in the red earth. A cold hand lay on them all. That was the price exacted. The pattern of their lives.

Within days of the disaster Hugh James was out again. It was all he knew. Fishing and the sea. *We lived off the sea*, he used to say. *And the sea lived off us.*

A flurry of wind drove at her. Whipped her hair about her face. Caitlín O'Malley hunched her shoulders. She thought of her father tending his grave. Hadn't she spent her childhood hearing him count the hours till he could lie beside his love? *And isn't a lover's child*, her grandmother sought to commiserate, rocking her in her arms, *always the poor orphan?*

She went on towards the old burial ground, brushing through eruptions of bracken, clumps of ragwort. Skirting the brambles, she clambered over a tumbled wall. Here, in the lee of the wall, well-nigh buried in bracken, was an ancient tomb of the O'Loughlins, lords of Irrul. With Liam and Francie she'd played here as a child. Crawled on hands and knees, scarcely daring to peer through the cracked slab at the darkness within.

She went on past worn, sand-blasted stones, their inscriptions long since effaced. She found her father gathering up his tools.

He paused, looking down at his handiwork, and sighed.

'Ach, the wound never heals, Caitlín. God keeps it open. It's very hard. But it's a consolation too. It keeps love alive. And memories can be a joy.'

He'd always kept them hidden from her. She thought of him getting them out from time to time. Rubbing his hands over them. The treasure he kept hidden. Kept for himself.

And couldn't I, she wanted to cry out, *have filled the gap? You had a child to care for…to love…her child.*

She bent, plucked a grass stem to stare at it, revolved it in her fingers.

'She was drowned in the whirlpool.' She turned to look at him.

'She was.'

'I used to dream about *An Cailleach.*'

'You never told me.'

'No.'

His face filled with sudden concern.

'She used to come in the shape of an old woman, and stand at the foot of my bed. I knew she was waiting for me.'

He began wrapping some sacking round the blade of his scythe.

'They say every picture tells a story, Caitlín. With us it is our stories that reflect a picture of the world.'

He straightened his back, and sighed.

'The sea is a place of chaos, Caitlín. It is not possible to control events at sea. What else are the old songs and stories but ways of teaching what we need to know?'

She looked up, directly at him.

'Why did you go there?'

'Why do young men do foolish, reckless things? Perhaps I wanted to show your mother what a fine fellow she'd married.'

'And did she not know?'

'Maybe I was the ignorant one. I did not know what I was.'

So it was that he began to tell her what he'd never been able to bring himself to speak of before. That he'd set out at slack water, on a neap tide. That Mairéad had gone with him to help to lay a string of creels among the inshore reefs of the Sound. Lobster were plentiful there. Everyone knew that. So why not catch them?

But he'd miscalculated the time. Before long the stream had begun setting north between the mainland and Inishmor. For a neap tide it was surprisingly strong, increasing in strength as they approached the point. Once round the headland his intention was to keep well inshore, making for Shark Island. But the stream had turned from north to north-west, making it difficult to hold his course, the sudden surges and back-eddies swirling past them an ominous foreshadowing of what was to come. For the westward stream had begun to flood into the Sound. Soon they were heaving up and down on the *fág*, pitching and tossing, the outboard lifted right out of the water, turned right round in the force of the stream. Within moments they were into the first of the whirlpools, the little boat swirling round almost onto its beam ends, tipping Mairéad out then righting itself even as she was swept away. The memory of her white, imploring face was with him still.

They sat long over their meal that night. Tomás O'Malley told of the wife who was loved by all who had known her. Of what she had brought to his life, and what her going had taken from it. He praised her beauty, the raven hair, the eyes green as the sea itself. He spoke of her strength of mind.

'She would have been a power to you, Caitlín, had she lived.'

It was past midnight when they got to bed, and Caitlín kissed her father before she went to her room.

A lover's child, her grandmother said. She thought of her mother. A young woman, no older than herself. And of her father, her lover, as Martin was *her* lover.

Sometimes, after they'd made love, she lay in a dream, no longer conscious of where he ended and she began. Her arms enclosed him. Her fingers moved in his hair. No longer was there any limit to the surface of his body. It flowed into hers.

To love, to be loved. That was the life that was happy, whatever the misery of the world.

Memories can be a joy... Though that was little enough to live on for a lifetime.

Why couldn't he have put it behind him? Got on with his life. Started again.

Yet she had only to think of the way his face broke apart as he finished his story to know he could never get over it, to know that in his own mind he would remain for ever the man who'd found a pearl of great price, and lost it. Thrown it away.

Her eyes filled with tears. Tears for the mother she had never known, for the father who had been restored to her. Tears for what she had, and for what he had lost.

As she sat there on the edge of her bed, she heard a distant rasping sound. Soft, yet quite distinct. It came again. A repeated *crrek...crrek...* laid upon the silence of the night. It was the corn-crake, the bird of home, calling from some secret place.

Rocking to and fro, Caitlín O'Malley began to weep.

The Convalescent's Handbook

by Evie Wyld

While visiting your loved one, we encourage you to remain calm and supportive to the patient. Make eye contact and provide encouragement. Don't be afraid to touch the patient.

Coming out of the anaesthetic was like coming out of the sea. I bobbed to the surface and wanted a drink. I could have slept a whole lot more but my parents were there and they wanted me to float. My mother was the colour of salt fish. My father's lips stuck together when he talked, like he hadn't opened his mouth in a while. I closed my eyes but I could feel them still there, leaning towards me like stalking herons. When I opened my eyes again my mother put her hand on my wrist.

At home I unpeeled myself and looked at the incision in the mirror. Horsehair stitches from the base of my throat to the dip under my ribs, like one long black sea urchin.

'You mustn't go taking your dressing off,' warned my mother, as she brought up a tray of out-of-season melon. She popped a thermometer in my mouth.

'You let the doctor worry about it. Don't go touching it, will you?' she said, like she'd been watching.

She looked at me and I shook my head a little.

'I'm tired,' I said.

'Well then, darling, you must go to sleep.'

I nodded, like the idea hadn't occurred to me. My room was cold, but I kept the window open. From not that far away I could hear the sea, rustling like leaves.

In a traditional type of incision, strong sternal wires are used to close the breastbone. The chest is then closed with special internal or traditional external stitches.

From my window I could see the beach stretching away around the northernmost point of the island. I pulled my blankets around me and sat up in bed, to learn to draw. I tried drawing the sea first, but there was no way of starting. I couldn't fit it all in, and when I looked hard, there seemed to be nothing there to draw. I filled a page with grey, and it looked like a grey page.

I drew my own fingers for a while, and then my feet – tried to do a drawing of my feet a day, but I got bored. My incision grew tight if I thought too hard about other parts of my body. I swallowed the pills my mother brought me and sometimes dozed with my eyes half open. A few weeks passed and I got out of bed and then walked up and down the stairs. Soon enough I was back in school: first half a day then a whole one. On what was supposed to be my first full week back, I put my head on the desk and held my shirt front, as if I was holding my skin together. The teacher sent me home in case my heart exploded out of me. I went to the beach and looked for cowrie shells, giving up after a thimble's worth. I left them in a small mound by the water's edge and took my shoes off. I stood in my blue woollen school tights that lumped over my pressure bandages. Standing in the wet sand, my feet and then my legs felt like nothing, just a trunk that attached me to the ground. One seagull flew above me, against the wind, not moving forward or backward, or making any noise. The seagull pointed out to sea and I looked too. The horizon was a flat, endless line, and the ribbons on my school hat flapped in the wind. I felt a thing in my chest throb like it wanted to come out.

If your sternum feels like it moves, pops or cracks when you move around, call your doctor.

On an afternoon when the sky was thick with brown clouds, I left school again and went to the beach. There was no one else there, no birds, just the muffle of snow falling on sand. The wind skimmed pale yellow scum onto the new white of the shore.

I wrote my name with a stick, punctuated it with a dead gannet that was frozen into the shape of a zigzag. I could feel the pinch on my chest where my skin was tight from the stitches. I moved my shoulders from side to side just to feel everything pull.

When I saw him for the first time I thought Roderick was a seal. The dark shine of his wetsuit tumbling in the white horses. He stopped at the shoreline and unhooked his flippers, doing a little dance to show how cold it was. It made me smile. I stood by my oily gannet and watched him approach. He came towards me, drawing his mask up so it sat on top of his head and showed a small pink face and the top of a large beard. He spat and then wiped his mouth neatly with the back of his wrist.

'Afternoon,' he called, still approaching.

I nodded and waited until he was close enough that I didn't have to raise my voice.

'What were you doing? It must be freezing in there.'

'Having a little swim,' he said. He pulled the beard free of his suit.

He looked at my name and gannet.

'Is that your gannet?' he asked.

'Not particularly,' I said.

'Mind if I…?' He pointed at it and I shrugged my shoulders, not sure what he meant. He picked up the bird and shook the new snow off it.

'Great,' he said.

I said, 'Aren't your feet cold?'

He said, 'Yes. How about you? Funny weather to be out in a shirt.'

It became my routine: sitting through registration and then leaving to go and breathe in the sea wind. Often I would see Roderick and we would talk for a while about what had washed up that day. I looked forward to seeing him. He never mentioned that I should have been at school.

I was pawing through the lunch my mother had packed me, a mixture of millet, grated carrot and leaf greens, and Roderick was collecting things out on the rocks, putting smelly urchins and bleached-out plastic bottles into a string bag. I left the food in the sand and used my lunch box to help him collect things. He held out a hand with a small white crab shell on it. It nearly blew away, and he shut his hand suddenly to keep it there.

'Ghost crab,' he said. 'Every time you think you see something out the corner of your eye, it turns out to be a ghost crab.' He opened his palm and this time let the shell be carried away on the wind.

I emptied my box of ring pulls and fishing line into his bag.

'Excellent.' He shook them to the bottom of the sack. He bent down to wiggle an old glove free from where it was lodged in a crack, and as he came back up he made a noise like the glove was heavy, a breathy hack in his throat.

'How long have you lived here?' I asked him.

'A while.' Sea spray dampened the hem of my skirt. An oyster-catcher landed not far from us and watched beadily.

'I never saw you before.'

'I only tend to come out in winter or after dark – beachgoers.'

'I don't often come to the beach. I'm not much of a one for it.'

'I'd say you were a one for it.'

I pressed my lips together, picked up a blue plastic bottle and handed it to him.

'Beauty,' he said.

His shack was behind the dunes, a beach hut really, not meant for living in, especially not in the winter. There was just one room. A coffin freezer with a small fridge attached, a zed-bed, a small electric heater with a battery, and a one-ring gas cooker. These were in the middle of the room, so that the walls could be free – and all over the walls, a collection of rubbish, seaweed and shells, fish bones, animal bones and feathers. The smell was not as bad as I would have thought. It was gas and drying gumboots, the small impression of tar and orange peel.

'You live like a mermaid,' I said, not sure if it was a polite thing to say. He didn't answer, but smiled as he offered me an orange from a box on top of the fridge. I took one and sat in the space he had cleared on the bed.

'Helps sweeten the air in here,' he explained as I began to peel. He took another and made a small dent in the skin with his front teeth, then gouged a hole with his thumb. He sucked noisily from the hole and then, clearing his throat, explained: 'I never have long enough fingernails to peel oranges, so...' He shrugged and I shrugged back and he carried on sucking.

'You live alone?' I asked, and he looked around at the walls of his shack and I felt stupid for asking.

'Ha!' was his answer.

I kept up a steady rhythm of putting orange pigs in my mouth and chewing six times. I was scared to choke. I pushed my chest forward to feel the tight skin there.

'What is it you do down here?'

He got up and crossed the room to the box freezer and motioned for me to come and look. It was full of dead birds, each with a tag around its leg, oiled and pointed.

'Every six months a guy from the mainland comes and collects them. Look, there's yours.' He picked up the zed-necked bird and showed me. The tag on its leg was blank.

'How come?'

'To see how many are dying, and what from. Our beach is like a full stop for lots of important currents. It's an important beach. Lots of interesting things wash up.'

It is okay to sleep on your back, side or stomach – you will not hurt your incisions. Make yourself as comfortable as possible while waiting for the night sweats to go away.

That night I dreamt that the sea was gone. That I went down and it had just dried up, and all that was left were fish and sharks all drowning in mud, armless corpses. I walked way out, looking at the horizon for a tidal wave. I stepped over great whites, tuber fish, jelly blubber. Against the horizon I saw Roderick. When I reached him, he was sitting in the sand cross-legged and he didn't speak to me. Crabs nestled in his beard, an eel took refuge in the crook of his arm.

I woke up and the room was hot and there was no sound of the ocean. Sweat made me itch. I got up to find that my mother had turned on my radiator and shut my window, but even with the window open and the cold sea air in my room, sleep stayed away until morning.

A letter was sent home concerning my continual non-attendance at school. I had to sit at the table in the dining room with my parents and they asked me why I hadn't been going in.

'I don't feel quite better,' I told them.

They didn't raise their voices, but my father patted my fist and bobbed his head down to look me in the eye.

'You must go to school, darling,' he said. 'You must get past this. You don't want to be held back another year.'

I nodded.

But there was still the cracking of my ribs at night, there was still the thing that plucked at me from inside like it was undoing buttons.

You may notice a swelling or lump at the top of your chest incision which could take several months to disappear.

'See this?' Roderick said, standing by the fridge door, holding a white and blue striped bowl with a tea towel over the top. He took off the cloth and handed me the bowl.

'What do you reckon this is?'

It was full to the brim with some kind of dark paste.

'Dirty butter?'

'Ambergris.' He looked at me for any kind of recognition, but got none. 'This is worth something. Really worth something.'

'What is it?'

'Like a whale pellet.' He came and squatted between my knees and pointed his little finger at the stuff. I could smell the kerosene smell of his skin.

'See these little shrapnel bits? Squid beaks.'

'Well, who would want to eat that?'

'You don't eat it – you make perfume, is what you do with it. The expensive stuff.' I sniffed at the bowl, but not much of a smell came out.

'I could sell this and retire. If I wasn't already retired.'

'So, it's whale sick?'

'Try some – rub it on your hands. Just a fingertipful.'

It felt like cold boot polish. I put down the bowl and rubbed it between my palms.

'It smells like the sea,' I said, breathing in my hand, uncertain of the right response.

'Well, it would do. This stuff's been floating out there for probably ten years. That's how come it's really good and black.'

'I see.' But I didn't see. I don't think I believed him.

I went home, all the time smelling my palm, thinking there was no way someone was going to buy a perfume that smelt like Roderick's hut. But I checked in the encyclopedia and it turned out it was true. I thought about all that money. I thought about the whale all that time ago, sicking up and the sick bobbing to the surface while the whale went back down deep under. I tried to smell the money in it, tried to smell the whale in it. It smelt like a stone rubbed smooth in the sea. I thought about what my mother would say if she saw me rubbing whale puke into my hands. There was some left under my fingernails; I imagined maybe a grand's worth. I picked it all out with a retractable pencil nib, and scraped it onto an old bus ticket, then I unbuttoned my shirt. In the places where my scar was still pink, I anointed myself with grease, and then I smoothed it all over. It shone like a snake in the dark.

You need immediate help if you experience the following: a new
irregular heartbeat, coughing up bright red blood, bright red blood
in bowel movement.

Late one evening, when it had gotten a little warmer, but not so
warm that we weren't done up tight with hats and windbreakers,
Roderick poured two mugs of treacly rum. We sat at the base of
a dune and watched the last traces of colour leave the sky and the
sea. We swapped jokes, bad ones.

Roderick asked, 'How d'you get a fat woman into bed?'

'I don't know,' even though I did.

'Give her a piece of cake.'

'*It's* a piece of cake.'

'Whichever way.'

Somewhere distant a car passed over a hill, and its headlights
shone dimly on the back of Roderick's head and then faded.

And then from nowhere: 'I lived in another country. Different
sea. I had a wife.' He sounded as if he was reading aloud.

'Oh?' The *had* is dead, I thought.

'We were rich. I hardly knew how to swim, truth be told.'

He refilled his mug, offered the bottle to me, but mine was
still full.

'How were you rich?'

'I sold the patent for those air-travel socks – you know, the
ones that stop you getting DVT? Sold at the right time – someone had just died from it.'

'So what happened to the money? How did you lose it?'

'I didn't. I suppose when you put it like that I'm still rich. A million-aire.'

I stayed quiet, waiting for the joke, but there was none. I had the feeling he was winding me up, like I'd missed something.

'Then why do you live down here?'

'I like to be close to the sea.'

'What's so good about the sea? In your opinion?' I did not want to get back onto the subject of Roderick's dead wife, but I felt her sitting in the dark around us, waiting to reappear.

'In my opinion? In my opinion, it's what's in the water.'

'Fish?'

'And the rest.'

'Like whales and sharks?'

'Whales are pretty good. But mainly just the water. It just moves everything about, like it's got this job which is just moving everything about.'

'Right.' I looked out past Roderick to where the shadows were too deep to see.

'You throw out a beer can – just out there, from our beach – you throw it out tonight, and in a couple of weeks she could be over the other side of the world, washing up in a place they don't speak the language or they don't have beer or something. All that stuff in the shack, all that's been brought to me for a reason. The tides, the currents, the wind. And what's in the water? Everything. There's rain in there, all the run-off from the earth. All the dead in the water.' He said it like it was obvious, and his words bled into each other.

He refilled my drink and I traced the outline of the pattern on the mug with my thumb until it was hot. With the other hand I fingered the topmost scratch of my scar, the sternum, it was called. It pulsed. He tapped the side of his mug with the back of his fingernail.

'We had our son. I moved us near the sea. He would have been nine by now.'

All the dead in the water. Roderick talked as if I wasn't there, like he was sitting talking to himself in a mirror. I tried to think of what I was supposed to say.

'We'd only lived there a few months. By the sea. I bought this boat. Speedboat. No idea how to drive the thing, of course. There aren't the same laws and licences in some places.'

I thought of Roderick done up in a smart suit. I couldn't imagine him shaved because I had never seen underneath his beard. In my mind he wore dark glasses and a white single-breasted jacket. A gold watch and a glass of champagne.

'It was a beautiful boat. Made me think I was a man of great import.'

An owl went *ooo-hoo* somewhere nearby and we both laughed, like it understood the beauty of the boat, envied feeling important.

In the dark I heard Roderick refill his mug. I had an image of his wife yellowed with illness, the boy flung up into the air by a car, drowned in a swimming pool within sight of the sea. One after the other they changed: murder, disease, blood, bone, hair and skin.

'We met these people who lived over the water some. Really rich, old money. Like that's important.' He grunted, more to himself than to me. 'I thought I was King Bum. Rich friends. Imagine that. Seems like a strange thing to hanker after, rich friends. But there you go.'

The owl sounded again but this time got no response from us.

'My wife. She was...very very good.'

A soft summer dress, long legs, dark hair. A wide smile and teeth. A wedding ring. My face felt hot from the rum, my throat thick and sticky inside.

'I don't know. She always wore her hair up. She had these blue lines on the backs of her hands.

'She was always.

'She smelt of, and long fingers.

'Soft cotton. Hot and soft.

'Turned earth. Our son was the same, so much of her in those long fingers. Funny little bugger. Collected feathers and threw them out of high buildings.'

Fell out of a window, was pushed, fell into a hole, choked.

'We were coming back one night, late, the three of us, from our new friends across the water. The boy was asleep in my wife's lap.'

Both at the same time then, the dead in the water.

'I was drunk. I was happy. There was a chain that attached lobster pots to this buoy, and the tide must've... Something like that.'

A smell of diesel oil, a fire on top of the sea, the dead in the water.

'Anyhow. I didn't see the. So anyway. I washed up.

'But not the other two. No.

'Not the other two.'

Ooo-hwoo, said the owl, *ooo-hwoo*.

I went to school and in school I recited the planets in sequence. I examined the growth of a bean sprout. I showed the math master where to find x and I conversed in French about a sandwich. And all the time my front was fixed to split.

I went down to the beach after dark, with no intention of finding Roderick. I walked out to the rocks and saw that water lay like ink spots in the rock pools. I knelt, feeling the pricks of barnacles on my knees and shins, and my face grew sticky with salt.

I unbuttoned my shirt, let the wet night air onto my skin. The moon caught in a pool of water and I guarded it until my legs fell asleep. When I walked towards home along the sand, I could feel eyes on me, I could hear the heavy silence of a person standing in the dunes, and I let him watch as if I didn't know he was there.

When you are upset, your heart works harder. It is best to anticipate and avoid situations, people or topics of conversation that make you tense or angry.

I went to the beach three days in a row, and Roderick was not there. On the third day I went to the shack. The place was torn apart. I could smell vomit, and something worse that meant the freezer had defrosted. The walls were bare, everything flung onto the floor and the bed. There was a dark bloodstain on Roderick's pillow, which was stuffed into the gap where a window had been broken. An ache in my chest reached a hand up my throat and held the start of my tongue.

My breath whistled through my teeth.

Something moved underneath the threadbare rug, amongst the seaweed and driftwood, the crab shells and beer cans. Roderick's face twisted from the mouth upwards and there was a deal of blood on his lips. My chest creaked with the sound of a night frog. Roderick choked a little, his eyes closed, and I stepped over to him, pulled the rug up, to find him dressed only in his underwear. He smelt like overripe meat. Sandflies rose in a squad to resettle on his legs.

'Roderick,' I said.

'Is it time?' He spoke but his mouth was slack, his eyes glassy.

'It's me.'

'The boy…?'

'You should get up. Should I get help?'

His eyes narrowed as he looked at me. I smelt through the meat smell of him, something like port. He looked at me, and leant on his elbow to reach at a can of beer. I kicked it from his hand.

'You're drunk,' I said, redundantly. He still reached for the space where the can had been.

'I thought you'd had a fit or got beaten up.'

He pulled his outstretched arm back with difficulty and put his thumb and fingers on his eyebrows.

'It's that flaming kid again,' he said and a red bubble burst at his lips.

I kicked him in the hip and went outside.

Then I turned around and went straight back in, took up one of Roderick's old net bags and collected all the half-filled cans I could find. I went to his fridge and pulled out a box of wine, a small tin of brandy. Most of the cans were pretty empty – he hadn't left much behind. The port had mainly spilled between the cracks of the floorboards. He watched me as I did it; I could feel his eyes on me, could hear his laboured breathing. Just like an old man, I thought, but I didn't look at him, and neither of us spoke. I left the hut and dragged the bag up and down the beach with me, making tracks in the sand. Then I went home, dumping the bag in the public garbage on the way. I said hello to my parents, and they were so surprised, they didn't say hello back. I went up to my bedroom and started a project for school, called 'Earthquakes in Colombia'. I coloured in tectonic plates and read about the demographic. I jotted down numbers in a notebook. My mother looked in just before she went to bed.

'Sweet dreams, darling,' she said.

'Sleep well,' I said. She stayed in the doorway before leaving.

The next day I went to school and a boy whose name I didn't know waved a hand for me in 'hello'. He looked away then, so that when I raised my hand he didn't see it, and I left it floating there like I had a question. I noticed for the first time that the hallways at school had been painted green.

At morning break I took myself to the bakery and bought a loaf of warm bread and a cinnamon swirl. I got a pint of milk and some honey and then I walked down to the beach. I went the long way, eating the cinnamon swirl and drinking milk out of the carton. The milk went cold down my throat, and I looked to see if it would reappear out of a hole in my chest. But it stayed put.

A bad smell whipped up from the sea and, looking down to the shore, I could see a heap of dead birds defrosting on the sand. Seagulls eyed them, unsure of how to begin. There was a deal of old stuff outside Roderick's hut.

I knocked and Roderick came to the door. His face was swollen under his beard, but he stepped aside and let me in. The freezer was open, letting go a breath of bleach. The bed was stripped, the mattress turned, the walls bare.

I passed Roderick the bread, milk and honey.

'Oh,' he said. He turned to his stove and lit the ring, put the kettle on top. I sat on the bed, waiting for something, but

Roderick didn't speak. He busied himself making tea, fumbling with the tea leaves, putting too much in and then taking too much out again. I watched as he dissolved a teaspoon of honey into one mug and emptied a small bottle of brandy into the other.

'Hair of the dog, mind,' he said, glancing at me as he poured. He handed me my sweet one and we both took a long swallow.

'I lost a tooth somewhere along the way,' he said finally. He bared his teeth at me, showed me the front left missing. 'Sorry if it looked bad.'

'Sorry I kicked you.'

'You kicked me?'

'In the hip.'

He rolled down the side of his trousers and showed me the sick yellowing of his skin there. 'I was wondering about that.'

'What will you do now?'

'Start again. Collect new birds.'

'Will you lose a lot of money?'

'How do you mean?'

'When the government man comes to get his birds.'

Roderick touched his lip where it was cracked and swollen.

'The government man never comes. I just said that so I didn't look bonkers.'

'Oh. What do you do with them then?'

'I suppose I haven't figured that out yet.'

When I got home I did the washing-up that was in the sink. I took a shower and blew my nose. I dried my hair and parted it in the middle. I sat in my dressing gown and old rabbit slippers, and I coloured in my school timetable, a different colour for each lesson. When my mother came home I kissed her cheek. She gripped my shoulders and then watched me pad upstairs. I put myself to bed in an oversized T-shirt with a cartoon of a sad dog on it. I read part of a novel for school and then I turned out the light and snuggled down in the duvet.

It quivered inside me like a fish.

It is okay to let warm water run down over your incisions; however, do not put the soap directly onto the incisions.

In the very early spring there were more people. They left their imprints on the beach, their sandcastles, their ice-cream sticks and orange peel. Roderick took me to a sandbar way out and taught me to snorkel. I wore a T-shirt and the cold salt felt good against my healed chest. Now it looked more like a line drawn in the sand. Going under the water was like having someone put their hands over my ears. I felt the anaesthetist holding my arm and I heard myself counting backwards from twenty.

I saw an eel, a thin one, and a mass of thumb-sized silver fish that you could see through when they swam in the light. I saw that Roderick changed underwater. His skin was blue, he glowed and his beard caught silver baubles of air. We held our breath and swam down to look at a rusted anchor that had broken off from its chain. Roderick picked up a handful of sand and let it fall through his fingers. A butterfish whipped around him, kissing the churned-up sand. A big air bubble sat underneath his armpit. I ran out of breath. I popped to the surface and trod water, but Roderick stayed and stayed until I thought something was wrong. I spat in my mask and held it over my face to look down at him. He was in the same place, watching the breeze of the currents spin the sand away from his closed hand.

When he came up I said, 'I thought you'd drowned.'

He laughed and shot water at me through a gap in his teeth.

'Don't worry about me,' he said. 'I've got whales' lungs.'

I didn't realise that Roderick knew where I lived. I picture him in his wetsuit padding up through the suburbs like some living thing from a lagoon, and leaving the box on the doorstep.

How else could he have said goodbye? Knocked on the door? Explained to my parents who he was? I can't picture it.

'The fruit man's been,' my mother told me with a small frown. 'I'm not sure it makes sense getting these boxes – I mean, all we got this week is oranges. I don't really know what to do with an orange.'

She emptied half the box into the fruit bowl, picking them over with a careful hand.

'They don't seem all that fresh either,' she said more to herself, the frown deepening. 'And what's this? Some kind of black butter?'

She held up a jam jar, wrinkled her nose and put the jar and the rest of the fruit on the floor by the bin.

The Boy

by Tessa Hadley

A woman lay on a bed in a darkening room: it was five o'clock on a winter's evening. She lay fully clothed on top of the bed, on her side; it was cold, but she didn't move to cover herself with a blanket, only clasped her hands for warmth between her knees. This was her father's house, although this wasn't the room she had slept in when she was a child, because her father used that now as his study; this had been her parents' bedroom. Her father had moved out to sleep in a smaller room when her mother died. She was watching the light change outside the window. The view – down long walled city gardens, mostly tangled and neglected, or crudely concreted, across to the tall patched scarred backs of other houses opposite, criss-crossed with fire escapes, spiked with television aerials – had been her childhood view, nursing her to sleep, hauling her awake: it was her old universe, seen at a different angle from the floor below. Not much had changed in the view, although the woman was almost forty. The ramshackle

Victorian houses in this corner of the city, with seven or eight bedrooms, were too big for modern families and the upkeep was too expensive, so they had never quite been gentrified. The same huge ash tree, growing at the bottom of the garden opposite, still uplifted its shapely black tracery against the weaker dark of the houses behind and the deep blue of the sky above, where the first stars showed.

Lit windows studded the darkened façades, rectangles of bright colour, or skylights showing as rhombuses in the attic roofs. Flickering behind the lace of the ash twigs she watched a girl dressing in one of the rooms, walking backwards and forwards, choosing something that sparkled and then changing it for something else; she had the illusion that she was watching her past self. The instant the girl extinguished the light, blackness sealed the space like an eye shutting. In his study upstairs, her father moved about too: he wrote something on his computer, she heard the keys tap-tapping, then he pulled open a drawer in his filing cabinet. He was supposed to have retired, but he seemed to be as busy as ever. He was a historian, he had taught the history of international relations at the university; now he was working on a new book. Also, he had told her he was going through her mother's papers, after all this time. He was waiting to eat supper, he was probably hungry, he sent the drawer in the filing cabinet slamming shut.

In the room behind the woman's turned back loomed the pale shape of the old cot, and the heaps of baby clothes and reusable nappies she had begun unpacking from her suitcase. In the cot her baby was asleep. He was new, a boy, only ten weeks old, and he didn't sleep much. She had got into the habit of lying down to rest whenever he did sleep, and sometimes she didn't fall asleep herself but lay acutely awake like this, her awareness sliding along on the taut thread of the baby's breathing, snagging on the tiny knots of his hiccups and snuffles and pauses.

Among her mother's papers Ken had found John Colley's memoirs. Vaguely, Abigail could remember her grandfather labouring over these: he had written them out longhand and then paid someone to type them up on a word processor. Ken said they were rambling and self-important: he hadn't got on well with his father-in-law. But he added in fairness that the old man did have some good stories to tell. Grandpa Colley had been in the merchant navy, and then in the Royal Naval Volunteers, where he was first lieutenant on an aircraft carrier; after the war he had ended up as chief of the docks police at Avonmouth. When he was a boy, aged only fourteen, he had been shipwrecked in a storm off Vancouver Island: they had run a line from the boat to the rocky shore, and one by one they had crossed to safety, hand over hand along the rope, sometimes dangling high above the waves, sometimes submerged below them. Lying still on her bed, Abigail tried to imagine this: because she was exhausted and hadn't eaten anything since lunch, if she closed her eyes she felt a vertiginous swooping. Of course there was no comparison between her private troubles as a new mother and the real disasters that could strike in the world outside. She remembered her grandfather telling her the story. The family had helped him in his old age to find newspaper reports of the shipwreck in the Canadian press, and even a photograph of his ship, the *Trojan Prince*, aground on rocks. Abigail began to imagine that this room she lay in was a boat afloat, and that the night outside was the dark sea.

The downstairs hall had its original black and white floor tiles, its walls were painted Chinese red; an archway led through to the kitchen and dining room, with polished wood floors, Turkish kelims, a light in a huge heavy ground-glass globe that looked like a full moon hanging over the long table of African yellow-wood. Abigail often dreamed about this big house, as if it was still her true home, in spite of all the years she had lived away. She and her brothers and sister had thought their father would probably move out when he was left alone five years ago, they thought it was a house meant for a young family; but Ken wouldn't even consider it. He offered rooms to a couple of graduate students in return for cleaning, and often there were several of them at supper. The place had begun to look unloved and dated; it wasn't dirty, but he lined up the chairs symmetrically in the rooms, laid out the cushions on the sofas in straight rows. He crowded miscellanies of family treasures all together at one end of the shelves to make for easy dusting.

When Abigail came downstairs, carrying the baby in a clean sleepsuit, Ken was tasting the coq au vin. Recently he had taught himself to cook, setting about understanding its secrets with his usual intensity, writing comments and corrections in the margins of the recipe books. As he aged he had come to look like a striking caricature of his younger self: the gaunt thinness, forward-thrusting lean jaw, weak eyes in deep sockets, the shock of silky white hair, the trademark jeans growing loose on his hips, on the concavities of his thighs. He talked to the baby in a joking loud voice, which Abigail thought meant he wasn't really noticing it.

—Awake again, wee mannie?

This wasn't his first grandchild, he had a whole clutch of them. But she had hoped to surprise him with this one; she had imagined bringing her baby to see her father over and over in the weeks since he'd been born, and in her thoughts the meeting had always involved some alteration between them, some recognition of her changed status, and new awe on his part because she was managing motherhood all by herself. The family had probably not expected her ever to have babies; she was the fourth child of five, given to dramas and self-destructive exploits, generally seen as needing to call attention to her overlooked self.

—I told you, he's always awake in the evenings, it's his worst time.

—That'll be colic. You should try gripe water.

—I've tried everything.

Ken was drinking red wine, but Abigail had to refuse it because she was breastfeeding. She put the baby down in his bendy seat which she could rock with her foot while she ate; with luck she might get through her plateful before he had to be picked up again, but she cut the chicken off the bone first so that if need be she could eat with her fork, joggling the baby on her other arm. She was hungry: along with the chicken and sauce there were potatoes mashed with celeriac, one of her mother's recipes, and she ate greedily.

Almost as soon as they had begun eating, Ken started to talk about the wars in Iraq and Afghanistan. This was what his new book was about. He couldn't know that since the baby was born Abigail couldn't bear even to listen to the news on the radio, let alone watch it on television. This wasn't a moral or intellectual thing, or a worry about the future her son would grow up in; it was physical, simply as if every layer of the skins that protect against real knowledge of what suffering feels like had been scraped away in the birth process, leaving her imagination exposed and raw. It wasn't just politics and war; it applied just as much to the ordinary disasters which would happen anyway, even in an ideal world: sick children and car accidents and cancers, shipwrecks. She had never felt quite like this before; she had always been good at knowing these things in a way that she kept sealed off from real awareness, although she hadn't realised she was doing that. In the past she might have joined in with Ken's raging, or she might have yawned and thought he was getting to be a bore. Now, when he told her about a bomb in a market-place in Baghdad where unemployed men queued for work, she had to shut this information out, push it back and back from her thoughts until it became mere sound, smiling slightly, prob-ably idiotically, bending her head over her plate, letting her hair fall down to hide her face. The government are launching a new US-backed security offensive, Ken said, and she had to press her mouth against her hand, to keep in horror. From time to time she made the right noises of assent, so that he went on talking. Of course she agreed with his outrage at these wars. She didn't understand politics and history: she had a small business buying and selling fashionable vintage clothing, and she played the cello. She was grateful that at least intelligent and informed people like her father were around to diligently research the truth and pile it up and define it, and know it. What else was there to do except know it? Only for the moment she could not afford to.

In his chair, the baby stared frowningly and kicked with his feet. At one point, to his own mild surprise, he sicked up yellow-white curds onto his sleepsuit (Abigail had forgotten to put his bib on). Because he didn't smile yet, she never knew if he was happy, and feared that he was not, because of some lack in her. She was almost broken with dread and panic at her enveloping new motherhood, and yet the sight of the baby in his existence apart from her claimed her; she thought he was singular, startling, baffling: his rather dark olivey skin, his faint drift of dark hair rubbed away at the back, his long slender hands and feet. She did not recognise herself in him. She was small and pale and fragile; he did not look as if he was going to be any of those things. Nor did he remind her much of the oboe player she had met on a music course a year ago. She had agonised a great deal to her friends while she was pregnant about whether she ought to tell the oboe player anything; now she was finding she didn't think about him very often.

When the baby began to writhe and protest in his chair, Ken told Abigail to finish her dinner. He picked him up and bore him off, limp over his shoulder, into the front room next door. She heard him in there talking to the baby in the loud chaffing voice: clearly he could switch without any difficulty between his news of doom and this pleased-with-himself brisk cheerfulness. It sounded as though he had put the baby down on the sofa and was making a fire in the hearth. When he and her mother had first bought this house, more than forty years ago and before Abigail was born, they had taken out the mean little nineteen-fifties tiled grate that was in the front room, and behind it they had found and opened up the old hearth, almost big enough to sit inside; they had always reminisced about this as if it was a symbolic act, a sign of the kind of family life they had gone on to make here, generously open and uninhibited, a warm blaze at the heart of the home. Their children had had some difficulty when they grew up, making families of their own to match it.

Abigail thought her father was showing her how to put the baby at its ease and not to fuss over it; she guessed he thought she was doing everything wrong, feeding too often, not establishing the firm routines that would allow the baby to feel secure. When she joined them, Ken was sitting on a cushion on the floor, with his back to one of the sofas; the baby was propped up against his knees, absorbed in contemplation of his grandfather's face, which must have seemed to be strangely flickering in the reflected light of the new flames. Between fires, Ken threw all kinds of rubbish into the hearth for burning: chocolate wrappers and orange peel and used paper hankies. Abigail didn't like to see this mess mixed up with the cold ash.

He talked to her about Grandpa Colley. At least the war Grandpa Colley had fought in was safely in the past: Abigail thought she could bear to hear about that, it ought to be safe ground, and might keep her father off the subject of the baby. She didn't understand why he was so interested in Grandpa Colley all of a sudden, when he had always been exasperated by him. Grandpa had been massive and handsome, his Gateshead accent with its cheerful overbearing unpretentiousness still robust, although he had lived for most of his adult life in the south; he voted Tory and he was a Mason, his opinions were all the contrary ones to Ken's opinions. In his last years he had taken to Christianity and changed his character, at least in its externals, making emotional confessions on family occasions of his former selfishness and pride; Ken hadn't liked that any better.

The baby began to cry and Abigail tried to feed it. The evenings were often like this. He would take the milk for a few minutes and then twist his head away and arch his back and cry loudly with dissatisfaction, screwing up his face as if the milk was curdling inside him, gulped down with too much air. She was aware of herself dishevelled and unbuttoned and leaking in front of her father, although he hardly seemed to notice, he had seen it all before. Usually she could appease the baby for a while by walking up and down rubbing his back, bouncing rhythmically on her feet to soothe him.

—He was quite a man, your grandfather, Ken said.

—You couldn't stand him while he was alive.

—He was what he was. But he had a lot of grit.

—What's grit?

—What men had to have in those days. To go to sea, for instance.

—Don't you have grit then, Dad?

—I don't know. I've never been tested, not in that way.

—Tested! What a strange way to think about it. Aren't you men strange?

—You'll have to learn about that, said Ken. Now you've got one of your own.

For a moment she thought he was talking about the oboe player, but of course he only meant the boy, her son. She held the baby face down on her two arms and swung him through the air: sometimes that worked. His eyelids would droop, his body would grow heavy and relaxed. She would lie him down in his Moses basket, and for a few minutes there would be peace. Then his whole body would convulse suddenly in some spasm of pain, his eyes would fly open accusingly, the desperate crying would begin again. These struggles could go on for hours before she finally got him off to sleep. While she walked up and down Ken read to her from Grandpa Colley's memoirs.

The weather was not good and although our night-time station was in the centre of the convoy, our captain preferred to take up a station outside the convoy because we found it difficult to maintain a position due to the slow speed of travel, and the force of the wind and the size of the carrier made steering difficult. One night, I was officer of the watch, midnight to 4.00 a.m., and I cannot recall a more difficult watch in all my sea experience. None of the ships were showing the usual navigating lights – all were in total blackout; entrances to cabins were shrouded with blackout material. It was late December, with overcast sky and heavy cloud. There was not even a single star to be seen, made worse with almost constant rain. I will never know how I escaped colliding with the vessels that were travelling in line abreast with me. With the ships ahead or astern, one felt a bit safer: the look-out on the forecastle and on the extreme poop deck equipped with telephones would alert me of the near proximity of a vessel and all I needed to do was to increase my speed or diminish it to escape a collision. All the vessels in the convoy were loaded to the limit of their carrying capacity and consequently deep in the water and harder to see. All were camouflaged and not so subject to the strong winds; our flight deck was almost forty feet above the sea and we bounced about like a cork. With our bulk, we would be easier to see, and I pay tribute to those merchant navy officers of the watch for their diligence in avoiding us. We did not suffer any collisions. Mark you, there were several close shaves, and taking off my oilskins at the end of the watch, I was completely exhausted.

For the next few days in the waters of the Atlantic Ocean, we exercised our pilots to perfection. Seafires were Spitfires fitted with a device like a hook which could catch, on landing, onto an arresting wire stretched across the breadth of the flight deck. *Battler* was also fitted with a device that was called a catapult – this was to be used when we were flying off Seafires and there was not sufficient wind speed to exceed the stalling speed of the aircraft, which was about 60 knots. A lieutenant RN who was the senior pilot in the Seafire section got into the cockpit and started his engine, and his plane was then connected up to the catapult. The Seafire was revved up and the 'Go' signal was given and the plane shot forward, only to fall over the end of the flight deck into the sea whilst *Battler* sailed over it. The captain ran off the bridge, down to the catapult area, and for once I did not follow him. Instead I remained on the bridge, knowing he would return there once he realised nothing could be done – all flying was abandoned for the day and we half-masted our ensign.

That night there was a quietness in the mess and not too much chatter at the dining tables. After I had eaten, I adjourned to my cabin to catch up with my log and at about 9.30 went into the wardroom and found it in a state of organised pandemonium. Two or three senior lieutenants from the squadron were being suspended by their shoelaces fastened to the hammock hooks, which were fastened to the overhead girders – others were playing a game like a pillow fight only using canvas bags stuffed with paper, whilst others were playing a tank game with a settee as a tank against an opposing settee. I realised it was no place for me and that this was no skylark or foolish prank but a relief of spirits after the awful accident causing the death of one of their officers. I saw the major of the marines, who were the party in charge of handling the planes on the flight deck, was trussed up, as was the senior officer in charge of all the flying, who signalled me not to interfere and I crept away.

The baby woke to feed only twice during the night, and then he slept until almost seven. After breakfast Abigail bathed him in the stained old bath where she had been bathed when she was a child. When she put him down for his morning nap, her father told her to go out for a walk and enjoy some time by herself. Usually the baby slept for two or three hours at this point; Ken reassured her that even if he woke up they would be all right, he would walk round the house with him and distract him until she came home to give him his next feed. Abigail hesitated, then she put on her coat and hat (a little black velour hat from the nineteen-forties), and went out to walk round the city streets. She was alone for the first time in ten weeks. She looked in the shop windows, bought herself a magazine, drank a coffee in a new place selling organic food. It was a cold day, the sky above the buildings was a pale china blue and the trees were stiff and bare: it surprised her that ordinary life had only been waiting here for all these weeks, ready for her to step back inside it. She was almost able to forget about the baby; when she remembered him she felt the milk pricking in her breasts.

She wasn't late home, but before she even opened the front door with Ken's key she could hear the baby crying: not fretfully but with anguish, in long drawn-out screaming assaults. Ken came hurrying with him down the stairs, harassed and anxious.

—I don't know what the matter is. He's got himself worked up into a state. There doesn't seem to be anything I can offer.

Abigail was dropping her coat onto a chair already, unbuttoning her dress, reaching out for the baby. His face around the yelling open mouth was congested with rage, puce-coloured, but he seemed to grunt in recognition as she took him, and the frantic protests deflated and were muffled as he bobbed his head down, puffing and scrabbling to find her nipple, closing his eyes in anticipation. Then he clamped on desperately, as if he was sucking for his life. She arranged herself in a corner of the sofa.

—It's all right, she reassured the baby amusedly, counteracting his end-of-the-world desperation. It really is all right.

The little body was still racked at first with quivering; then gradually the breathless gulping subsided into an intent, rhythmic absorption. Seeing him again after her absence from him, Abigail was astonished at the baby's reality; she tumbled into surprised love. He was so mysteriously complete, with his blueberry-dark eye staring up into hers, and his tiny perfect fingers puckering the skin of her breast or closing round her finger; she felt them separate from each other and yet joined where he drew milk from her, closing a circle. Mother and baby both started at a flash of light; Abigail looked up to see that Ken had taken a photograph of them with his new digital camera.

—I love to see you breastfeeding in your hat. Good that standards aren't slipping.

He made a fire in the grate again, and while the kindling blazed up he went into the kitchen to make coffee. Outside the windows the day had clouded over, but it was cosy inside. Abigail didn't tell her father she had had coffee already. He made hers milky and sweet, although she didn't take sugar, and brought her biscuits too, telling her she needed the energy, and to feed herself up. The baby sucked himself to sleep.

—He needed his mum, Ken said. I'd forgotten how that

crying fills me with panic. I'm really only any good once they arrive at the age of reason.

Abigail felt her own eyelids growing heavy under the influence of her morning walk and the milky drink and the crackling of the fire; her weeks-long deficit of sleep began to overwhelm her. Ken was reading the newspaper. But as she closed her eyes and sank away, a picture popped into her awareness as precise and real as if she was seeing it on a film: of a young man small as a doll, in a miniature plane, shooting along the deck of a long ship and popping off its end, plummeting straight down into the sea, and the ship sailing tranquilly on over the place in the water where the plane had disappeared only a moment before, and the helplessness of anybody to do anything. Firmly, patiently, she pushed the picture far away, out of her thoughts, down into oblivion.

The Anniversary

by Martin Stephen

Frank had found himself going to the museum more and more in the year since Madge had died. It was a long haul for an old man, from his tiny little house in Westcombe Hill, Blackheath, to Greenwich, and too often he found himself being extravagant and taking a cab. Not a black cab, of course. One of those mini-cabs. Frank now asked if he could get the young bloke with that funny hairdo and the cap set on top of it all to drive him. Always laughing, he was, and he called Frank Grandad. Cheeky bugger. Still, he opened the door for Frank, which was more than most people did for you nowadays, and every now and again he'd wave away the fare, grinning and saying he'd enjoyed the chat. Well, Frank wasn't that short of a bob or two, but you didn't say no to a favour, did you?

He liked the museum. He was a northern lad, never been in London never mind about living there until he met Madge. They'd given them leave, after training, and there was nothing for him back up north, so he'd gone with his new mates to London. Serving tea, she'd been, from a WVS stall. She'd been closing up, and he'd been feeling lonely, despite his mates. It wasn't home. He'd cadged a cuppa from her, although the stall was closed, and she'd passed him a rock cake when the old cow who ran the stall had her back turned. And that had been that. He'd fallen head over heels, and it was her who'd first taken him to the museum. You're a sailor, she'd said, you should see it. Well, he'd been seeing it ever since. They'd done it up a treat, all light and airy. Bit different from when he first saw it. Not that he'd anything against the war museum, or HMS *Belfast*. He'd been to both often enough. It was just that this place made him feel less like a young idiot who'd joined up for excitement in 1939 ('Hostilities Only'), more like a member of the club of sailors. He needed to feel he'd been more than just cannon fodder or fish bait. It helped him to think he was part of something bigger, like that poet said, men going down to the sea in ships. Stretching back thousands of years, not just five or six. There were warships aplenty in the museum, of course. But there were other ships too: passenger ships, stumpy little coasters, ancient trading vessels, whalers, discovery vessels, fishing boats…and all of them needing sailors to man them. Sailors who more often than not, he guessed, hadn't made a choice to go to sea or made a choice as to whether they manned a slave ship or an ocean liner. Working folk. Seasick like anyone else, felt the cold and the wet like anyone else. They took what came up. They were working class. Working class didn't choose. Working class did what they had to, or starved, and if some upper-class bastard of an admiral ordered a turn to port when he should have ordered a turn to starboard then thousands of them took a 15-inch brick in the guts, or a bomb or a torpedo, and like as not drowned if they weren't torn apart. Those six years in the Andrew, they'd marked him for life. Only six years it'd been, before he'd taken the first chance to come out and join Civvy Street.

He'd done well, there was no hiding it. The training he'd got as an electrician had let him set up in a tidy little business. He'd no one else to care for except himself. His mum and his dad had gone when Jerry had bombed Sheffield, along with his brother. That's why he'd been in London on that first leave. He couldn't bear going back up north. Funny, that: him a sailor, a wartime sailor, and he'd lived, and those at home had died. As for the electrical business, he had done all the real work, and Madge had done the bills and the paperwork. She was good with figures. He liked knowing his customers, and he never took on more work than he could manage on his own. A good job at a fair price, that was his motto. He'd worked till past 65, not so much because he needed to but because he didn't have much else to do. He'd never been much of a reader, didn't like dancing, was bored by the pictures more often than not. Then the work had started to dry up a bit, and he'd just started to get that feeling that some of his remaining customers were doing charity, not business. And the old hands weren't so steady any more. So he packed it in, and he and Madge had got on surprisingly well, with him not out at work all day. Then one day it had all ended. Out of the blue. He'd been woken with Madge moaning, clutching her chest, her face a horrible colour. Poor old girl. It'd ended before the ambulance came. He knew she was dead. He'd seen enough dead people to know.

They'd one son; something had broken inside Madge after him, and they'd had terrible warnings about what would happen if she got pregnant again. Sometimes he thought he'd spent more time worrying over whether the damned condom had broken than he had worrying about losing his life in the war. He was a good lad, his son, though he'd married a bossy wife who demanded more and more of his time. She tried to organise the funeral, of course, the wife. She tried to organise everything. Still, he'd got his way in most things. No sign of the pair of them having a child, more's the pity. It might calm her down a bit.

Well, it'd been a year since Madge had gone, and things hadn't got any better. You kept going, didn't you? But it was like someone had drilled a hole in his head, where Madge had been, and there wasn't ever going to be anything again that could fill that hole. Problem was, whatever bastard had made that hole hadn't used any anaesthetic.

He'd got into the habit of going to the museum just before lunch. By that time, he'd got up, done himself a bit of breakfast and read the paper. The few jobs he could find to do in the house were done by twelve. He'd get there, walk up to the entrance by the anchors and go and buy a sandwich at the café, glad to sit down if he'd made it by bus. He'd make the sandwich and the cup of tea last and read again the paper he'd carefully packed. Later he'd pack it away carefully yet again to guide him through the telly, the thing that saved him in the long evenings. That left the afternoons. He'd divided the museum up into sections, and varied the order in which he went round them. New displays were always a treat, but he always saved the best until last.

He'd often thought that he'd stop coming to the museum if they put both his exhibits back into storage. They were tucked away rather, big as they were, in a corner on the first floor. *King George V*. It was a huge model, so big that it actually gave a hint of the real thing, that vast steel monster he'd spent all those years in so long ago. He liked the way its stern pointed at the other, smaller model – not much smaller, mind. *Bismarck*. That was how it had been. *King George V* had turned away from *Bismarck*. Not the gleaming, massive, powerful *Bismarck* shown in the model, but a burning, bleeding hulk, red-hot plates sizzling as they met the freezing waters of the Atlantic, sinking for ever beneath the waves. Old *KG5* had turned her back on *Bismarck*, all right. Sunk her, pulverised her and left her to the cruisers, whose torpedoes would tear out what was left of her metal hide and finally send her to the bottom, as she'd sent those brave lads in the mighty *Hood* to the bottom, only a few days previously. Not so mighty then, *Hood*. Good-looking on the outside, too old and clapped out on the inside. 'Just like you, then,' Madge would have said, and he grinned at the thought of her.

And Frank had been there. Barely turned nineteen, he'd been on the old *KG5* right from the start, August 1940, right from when she came fresh out of the dockyard and was commissioned. He'd been there when they worked her up, or at least did all the working-up the Royal Navy was allowed to do in those days. They did say the Germans gave their ships months and months to work up, never sent them to sea until they were pitch perfect. Well, that was not a luxury the old Andrew could give itself. You were lucky, when a ship commissioned, if more than half the crew were experienced. The rest were fresh-faced lads who just had to learn on the job. That was part of the problem with their sister ship, *Prince of Wales*. She was a jinx ship, they all knew that. The Navy had always had 'em, would always have 'em in the future and had one now. There'd been deaths on her when she was building, and she'd never really worked up. Course, she had the same problem as all the rest of the class had. It was quite a big problem, when you thought about it. *The bloody main armament didn't work!* Well, didn't work properly. The ships had been designed in the 1930s, hadn't they, when there were all these bloody treaties trying to stop the 'arms race'. They'd put limits on the size of ships, and battleships in particular. It hadn't stopped Jerry building bloody great monsters with 15-inch guns and enough armour to stop a meteorite. They'd just lied about the tonnage. But the bloody British had played it by the rules, hadn't they, played it fair? To save weight they'd gone for 14-inch guns. They'd tried to put twelve on *KG5*, in three bloody great quadruple turrets, but they found it made the ships too heavy, so the second bow turret of three had to be redesigned in a real hurry as a twin turret only. Fact was, the whole design of the guns was shit. The Navy had got so scared by ships blowing up at Jutland in the First World War they'd gone overboard on safety. Result was so many bloody safety systems you'd think the damned things were never meant to fire. And the clearances were too low, so lifts and shells got jammed. In firing practice, you were lucky to get a salvo of seven guns out of the ten, and he'd known it go down to less than half under pressure.

Funny, weren't it? The model didn't tell you any of that. Superb, it looked, like no wave could ever move it. When he'd first seen it, all that detail (except he was sure one of the boats was wrong: hadn't they had two small cutters where the model maker had put one great motor launch?), he had a fantasy that maybe they'd let him take the top off it, and build a sort of doll's house inside, showing all the rooms and passageways. Those steel walls that had been his home for so long. The mess room where he'd eaten, slept, pissed and shat alongside his mates, shivered in the cold and sweated in the heat as the condensation had sprung down the walls. They'd never got the heating right, and they could whistle for anything to cool things down in the tropics. British ship designers had only heard of the Atlantic, and even then they couldn't keep a sailor warm. The galley was about the only place where you didn't shiver. It was the smell he most remembered. Hundreds of men cramped together, with bloody basic washing facilities and never enough fresh water. The serge uniforms they wore never got properly dry, and they sent out a warm, musty smell even before the sweat got to them. Then he'd thought, no. There probably aren't even plans anywhere for the inside of a *KG*5. Who needs to know how to plan the innards of a battleship nowadays? It's only us who lived in her know what it was like, and we'll soon all be dead. And he'd wanted to tell the people who looked at the model, write a sort of paper to go on the case, telling them about the water running down the steel walls, and how the whole bloody ship vibrated something rotten if you was anywhere near the stern, because some stupid bastard had designed the props to overlap. They'd scrapped her in 1957, and he bet she were still vibrating as they took off the last plate.

Any road, they sent *Prince of Wales* out with *Hood* to find *Bismarck*. Even Frank could see why they did it. 'The mighty *Hood*' was a symbol for the Navy, a kind of flagship. She was a right stunner to look at. Twin funnels, hull like a greyhound, eight 15-inch guns in four twin turrets and 30 knots of speed – she went like a greyhound too. Lots of armour as well – but the problem was a lot of it was in the wrong place. Frank knew. He'd read about it, the only reading he did do. She were just a First World War design really, like all those battlecruisers that had blown up at Jutland, too far built on the stocks to be cancelled and a new start made. So they'd bunged armour on here and there, and made her look like a battleship, but she weren't. Not really. She were a battlecruiser – bloody great guns and bloody fast, but thin as a tin can if she ever had to stand and fight. Still, *Hood* was a sort of symbol, so she got the best crew, and they let her crew stick together. She probably had the best-trained lot in the Andrew when *Bismarck* came out, and they'd seen some fighting in the Med as well. There's nothing helps a crew do their job as much as having some bastard chuck things at you. Whereas old *Prince of Wales*, her crew were as green as cabbage, half her guns didn't work – there were civvies on board when she sailed, people from the builders, trying to get the bloody guns right – but she weren't going to blow up in a hurry, not with all that armour. So they must have thought that together the two ships could do it. After all, the British had eight 15-inch guns and ten 14-inch guns against *Bismarck*'s eight 15-inch, and the eight 8-inch guns on the Jerry heavy cruiser *Prinz Eugen*. No one had asked Frank's opinion on the battle, but he'd read quite a lot of the books, not that they'd mentioned him. He'd never understood why the British hadn't put *Prince of Wales* at the front in their rush towards *Bismarck*, let her absorb the punishment (everyone knew the Jerries got the range quicker than anyone else) whilst *Hood* with her weaker armour stood back and let her experienced gunners wound *Bismarck* with eight 15-inch guns that actually bloody worked. Well, it hadn't been like that. *Hood* had gone in first, taken a hit in her magazine from *Bismarck*'s third or so salvo and blown up, leaving only three survivors. This had left *Prince of Wales*, with half her guns not working, facing the combined fire of eight 15-inch and eight 8-inch guns. She'd taken several hits, including one that wiped out most of the people on her bridge, and had to turn away before Jerry put a second British battleship on the butcher's list. And that was when Frank had heard, with a sickening jolt in his stomach, some posh-voiced bastard telling them they were going out to sink the *Bismarck*. Whoo-bloody-pee. They were just lads, after all. The *Bismarck* was like one of them devils his parents had used to frighten him as a kid.

He'd been hurting more, these past few weeks – pains down his side and in his arms. Doctor had said it was just old age. It was May now, and warmer, but he hadn't warmed up inside. He'd done something he didn't usually do that afternoon, feeling tired and hurting just that bit too much. He'd gone back for another cup of tea instead of paying his ritual visit to the models, sat down for fifteen minutes. He realised with a start that the museum would be closing soon, and he hadn't paid his regards to *King George V*. The pain had lessened now, and he got up feeling oddly guilty at the delay in visiting his shrine.

A light had gone in the corner where the models were, and it was darker than usual. There was a man standing by the window, back to the models, looking out. Gave Frank quite a start it did, when he first caught sight of him. He was wearing a long black coat, and for a moment Frank thought it was one of those the officers used to wear in the Andrew. He didn't recognise the man, though he caught sight of just the side of his face. Nagging echo, annoying. Did he know him? Frank knew all the regulars and a lot of the staff by now. He didn't think he'd seen this man before. He'd have remembered. But that half-glimpsed face…old, though not as old as him, and you could see he were a toff even with his back turned. There was the coat for one thing, the carefully cut grey hair and the black lace-up shoes polished like an ice rink. Military, must be, with shoes like that. Either that or he had a bloody good servant. Lots of the officers had servants, back when he was a sailor.

He stood by *King George V*, and a wave of tiredness came over him. God, he felt old. It was the anniversary today, now he thought about it. The anniversary of the day *Bismarck* had gone down. Couldn't be many of them left now, those who'd been there. Brits or Jerries. He'd never liked reunions. Load of nonsense. Life was to be lived, Madge had said, not just to be remembered. And there were too many memories he wished he didn't have.

Christ. All those bloody years ago. He looked at the gleaming deck, hearing the petty officers barking orders as he and his mates cleaned and cleaned and cleaned it, and then cleaned it again, as if the sea didn't do it for them. Bloody awful sea boats, the *King George V*s. They'd got this flat bow, so as to let them fire straight ahead, but the sea just came over it in buckets. 'SEALS IN THE SHELLROOM!' they used to cry as the ventilation vents for'ard were swamped and the sea got 'tween decks.

Then something happened that had never happened before.

He saw, yes he actually saw, a tiny figure walking across the deck of the model. Bloody hell, he really was losing it, for sure. But the figure stayed there, kept on moving.

'George!' he found himself whispering. 'George! Don't do it! Don't be a daft sod! Come back here!'

George was his best mate, right from the first night in the training camp at *Frobisher*. He'd got drunk for the first time with George, tried to lose his virginity alongside him, until they'd seen the two whores in proper light and run from their raddled faces. They were everything to each other, George and him, right muckers. Then on exercise, in a bloody Force 10, they'd gone on deck. The ship was rising and falling what seemed like 50 or 60 feet, digging her bow into the waves and shipping hundreds of tons of water every time. He couldn't even remember what they'd been called out for, he was half asleep; some drill or other. They were sheltering by 'B' turret, hanging on for grim life, when George's cap blew off. God knows why he had it on in the first place; no one bothered much about caps in a Force 10, not if they had any sense. Any road, George saw his cap fly off, roll along the foredeck. It was a right bugger if you lost a bit of kit, not least because you had to pay for it. George turned round, grinned at Frank and set off up the deck. He had no line on, and they'd been struggling into those bloody life jackets when George had set off. He could remember the stupid bugger's face even now, a cheeky grin on his ugly mug.

'*George!*' he screamed. '*George! Don't do it! Don't be a daft sod!*

Come back here! The words were plucked from his mouth by the screaming wind, torn apart before they'd even lived.

It was no use. Appalled, Frank saw the vast wave surge up and hang over the bow, like some monster towering over its prey. George didn't see it. He grabbed his cap from the stanchion it'd come up against and turned to wave it in the air at Frank before ramming it on his head. He was chuffed he'd got his cap. Then the wave broke, and a massive surge of grey and white foam smothered the foredeck, picked George up like a doll and sucked him over the side. Frank caught sight of his face as the wave grabbed and lifted him. It was confused, startled, like the face of a child whose grandma has just turned into a wolf. This is daft, that expression said, but there'll be an answer, there's always an answer. That was the last Frank ever saw of him.

Frank was panting, clutching at the glass of the model case to keep himself upright. Christ! The staff would have him! There were grease marks, his grease and sweat, scouring the glass. The figure was gone now, the ship not a great beast fighting mammoth seas, just a model. What had come over him? Bloody hell, that had been real! It was as if he'd been there, all those years back, like the kid he'd been all those years ago.

He sensed a presence beside him, felt confused at how he must have looked to someone else. Someone who didn't understand. He'd had a turn, that's all; just a turn. If he could just find a seat... He tried to turn round, but it was harder than it should have been. In trying to turn, his eyes fell on the model of the *Bismarck*.

Beautiful ship. Not like *KG*5, ugly bugger that she was, two squat funnels and a bloody great gap between them, like someone with a middle tooth missing. Truth was, he'd never really looked at *Bismarck*. Not as a ship. Foreign territory, wasn't it?

Did they lose men overboard off the *Bismarck* as well, when the sea went wild? Breathing bodies smashed to a pulp, or the life frozen out of them in minutes? He was looking at the *Bismarck* now, and all of a sudden it was like a light had been dimmed inside his head. His vision went all funny, as if there was a sheet of gauze behind his eyes. He was falling, falling... Christ! Where was he? There was strength in his legs, youthful strength. He was on some sort of sponson, and he was behind a gun, but it was like no gun he'd ever seen. Then he knew who he was, though God knows how he knew. Hans. Not Frank. Hans. He was Hans. It was as if every letter of the name was being embossed in white-hot print on the inside of his eyes. Hans. He was 19 years old and the second proudest day in his life had been when he was selected for the *Kriegsmarine*. The proudest day in his life? Being assigned to the *Bismarck*, the pride of Germany and the greatest battleship the world had ever seen.

And now Hans was scared. More scared than he had ever been in his young life. He was an anti-aircraft gunner, and they had joked that he and his fellows were the only unemployed on board the ship. He'd seen the *Hood* blow up, a dim pyre of smoke on the horizon, the pride of the Royal Navy, blown to pieces by the firepower of the *Bismarck*. He'd seen the other British ship turn away, smoke pouring from more than her funnels, and joined in the cheering. Then they'd ploughed ahead, and as the lack of sleep caught up with them had heard with increasing worry the rumour that they were still being shadowed by British cruisers. Then there'd been the moment when in the mist *Prinz Eugen* had been ordered to go her own way. Later *Bismarck* had taken a hit for'ard, minor in itself but cutting off access to some of her fuel tanks. She would head for Brest, whilst the undamaged *Prinz Eugen* would detach for commerce-raiding duties.

They were heading for France! The elation among the crew was palpable, almost a physical thing, compensating for the sense of loss they felt when *Prinz Eugen* detached. They thought they'd made it. The captain had announced that U-boats were being sent out to cover them, that they'd be surrounded by them at dawn tomorrow. Then that hellish noise of the klaxon, the one that froze you. It was almost dark, and the aircraft had come, the pathetic biplanes the Tommies called 'Swordfish'. They looked so slow and so frail. What must it be like to fly one of those things at an enemy belching fire, fly something like a pram that had lost its wheels, have to keep slow and low so as not to damage the torpedoes when they were released and hit the water? They had fired until the rain bounced in steam off the barrels of their guns. Someone had shouted that the planes were too slow, that the calibration on the guns had allowed for a minimum speed of 90 knots through the air. The ancient Swordfish were flying at 70, 80 knots, and the German guns could not seem to centre on them. They'd seen the British launch some of the torpedoes, but they were too busy firing through the rain and smoke to see the tracks. Then there'd been a massive bang amidships, and the ship had stumbled for just a second but carried on. Good! Good! Their ship could take any number of hits on its main armour belt! But then there was another huge explosion at the stern, different this time, longer and with aftershocks, as the ship was heeling over in a mad turn to avoid the last torpedoes. They'd stayed turning, locked into it, even though the aircraft had gone.

It was ages before anyone told them. A hit on the rudder. Divers were going over, and they would make a repair. Yet the ship had slowed, was following an erratic course. He was sure they were heading away from the coast, not towards it.

Hans was going to die, he knew that, and so did Frank, and so did the part of both of them that was every sailor who had looked Death in the eye and known Death for what it was. Those aircraft must have come from a carrier, and they'd be back at dawn, refuelled and rearmed. And what would come along behind them? Every ship the bloody Tommies had afloat, to avenge the sinking of the *Hood*. Suddenly as he felt the sea slam against the metal ribs of the ship, he felt how frail and vulnerable it seemed, what before had seemed so strong and unsinkable. He hadn't even made love to a girl, just kissed a few and managed to get his hands on one girl's breast, briefly. And there, in the dark, in the bitter wind and on what had ceased to be a warship and was now simply a steel coffin sailing to its execution, a coffin for over two thousand men and boys, he cried. Cried and felt the warm tears turn to cold almost as soon as they dropped onto his cheek. Cried for his own sadness. Cried for all he had hoped to be and do. Cried for his mother and father, who he would never see again to tell them what it had been like. Cried because he did not know what he feared most, being torn apart by red-hot metal or drowning. Cried because youth is a fine thing, and a thing that most of all wants to live.

Frank was on the floor, looking up at the ceiling, sweat staining his collar, running down in front of his ears, cold. The ceiling was moving, and he knew there were lights there but couldn't see how many of them, they kept changing. Why did nobody come? Why had nobody seen him fall over? He realised he was being held, cradled almost, by the man in the long black coat who was kneeling down beside him. He was stroking Frank's brow, and the gesture was both childlike and, in some way he did not understand, threatening.

'Call…call for…call for an ambulance…' Frank croaked. His voice seemed to have gone. He knew what he wanted to say, but it wouldn't come out. His eyes flicked across, caught sight of *King George V*.

All around him such living men as could tried to sleep before the action they knew was only hours away, as many as possible stood down to conserve energy. They'd go for *Bismarck* at dawn. God help them, and us. Hundreds of faces stared, silent, into the dark, just as Hans, a young German anti-aircraft gunner, was doing not so far across the heaving sea.

He was back in the museum, but it was dimmer now, darker.

'I know who you are,' Frank gasped, his breath coming in short bursts, the pain in his chest almost too much to bear. 'You're Death, ain't you? You're Death!'

'We are all Death,' the old man said, with a fathomless expression on what could be seen of his face, blurring again now. 'Death is the only thing that unites us. The only thing we all carry within us from birth.'

And then the lights went out for Frank Carter, and mercifully so did the pain, and he slid effortlessly down and into the vast chute of darkness, that same darkness down which George and Hans and so many thousands upon thousands of sailors had gone before.

A Snow Goose

by Jim Perrin

J*une, 1848.* As the main body of sailors hauling the boat on its sledge across the sea ice – smoother now than where their ships were beset a hundred miles round the coast to the north – disappeared behind the island in the strait, Solomon was the first to speak, voicing all their concerns:

'I wonder if we shall see those men again on this earth, Captain?'

'Better that they head south to the Fish River,' Crozier replied, a memory of his Irish upbringing in the throaty tones. 'If another winter is to be endured, Sergeant, the hunting there is what will see those men through. We all hunt for our lives now. As to the field hospital, Mr Peddle and Mr Stanley will do what they can to restore the men to health, and Commander FitzJames and Lieutenant Irving will get them back to the ships in due course.'

His words tailed off into a forlorn silence, as though unconvinced of their own meaning. With a shake of his head he gathered himself and picked up the train of thought again:

'The stores we left they might eke out for another year. If all goes well, the men at the river can return to provision them, and once we ourselves get free of this fearful place and send out word...'

Even as he spoke, he was weighing again the decision to split his surviving men into three groups. From being a newly enlisted boy sailing out of Cork on the *Hamadryad* thirty-eight years before, he had been used to his every action being dictated by custom, order and regulation. In the year since Sir John Franklin had died – with the crews on half-rations now, and the paucity of those but little augmented by what they had been able to shoot or snare on the frozen northerly coast of King William Land or amidst the ridged and tortured ice close to the ships – ingrained habits had seemed to maintain not only the discipline but even survival itself.

Now, all was open to question. It had been five weeks since *Erebus* and *Terror* were deserted. In that time they had covered barely three miles a day, and nine more men had died. To separate was imperative if any were to live. His second in command, FitzJames, of whose mental fortitude Crozier harboured grave doubts, was too weak physically to travel much further. Despite which, he had to take overall charge at the hospital tents in Terror Bay. Crozier knew it to be a bad option, but it was the one that regulation and necessity decreed. Three of the five remaining lieutenants were among those who had succumbed to scurvy or pneumonia on the march south. Of the two still living, Irving would stay with FitzJames and Hodgson was leading the men across the ice. Splitting the party, Crozier had reasoned, and sending the strongest ahead in two groups – the larger one to establish a camp on the mainland to hunt, his own to find some way through the Arctic maze – was surely the last and only chance. If he and the six men here under his command were to survive, he knew that another model of conduct was needed, at odds with all his training. They must move light and fast through this alien land. Continually this last year, flickering through his mind had come the images of the Eskimo community at Igloolik, and the winter he had spent there with Parry twenty-five years before.

Ignorant and uncultivated savages, unspeakable in their personal habits and morality, his fellow officers would always opine (though those same officers, the Irishman noted, were not above availing themselves of these 'savages" favours, be they men or women). But in Crozier, himself at a distance from established attitudes through his Irish accent and long ascent through the ranks, the memory of Eskimo friendship and resourcefulness, the recognition of what was entailed in their long survival here, was growing daily now into admiration, curiosity, respect. He remembered his excursions from Igloolik with the hunters, strove to recall the Inuk word old Aua had taught him. *Quinuituq* – that was it – deep patience! The patience of a hunter, harpoon at the ready, waiting by an *aglu* – the breathing hole of a seal;

the stillness of a man as he draws his bowstring and watches the inquisitive approach of a caribou. *Quinuituq* – he mouthed the word to himself again. If there were a key to his men's survival here, surely the Eskimos and not the traditions of the Royal Navy were its custodians?

As their captain sat in silent thought, as if to dissipate the pensive mood descending upon them, his men set to loading their scant equipment, supplies and the gutta-percha Halkett boat onto the lightened sledge. Close by, a wheatear bobbed and scurried over frozen gravel. Blankey, the *Terror*'s ice-master, watched its progress, catching his captain's eye and exchanging glances as he did so.

'Come, Sergeant,' the captain spoke, 'and you, Mr Blankey, let us spy out the lie of the land.'

The marine picked up his musket, the ice-master a fowling-piece, and they followed Crozier as he climbed the brief slope. At its crest, Crozier suddenly crouched and gestured the two men urgently down. They crawled on to join him, small stones trickling into the heels of their sea boots through split and abraded seams. In front of them as they peered over, drumlins ranged north-west and south-east like shorn sheep flocking away over the mottled plain. There, a hundred paces beneath them, a first migratory caribou nuzzled at the snow, unaware of their presence.

'Watch now, Sergeant,' he whispered, 'and I guarantee it will come within twenty paces – aim for the heart.'

Slowly Crozier raised himself to his knees, head bowed and arms held high above as though he himself were an antlered beast. The caribou ceased browsing under the snow and turned quizzically to watch. It moved towards the men's hiding place, stopping here and there to nose at the ground, then lifting its head again and fastening a myopic gaze upon the sentinel at the hilltop. Hammer of his musket cocked, Tozer sighted down the long barrel. He remembered the contorted face of the first man he had killed – the soldier of Mehemet Ali's at Acre eight years before – remembered that then too life and death were in the balance; not slowly, as here, with disease and starvation its agents, but hovering on the point of a spear.

Barely resolving themselves into thought, his instincts turned from heat-of-the-moment action back to this watchful, silent intensity. The caribou ambled a few more paces towards them, sniffing at the air. The three men held their frozen tableau. The caribou trotted closer, halted, lifted a rear leg and turned to rub muzzle against flank as Tozer eased back the trigger, stock firm against his shoulder as the hammer struck. Powder fizzed, and the spinning ball grazed past bone to burst the animal's heart. Feet flailing, it rolled, twitched and was still, echo of the shot rolling out across the island.

'Well done, Sergeant – call the men and haul it down. We'll gralloch the beast, eat and then press on.'

Soon the caribou's belly was slit and its viscera spread out by the sledge. 'The stove, sir…?' asked the sergeant.

In reply, Crozier took his knife and hacked the steaming liver into seven chunks. When he'd finished he raised one to his mouth and bit off a piece, gesturing the men to follow suit. Hesitant, almost aghast, torn briefly between hunger and habit, they each picked up their portion and fell to.

'On all my voyages, I never saw an Eskimo with the scurvy. And yet we sailors always suffer. Think on that... I'm sorry, gentlemen, that we have no dinner service, nor lemon juice left to dress your meat. But nor did I ever meet the Eskimo who had use for those items, and it seems to me that we must now copy their ways. I oftentimes saw them stuff their mouths with blubber straight from white whale or seal, have tried it myself on occasion and suspect it has qualities of which we stand here sorely in need. Hot liver and raw heart for our luncheon then, friends, rare steak when we sup tonight, and we shall live to see England's shores again. A little fortitude in the matter of diet now, and Greenhithe will soon enough see you carousing along Grope Alley once more.'

And so the men dined – the marine sergeant Tozer; the whaling-fleet ice-master Blankey; seaman Manson from Whitby, who had often been north with the latter; *Terror*'s captain of the maintop Tom Farr, its coxswain John Wilson, and Osmer, the paymaster from *Erebus*. Apart from Osmer, who had been urged upon him, these were the few men still living whom he had come to trust and respect from among the assembly of Arctic tyros and those favourites of the Admiralty favourite FitzJames who had so dismayed Crozier before the expedition set sail three years ago. Smooth young gentlemen adventurers they were in Crozier's view, untested in battle, without instinct for this elemental place where his own rough and hard-won knowledge surely demanded precedence – and would now take it. His responsibility as captain apart, every step away from FitzJames and the continual reproach of his polished manners and brilliant conversation assuaged bitter pangs of resentment.

Wiping the blood from cracked and blackened lips and greying beards with handfuls of snow or tattered cuffs, they loaded the carcase onto the sledge, and with a new vigour in their steps bent to the traces and hauled it back onto the ice. Behind them, a flash of white beneath the wings and the high, pealing cry of a skua caused Blankey to glance over his shoulder to where the dark bird had swooped and snatched a length of the caribou's discarded guts, trailing it across the snow. With an involuntary shudder, his cleated boot soles slipping briefly, he fell back into step.

Their captain out in front, they turned to the north-east and set a steady rhythm. The ice here in the great bay that stretched across to the mouth of the Fish River, away from the jostling and shrieking stream of pack that surged down from the Beaufort Sea, was glassy and smooth. Here and there they splashed through puddles that told of encroaching spring, or skirted round meltholes from which, at a distance, seals watched. The sledge slid easily and the labour was light compared with hauling the boats down from Victory Point over the pressure ridges and the fractured leads. Tom Farr sang to himself as they pulled:

'The sea, the sea, the open sea, it grew so fresh the ever-free…'

'What's that you're groaning out, Tom?' asked Sol Tozer.

'Why, 'tis a little lament in the key of C for the delights of a life upon the land that my captain of the foretop, Mr Peglar, and I would often sing – the slip of that warm liver down my throat has put me much in mind of it.'

Before the sergeant could voice his ribald reply, Captain Crozier gestured shorewards to a shingle beach at the back of a rocky cove, sheltered from the winds.

'We shall camp there and eat well tonight, men. Come…'

The ice of the cove gleamed in morning sunlight as Tom Farr pissed against a rock wall. He looked at the dribble of thick yellow and viscous liquid that stained a shadowed drift of snow with distaste, fastened his breeches and walked down the shingle, his six companions still sleeping behind him. He gazed over the ice, studying its fractured patterns and monotone textures – gauzy, clear, opalescent – and wondered how so beautiful a substance could be so cruel, unpredictable, entrapping. How often had the same dilemma exercised him through the long months of imprisonment in the northern pack? He remembered climbing time after time to the crow's-nest to scan the horizon, seeing always the same infinite variety within monotony and emptiness. A rock round the corner of the cove shone strangely. He walked on to look at it, losing sight of the camp. Further on still, he knelt by another rock to examine the contained and exquisite vigour, the brilliant colours of the lichens that had caught his attention, their names unknown to him: jewel lichen, map lichen, sunburst lichen. In a moment of vision, their seamed and flaky growths, slow-colonising, rustling out from dead and hollow centres in ages of infinite patience, seemed to him the true Arctic hearts. As he was absorbed, lost and insentient to all but the focus of his thought and eyes, where these and the forms of beauty he had known, whether of ocean skies or the green life of land or the secret and exotic petalled flesh between a woman's thighs, seemed entirely as one – suddenly, in that moment of reverie, without uttering a cry he was dead, his neck broken by a single blow of the stalking bear's paw as it pounced. Before his companions were awake to his absence, he was torn and chewed meat digesting in the belly of the beast as it padded silently away, back into the frozen land.

Manson, who had survived the press of 1835 in Baffin Bay, made the discovery. He saw at once what had happened, and that Farr was beyond help. Blood was spattered across the snow-patched beach where the bear had hurled his lifeless body around like a terrier with a child's toy. The seaman hastened back across the shingle to rouse and inform his captain. All six men gathered, silently building a cairn of splintered rocks over their companion's remains. When they had finished, they stood bareheaded in a cold, crystal wind as Crozier stumbled through words by now known almost by heart. At the camp they lit the spirit stove, thawed and breakfasted with scant appetite on what remained in the iron kettle of last night's feast. Would they track and kill the bear? asked Manson's old shipmate from the *Viewforth*, Blankey. But he, the captain, all of them, knew that their strength was too fragile for that, and their supplies too scant. They would press on eastwards, hoping for better hunting grounds beyond the land-bridge they believed led across to Boothia, Fury Bay, Igloolik and perhaps even home. Henceforth, muskets would be loaded and no man would venture alone out of sight. They rattled the sledge out onto the ice once more, and headed into the sun.

After four hours of hauling along a coast that ran northerly now, the men's breeches and boots soaked with splashing through meltwater shallows, they pulled out onto a rackety stone beach down which ran a freshet of good water from the thawing ground behind. As the men filled the stove and set the great black kettle to boil, Crozier took out his telescope and scanned across the bight. Fixing on a point at the back of the bay, excitedly he called the ice-master Blankey and Osmer across, handing Osmer the telescope as he arrived.

'I was told, sir, by men that have spoken with them of something the Eskimos of Baffin Bay believe. Far to the west of Igloolik and the lands of its people, they say there lives a tribe called the Netsilik. The people at Igloolik, I'm told, hunt walrus, but the Netsilik are expert at catching seal – a more difficult, albeit less dangerous task.'

'Indeed, Mr Osmer, I heard a great deal about them in my time at Igloolik. It is a great mistake to assume likeness among all those we choose to term "savages". My friends of Igloolik, for example, were a good-natured and playful people, uxorious and happy. But I heard from them that those of Netsilik were quarrelsome, warlike and conversant with all the forms of Eskimo magic. They live in a place known as Uqsuqtuuq, which I was told translated as the place where plenty of blubber was to be had. From the look of the encampment yonder, I would say, Mr Osmer, that the soubriquet is apt.'

'That sounds like the language of Commander FitzJames,' responded the former paymaster of the *Erebus*, to Crozier's obvious displeasure, 'but if I understand your meaning aright, then this encampment surely is Uqsuqtuuq, and if their reputation is deserved, we do well to keep our weapons primed. Perhaps by means of that magic we shall ensure their cooperation?'

'I think, Mr Osmer, that a watchful diplomacy will be our first line of defence. Another haunch of caribou tonight, and tomorrow we shall introduce ourselves, I fancy.'

The men hauled the sledge up to a sheltered recess in the rocks, propped loaded guns against it and made camp. Manson, with studied delicacy, peeled back hide, removed a leg from the caribou carcase and carved chunks of it into the kettle to boil whilst the others stamped cold feet and smoked short pipes. It was Osmer, standing apart from the other men and reflecting on the captain's quick rebuff, who saw the bear first. It was ambling along the ice, and it was coming in their direction. 'Sir!' he called, and gestured towards it.

Crozier assessed the situation and calmly gave out orders:

'Sergeant Tozer – move forty paces down the beach to the right. A shot from the side for its heart. Manson, on the left thirty paces; wait until it's broadside to you. Mr Osmer, Mr Blankey – behind the sledge with the fowling-pieces, and you and I, Mr Wilson, must rely on sword and pistol to give the men time to reload if it comes to that.'

The bear, as he was speaking, shambled on purposefully towards the scent of cooking meat, its low head moving from side to side, breast still red from its morning feast.

'So, Mr Blankey, your friend will have his revenge,' the captain murmured, as the soft shift of shingle under the bear's weight whispered closer. It hesitated, sensing men to the left and right, and began to lope forward. Unerringly, the marine sharpshooter's ball crashed through its ribs to the heart, and as it flailed and reared Manson's bullet pierced the belly and shattered its spine. Suddenly Blankey was vaulting the sledge and running to where the animal writhed. From ten feet he stood and delivered both barrels of heavy shot, punching through its ribs into its heart. With a last surge of strength it lunged for the ice-master, pinning him to the ground as the captain's sword sliced through its throat and Wilson's pistol discharged through its eye into the brain. A great tremor shook the vast body, coughing gouts of blood across Blankey, and with a final faint convulsion the creature died. Wrenching out his sword, the captain wiped it across the dingy yellow pelt as Tozer and Manson ran across, muskets reloaded.

'Mr Blankey...?' called the captain to the crushed and blood-sodden figure under the bear.

'Aye, Captain,' came the response. 'All's well, but 'tis a heavy kind of blanket I'm lying under and I'd be grateful if you'd get me out from under here.'

The men sobbed out sighs of laughter and took position to heave away the animal's corpse. As they did so, with unanimous instinct they glanced over at the sledge, from behind which peered the pale face of Charles Osmer.

Orpingalik arrived that night. He pushed back the pointed hood of his caribou-skin coat and called the white men, whose language he spoke, *qallunaat*. He himself, he told them, was an *angakoq* – a shaman, as they eventually came to understand. All of them would later swear that as he walked unexpectedly up the beach in midnight twilight, making them reach for the guns, he was surrounded with a shimmering and fiery light which caused the superstitious among them to believe they were encountering a ghost. But he ate the remnants of their evening meat with corporeal relish, and later withdrew a small distance to converse with Crozier, whom he addressed as Aglooka. He told of how, days earlier, hunters of his tribe had met with the other Aglooka, the weak boy in the blue coat with gold at the shoulders, who had begged seal-meat of them for himself and his three companions. He was going to die soon, Orpingalik stated, and that was his fate.

'But you, Aglooka the man, known by our people to the east, who has brought Nanuq as gift to our tribe and can hunt for yourself in this land – you will stay with us through winters to come and father children of our tribe. Though you will not see them grow into men, for like the snow geese, you will fly south before your bones whiten here. Now I will dance for you and your men, Aglooka.'

Orpingalik stepped down to a flat stretch of shingle, stilled himself and started to dance. At first he was slow, the movement studied, cautious, stealthy, deliberate, but building into a sinuous, sure, rhythmical, intertwining ecstasy, stooping, coiling, circling, pirouetting low above the beach, his expression rapt, hypnotically intense, hands always describing, floating, shaping pictures for his watchers' imaginations to grasp; of his prey, conjured up for them, immanent, there. Later the white men would talk of the presences they had seen. All around Orpingalik as he danced, the same shimmering light, as though he had stepped straight from

the waves, dripping phosphorescence. And as he danced, he sang
this song:

> I remember Nanuq, the white one,
> The great white bear.
> With back and haunches high
> And snout in the snow he walked,
> He alone in the belief of his maleness.
>> He ran towards me.
>>> *Unaya, Unaya!*
>
> Down I was thrown, again, again,
> Until, breathless, he lay to rest,
> Ignorant that I was his fate,
> Through whom his end would come,
> Fooled in thinking he only was male.
>> I too was a man!
>>> *Unaya, Unaya!*

When Orpingalik had finished, he turned to Crozier: 'Aglooka,
tomorrow you come with your hunters to Uqsuqtuuq. Bring your
gift on the sledge for my people to see, and we will welcome you
there.' With that, he walked down the beach and onto the ice,
where his mercury shimmering was absorbed into the shadowy,
pewter dim.

As they approached the village, dogs along the beach left off gnawing the bones of caribou and bellowed their protest. Men, women and children ran down onto the ice, calling out to Nanuq where he lay, jaws agape and snarling atop the sledge. They crowded onto the traces and heaved the load up into the village, where women using the *ulu* were scraping fat from the skins of Arctic foxes stretched on frames. A smell of boiling seal meat hung round the low stone houses. Where the ice on the sunlit side of the bay had melted, scalloped and glistening little icebergs with turquoise melt-pools on their tops floated in the sea. The women unloaded the bear and the caribou carcase and immediately started dismembering them, teasing out sinews from flesh, scraping fat from hoof and paw into bags of salmon skin, butchering the meat into ever-smaller joints, discarding only the liver of Nanuq. The six white men were ushered into the *qaggeg* – the largest dwelling in the village, where the smell of burning seal fat from the *kudlik* was overpowering and a flickering light from its moss wicks cast strange and moving shadows. Orpingalik was waiting for them there, seated on a stone bench covered with the winter hide of caribou. He gestured Crozier to walk with him to the door of the hut.

'See there, Aglooka, that far hill?'

He pointed west to where an ice mirage, a long, low chimera of a sky-hill, glimmered along the horizon. 'That is Uvayok. Before death arrived on earth a race of immortal giants lived in the north of Qiiliniq. But one summer there was no food, the walrus and the bowhead whale had disappeared, so the giants set off towards the south. South took them further from food, and so they starved. Uvayok was the largest of them. In time his body sank into the soil and the small flowers of summer grew over him until only a rib showed here and there and he became a hill. Lakes formed from the liquid that drained from his bladder. Fish swam in those lakes, and the loons called from them. Aglooka, these are our stories, the stories of the land to which you must listen now. You, and the *qallunaat* with arrow feathers on his coat…'

Orpingalik glanced and nodded to the marine sergeant.

'…you will stay here with us, hunt seal and the white whales and geese. Those other men will cross the ice before it breaks up, and will live at Taloyoak. They will kill caribou. This way, all will eat. We have lost many hunters in two springs. My daughter's husband was one of them. The women become dangerous when they have no husbands to lie with them. You white men who are strong and can hunt will take their place.'

That night, as they feasted in the *qaggeg* on seal meat, and caribou, and fermented walrus intestine that tasted within the skin like strong cheese, Crozier reflected how easily responsibility gave way to compliance in the face of greater knowledge. His fate was to have arrived here. That of those others who might still survive was now in their own hands, and he was absolved of it. After all had eaten, the women removed the blackened kettles from the *kudlik*, trimmed the wicks and recharged the trough with seal fat. Story-songs and dancing entertained them, and between the *qallunaat* and the young and widowed women glances flickered. Crozier remembered his proposal to Franklin's niece Sophie, the disdain with which it was received, the averted eyes and the sidelong quick glances as she talked later with her Aunt Jane, the scalding tinkle of their laughter. He caught a young woman's eye and thought how different was the frank and unabashed interest of her gaze. Observing them, Orpingalik whispered to him: 'Aglooka, this is Uvlunuaq, my daughter.' Later that night, she led him back to her house, where, by the light of the *kudlik*, she took the long sticks called *tuglirak* from her hair so that it fell over her shoulders, and slipped out of her fur clothing to stand naked in front of him. Laughing, she unfastened the buttons of his frayed uniform, pulled down his breeches, helped him out of stained and ragged linen. His arms encircled her as she stood close, her breasts against his chest, feeling him rise against her. With a cracked hand, he sought out and caressed the velvet moist of her, her salt savour stinging in the split tips of his fingers: 'A man must be patient to give a woman pleasure,' she pouted, squirming away, pushing him down merrily onto the sleeping platform and tumbling with him between the heavy winter hides of caribou.

A decade passed as quickly as the bloom of fireweed in a summer season.

Aglooka and the *qallunaat*-with-arrows-on-his-coat lived with their wives in Uqsuqtuuq, knowing from the other hunters that the ships had drifted away and sunk and their erstwhile companions along the northern coast were all dead. But they shunned those places where their uncovered bones lay. Children were born, as Orpingalik had promised, and when the attending women called him in to hold the squalling bundle, black-haired and red of face, Aglooka was amazed by the overpowering rush of love he felt for each one of them. Between him and Uvlunuaq too the warm laughter, the cooperation and the mutual learning flowered into understanding and a slow fondness of passion. News came from Taloyoak, to the north across the long strait: of Wilson's uncanny expertise with a dog team ('What's a coxswain but the handler of a bunch of old sea dogs?' chuckled Aglooka, remembering a former life); of his and Blankey's journey to Fury Beach, from the cache of stores at which they had brought back muskets, and a great quantity of black powder and shot, some of which made its way back to Uqsuqtuuq in the *umiak* – the women's boat – in the summer Uvlunuaq's first-born had died. One spring Wilson and his dogs sledged over the ice, and filled out detail for Aglooka of the rumours he had heard about Osmer's death: he had forced the wife of Ugarng whilst the latter was hunting. Before the men came back, the women had overpowered him. They had stripped him, tethered him spreadeagled to stakes of sharpened caribou bone, had cut off his genitals, put them in his mouth and left him on the slope above the summer camp in the hills for predators. The parasitic jaegers had taken out his eyes. Nanuq and his attendant daemon, the little Arctic fox, had feasted on what was left. Manson had been killed by a charging musk ox. Blankey had a wife and many children. One year a strange *qallunaat* had come by land from the south with dogs, and the village had sold him useless things from the ships, but told him nothing of the two *qallunaat* married to women of the village who had just left for the summer camp to hunt caribou, nor of those across the water. He went away, but Aglooka knew he and his kind would be back, and Uvlunuaq knew too, as they and their children held close under the heavy hides in the dark of winter. She knew that the autumn of his life was settling on her man. In their tenth spring together, she sewed new boots for him, lined with the fur of Nanuq, soled with the skin of bearded seal and stitched with caribou sinews, which swelled when wet to make them waterproof. She fashioned his coat of sealskin because she knew he would be going south, and on the morning when she heard the skeins flying high over the bay she slipped from the bed, stood so that he might see her naked for the last time and sang him this song:

I will walk with leg muscles
Strong as shin-sinew of the caribou calf.

> I will walk with leg muscles
> Strong as shin-sinew of the white hare.
> Carefully I will turn from the dark.
> I will head into the light of day.

She dressed him, tied packages of seal meat on his sledge, drums of powder and shot, a snow knife and a heavy sleeping hide. Months later, by Angikuni Lake on the Kazan River in Keewatin, Aglooka lifted the heavy fowling-piece to the hole in the canvas screen as the snow geese, black primaries stark against their brilliant white, wheeled in to land in the shallows. The largest of them began to walk towards his hiding place over stony slopes, ground thawed billowy and summer-soft, the surface litter of stone graded into parallel or polygonal abstractions. A pair of snow buntings scurried past. The goose paused to graze the minimal low plants that crouched beneath a dry, harsh wind – saxifrages and sedums, the roseroot and mountain avens, the cinquefoils and grass of Parnassus and fragrant shield fern, bog cotton ever-moving, the polar willow, slender-shooted, its leaves a muted, dark and unassertive green. It scratched its long neck against an old bone from the caribou herds, honeycombed and grey, mottled, with the appearance of bleached and seasoned timber, the mosses growing over it. As it did so, Aglooka's finger tensed on the trigger and squeezed.

The flash as the worn and rusting barrel split seared his eyes, a splinter of pitted steel bedded in his throat. He wrenched it free, and in doing so the razor edge cut the artery and his blood pumped out in a dying rhythm. The high tumbling calls of the geese as they hurled away across the sky, heading south, registered faintly in his fading consciousness. His last breath rattled out in a red froth. Coyote and wolf spread his bones, the snows of winter shrouding them, and those of all the lost who would never be found.

The Museum of the Sea

by Nick Parker

In the early days, we were mainly engaged in attempting to clarify what the Museum of the Sea was to be. Which is to say, we mainly followed Mallard around with our notebooks, while he extemporised on his vision. He spent a lot of time in his rowing boat, out in the bay. We followed him in boats of our own. Making notes while rowing at the same time was quite tricky, we recall. It was also difficult to hear Mallard above the breeze – the sound of waves lapping is surprisingly loud. Mallard seemed oblivious and went on talking away, and waving his arms all over the place. We tried to draw conclusions from his arm gestures. Charles wrote down 'jellyfish', 'harpoon' and 'oscillating water column'. Mallard would frequently lean over the side of the boat and dip his hands into the water, bringing up palmfuls of brine, and proffer it as though by way of explanation. We would nod and make it look as if we understood perfectly well what he was on about, and try not to let the laptops get too wet, or let the oars accidentally slip into the water. Later, when we were back on shore, I asked Charles how he had known what to write. He said he was just 'riding the wave', whatever that means.

The coastal hike was also rather fraught, if we're honest. For some reason Mallard chose an exceptionally windy day to head out. The coastline that is closest to us is treacherous, to say the least. Loose shingle followed by crumbling chalk followed by stretches of path strewn with boulders and boot-snagging heather. Mallard marched on ahead, his umbrella raised in the air. We followed, the winds that whipped around the headland snatching the air from our lungs as we stumbled along. With our hearts crashing in our ears and the waves crashing against the rocks, the last thing on our minds was getting a handle on what exactly it was that Mallard was driving at. Occasionally he would stop and gesture expansively out to sea. We would write a few desultory notes in our notebooks and then plunge onwards. When we arrived at the cove, Mallard picked his way deftly down to the shore, his sights fixed on the cave that was half obscured by fallen rocks. We caught up with him just as he was concluding what must have been some kind of rousing oratory. His words echoed back at us from the mouth of the cave. So as Mallard stood with his arms folded, beaming at us, his words boomed all around us: 'None none of of this this is is the the sort sort of of thing thing that that will will appear appear in in the the Museum Museum of of the the Sea Sea.'

The day at the Aqua-Park was really quite eventful. We set up the video cameras and got some excellent footage of the penguins, and the fast shutter speeds really came into their own when capturing the seals mid-backflip. Mallard paced up and down behind us shouting encouragement. We all had a go holding out the bait, and the close-ups of the killer whale leaping up and brushing against our fingertips were spectacular. It was a struggle for some of us to get the wetsuits on, but it was worth it to swim with the dolphin. The keepers said that it was the first time they had ever seen twenty-five people all swim with one dolphin, and it's true that the little fellow did have to thrash up a fair old foam just to get moving. Afterwards, as we sat on the side of the pool, catching our breath and bandaging Peter's arm, the keepers said that it was highly unusual for a dolphin to turn like that, what with them being so highly evolved and all. But we could tell that they were laying the blame pretty squarely at our feet. We stared at our flippers and didn't say much until Mallard brought the minibus round. Back at the studio, we stuck the photographs on the walls and pointed out the ones we thought captured the events of the day best. Mallard seemed quite drawn to the picture which caught Peter's unfortunate run-in with Slippy. He remarked on how he had never imagined dolphins to have so many teeth.

Then he said, 'Of course, none of this is suitable for the Museum of the Sea.'

As soon as we arrived on the beach, Mallard unloaded twenty-five sets of buckets and spades from the back of his beach buggy, and set us to work on building sandcastles. He also said that we should remove our shoes and jackets, and advised that our silk ties might suffer a little if they came in contact with the salt water. We appreciated the warnings. As we beavered away, shaping and perfecting our castles, sculpting ramparts and turrets, and digging moats for the tides to fill, Mallard clambered up onto the lifeguard's tall chair, and bellowed through the lifeguard's megaphone: Volume, gentlemen, is all. Context, gentlemen, is all. Faith, gentlemen, is all. Two-for-one entry on Mondays, gentlemen, is all. Never forget these principles when thinking of the Museum of the Sea. We have to admit that we were too busy with the castle building to write any of that down, but Mallard bellowed it so often that there was no chance of us forgetting any of it.

By the end of the day, the array of sandcastles was truly impressive. Some were enormous high towers, bold structures encrusted with shells and dried starfish that stood taller than a man. Some were precarious constructions of pillars and platforms, which seemed to defy the natural properties of sand. Some were long and wide, collections of dozens and dozens of smaller turrets and ramparts, with intricate patterns of pebbles adorning the outside, and moats that ran for several metres in all directions. All day we ran back and forth through the soft waterlogged sand, fetching shells and seaweed and pebbles, leaving those little sucking footprints behind us. We have to say that we surpassed ourselves. Charles was so taken with his own creation that he tried to scoop some parts of it up and put it in his briefcase. He soon realised the error of his ways; grains of sand got lodged in the clasp mechanism and made an unpleasant crunch when he tried to close it. Mallard strode among the castles nodding seriously to himself. As the sun began to set he sent us all off to buy ice cream, but alas we had left it too late, and although we found a waste bin overflowing with Cornetto wrappers, we realised that the van must have already gone home. We returned a little downcast to the beach, to find that the castles had vanished. At first we thought the tide had come in and washed them away, but one glance at Mallard and we knew the truth: he had destroyed them all. We looked around. All that was left of our day's handiwork were little sandy mounds, with Mallard's flip-flop prints all over them. 'I hardly need to say, gentlemen, that none of this is at all fit for the Museum of the Sea,' Mallard said flatly, and stalked off to the car park.

Mallard hired a beach hut and called a meeting. We had dried our notebooks on the radiators in the studio, and were ready and waiting. He wished to clarify, he said, a few further things about what the Museum of the Sea was not. He wasted no time. As soon as the wooden doors were shut and his overhead projector had hummed into life, Mallard began to elucidate: The Museum of the Sea is not an aquarium. The Museum of the Sea is not a theme park. The Museum of the Sea is not a repository for artefacts pertaining to exploration, sailing, shipping, or maritime endeavours. The Museum of the Sea is not an educational facility aimed at addressing environmental 'concerns' in an 'accessible' way. The Museum of the Sea is not a curiosity shop for the display of aquatic artefacts, nor a storehouse of a taxonomy on the seas, such as comically ugly fish which have been rendered thus by the crushing pressures of the ocean deeps. The Museum of the Sea will not mention in any way the crushing pressures of the ocean deeps. The Museum of the Sea will not be a place for re-enactments of early attempts to cross the oceans, by means of canoe, raft or otherwise. The Museum of the Sea will not countenance the display of ocean-related painting, sculpture, tapestry, poetry, myth, song, or dance. The Museum of the Sea will not contain any signage written in easily digestible factoids; the Museum of the Sea will not, in fact, contain any signage at all. The Museum of the Sea will have no interactive display units; in the Museum of the Sea, there will be no audio guides. I'm sure it goes without saying that the Museum of the Sea will certainly not have a shop. There will be no pencils with 'Museum of the Sea' written down the side in gold lettering; there will be no Museum of the Sea erasers or pencil cases.

We all sat in silence for the longest time. Eventually, Peter raised his good arm, and went to ask the question that we were all thinking. But Mallard raised a hand and silenced him: 'Let me say only this,' he said. 'When I go to an aquarium I do not marvel at the fish. I do not marvel at the crustaceans. I do not marvel at the anemones. When I walk through the glass tunnels, I do not marvel at the sharks overhead. I marvel at the water, the beautiful tanks of water. I see the wood, not the trees.'

We were chastened by these words. Although out of the corner of my eye I noticed that Charles had jotted down in his notebook 'Trees made of *water*?'

One morning, we all received through the post the following note, torn from an encyclopedia. We sniffed it carefully. The paper smelled faintly of brine. It read: 'Seawater is about a 3.49 per cent salt solution, the rest is fresh water. The more saline, the denser the seawater. As the range of salt concentration in the ocean varies from about 3.2 to 3.8 per cent, oceanographers refer to salt content as "salinity", express salt concentration as parts per thousand; 34.9 ppt is the average salinity. As seawater evaporates the salt remains behind; only the fresh water is transferred from the ocean to the atmosphere. A region of excess evaporation, such as the subtropics, tends to become salty, while the areas of excess rainfall become fresher. Sea ice formation also removes fresh water from the ocean, leaving behind a more saline solution. Along the shores of Antarctica this process produces dense water. Salinity reflects the workings of the hydrological cycle: the movement of fresh water through the earth/ocean/atmosphere system.'

On the other side of the piece of paper was written: 'Wind-induced upwelling and sinking has an effect on the chlorophyll within the ocean surface layer, a marker of phytoplankton (Fig. 25). Upwelling of cool sub-surface water provides nutrients promoting the growth of phytoplankton, beginning the food chain. The light blue, green and red areas of the ocean (Fig. 25) denote regions of high chlorophyll. Low chlorophyll areas are shown in dark blue. Compare the chlorophyll map with the SST map (Fig. 11).'

Figs 11 and 25 were not included in the envelope.

Scrawled on the scrap of paper, in Mallard's unmistakable handwriting, was a note saying, 'The Museum of the Sea will naturally make no mention of these facts.'

One night over drinks, Mallard gathered us all around the table. He asked us to put down our drinks, close our eyes and make ourselves comfortable. He said, 'Imagine that you are floating in the ocean, right out in the middle of the ocean, where all you can see in any direction is just ocean and more ocean. Now imagine that you begin to sink. First of all, you sink down through the warm water to a depth of 200 metres. When you look up, you can still see the glow of the surface above you. You have sunk through the photic layer. You keep on sinking down. You are now sinking into the mesopelagic region. The water is colder. The light is almost gone. At one thousand metres, you will find yourself sinking into the bathypelagic region; there is no light at all at this depth. You sink further, into the abyssalpelagic region. The temperature is just a few degrees above zero. You might see a giant squid at this depth, or perhaps a black swallower. Except of course you won't actually be able to see anything at all, because it is pitch black, an utter freezing blackness the likes of which it is not possible to experience anywhere else in the universe. A blackness that is crushing you to the tune of nearly five long tons force per square inch. You are now nearly six kilometres from the surface, and still sinking. Take a moment to imagine just how far six kilometres really is. But you haven't come to rest yet, you keep sinking, past even the bed of the deepest oceans on earth, into the hadal zone. That's hadal, from the French for house of the dead, in case you were wondering. This is the water in the deepest trenches at the bottom of the deepest oceans. If only you could see, you might glimpse perhaps a blind tube worm leeching an existence on the side of a black smoker, a hydrothermic vent that spews out a toxic chemical brew at scorching temperatures. The tube worms live on sulphur. Their bodies are transparent. If any of the few creatures which scratch out a living down here were to float up to the more hospitable regions of the sea, the lack of extreme pressure would kill them. Imagine what it must be like, to need that crushing pressure on you at all times, just to stay alive. You may open your eyes now.'

We opened our eyes, gasping for breath and sweating with fear. Several people had passed out, and others dashed for the door to take in fresh air or be sick. Mallard seemed rather pleased with himself, even among the cacophony of complaints. The evening's drinks had been utterly ruined. 'Anyway,' he said, 'we won't be making reference to any of that in the Museum of the Sea either.'

By now, we had many volumes filled with our notes concerning items which would not appear in the Museum of the Sea. I had spent several weeks painstakingly colouring a map clearly showing the designations of all the oceans and the seas: the Atlantic, the Pacific, the Indian, the Southern, the Arctic, the Caspian, the Dead, many others. Next to each ocean, Mallard had written 'Don't mention this in the Museum of the Sea', and appended a little arrow, pointing from the words to the names of the various oceans. Then there were the meticulous diagrams detailing all tidal movements across an entire lunar month. I had copied each diagram out by hand, and Mallard had added, in neat pencil writing in the top left-hand corner: 'This will not be appearing in the Museum of the Sea.' The scientific papers were also piled high, each one printed out on the special paper Mallard had ordered. Pick up a copy of, for instance, 'Rupture of the Cell Envelope by Decompression of the Deep-Sea Methanogen' by C. B. Park and D. S. Clark (2002), and hold it up to the light and you'll see the watermark: 'This information must not be included in the Museum of the Sea.' The same goes for printouts of the complete transcripts of every single shipping forecast. Our store rooms are filled with coral, shells, fossils of ancient sea creatures; maps from almost every century, showing the locations of trade routes, or treasure, or sea monsters. We have a complete set of all the uniforms of all the naval forces around the globe. Each artefact bears a tiny laser-printed tag, saying, 'Not for inclusion in the Museum of the Sea.'

And then Mallard convened us all on the derelict oil rig. It had been derelict for some time, and in truth we all admired its shabby grandeur, the casual atmosphere of menace. As we slipped past the DO NOT ENTER signs and over the barriers with DANGER written on them in orange lettering, we wondered to ourselves whether the oil rig itself might warrant the honour of being excluded from the Museum of the Sea. Mallard was already standing up on the main viewing platform, watching the ocean thunder beneath us. As usual, we had to gather close, in order to hear Mallard's words, before the salt air snatched them from his mouth and flung them out to sea. Mallard said:

'I have a story to tell you. There was once an island in the Pacific Ocean. It was a small island, no more than a mile across.

It was blessed with golden beaches and rich soils and a rotation of rain and sunshine which presented the islanders with an embarrassment of bounty. All who lived on the island were content, and the island's chief saw to it that this happy state of affairs was given every chance to prosper. He made sure that the islanders were generous towards one another and when he was, infrequently, called upon to adjudicate in a dispute between two islanders, he was regarded as just and fair. The islanders had no knowledge of life outside of their island, and in every direction their horizon showed unceasing, unbroken ocean. They passed their days fishing, dancing, tending their crops, raising their children and racing each other to see who could swim around the island the fastest.

'And then one day, after a terrible storm had raged for three days and three nights, the islanders noticed that there was a ship floating in their shallows. It had been much abused by the storm; its sails were in tatters, its masts were broken, it was listing heavily. The islanders were curious and sailed out to the stricken vessel. On board they found a dozen survivors, who had been violently abused by the storm. Everyone else on board had been lost. Thinking only to help these poor sailors, the islanders loaded the survivors onto their canoes and took them back to their island, where they fed them and tended to their injuries. Soon the survivors were much recovered, and wished to thank their rescuers, but the islanders had such a bountiful life that there was nothing that they wished for. The sailors felt that offering the islanders the ship's three remaining barrels of salt beef was a poor exchange for their lives, and just about everything else had been lost in the storm. So the captain and his bosun returned to their stricken ship and searched the remains of their cargo for something that they might offer the islanders. And there in the hold, they saw the very thing: a meteorological balloon. It was a small balloon with a seat slung beneath it, in the French style. Also in the hold was the sack of iron filings and the vessels of hydrochloric acid required to create the hydrogen gas which the balloon needed in order to take to the air. These were loaded onto the canoes and brought ashore.

'Through much arm waving and smiling, the captain managed to communicate that the men and women of the tribe, should they wish, could sit in the balloon, and by means of a gas that was lighter than air, they would rise far above the island, up to where the gulls flew. The islanders were excited, and milled around expectantly as the sailors set about mixing the iron filings and the acid, and filling the balloon with gas. In the few hours that this took, the chief of the island made it known that he wished to be the first to ride in the balloon.

'Once the balloon was fully inflated, the sailors secured it to a large tree, and the chief, grinning from ear to ear, took his place in the seat. It was an extraordinary sight, this serious-looking tribesman, in full ceremonial headdress, sitting under a bobbing balloon as if he was sitting on a child's swing. And then slowly the sailors began to slacken the rope, allowing the balloon to rise. For nearly a minute the balloon floated up, hardly deviating left or right on that sunny and windless day. All seemed to be going well. The chief waved down from the balloon. He seemed relaxed.

'And then suddenly, as the balloon reached the limit of the rope, the chief of the island started screaming. Even over two hundred feet in the air, his screams could be heard clearly by all those below, who quickly hauled on the rope and brought the balloon back to earth. Had the chief had a fit of vertigo? Was he terrified of falling? Perhaps he had decided that the balloon was some terrible piece of black magic? Was he mistrustful of flight? As soon as his feet touched the ground, he fled into the forest. The islanders and the sailors stood frozen, watching each other, as the chief's screams slowly faded into the distance.

'Perhaps everything would have been all right if the sailors hadn't panicked and tried to make a run for it. They dashed into the shallows and tried to clamber into one of the islanders' canoes. Perhaps they were trying to flee back to the safety of their own ship. Whatever their motive, the islanders, fearing that their chief's screams signalled something terrible, fell on the sailors and killed them with spears. Then, revolted by their own actions, they too fled into the forest, leaving the bodies to be washed back onto the beach by the tide. As the bodies came to rest, their blood stained the sand.'

We held our breaths expectantly. Mallard was beckoning us towards him. 'It is said,' he almost whispered, 'by others who visited the island later, and found its lands untilled, its people dishevelled and drunken, and its shorelines littered with debris, that what happened to the chief up there that day was that he saw with his own eyes the insignificance of his island in the vast ocean. He saw the ocean stretching off for ever in all directions. He saw that his own island, all the people he knew, his entire world, was a mere yellow speck, a precarious blip, a mere nothing. It is said that the realisation of it drove him mad. He tried to hide this terrible revelation from his people, but they didn't need to have it explained to them. They picked up on his terrors. The whole island fell under a terrible pall from which it never recovered.'

Mallard stared at us with a look of soft-boiled resignation in his eyes. The sea boiled behind him. The wind ripped at the pages of our notebooks, which flapped in our hands like angry seagulls.

'The question is,' said Mallard, 'does such a story belong in the Museum of the Sea?'

Some say it was Peter who snapped first. Others say it was Charles. I have to admit that even though we all rushed at Mallard as one, I felt that it was my hands which were round his throat first. And yes, we know that such an act is indefensible, but all we can say is that as we heaved Mallard over the railings and watched him plunge down into the sea, several of us would swear that we saw a smile on his lips. And as he surfaced for a second time between the waves, was he trying to say something to us? Did he perhaps shout, before he went under that final time, 'Put this into the museum'? We rather think he did.

Contributors

Desmond Barry

Des Barry has published three novels, the most recent being *Cressida's Bed* (Jonathan Cape). He teaches Creative Writing at Glamorgan University.

Chris Cleave

Chris Cleave stopped delivering yachts for a living after the voyage on which *Fresh Water* is loosely based. His debut novel *Incendiary* won the 2006 Somerset Maugham Award, was shortlisted for the Commonwealth Writers Prize, and will be released as a feature film this year. He has recently delivered his second novel.

Margaret Elphinstone

Margaret Elphinstone has published eight novels, including *The Sea Road, Voyageurs, Hy Brasil* and *Light* (all with Canongate) and numerous short stories. She is Professor of Writing at Strathclyde University.

Niall Griffiths

Niall is the author of six novels, the most recent being *Runt* (Vintage).

Tessa Hadley

Tessa teaches literature and creative writing at Bath Spa University. In 2007 she has published a new novel, *The Master Bedroom*, and a collection of stories, *Sunstroke* (both Jonathan Cape).

Roger Hubank

Roger is a past winner of the Boardman-Tasker Prize, and the Grand Prix award at the Banff Mountain Book Festival. His novel *North*, about the ill-fated 1881 Lady Franklin Bay polar expedition, was described by *The Observer* as possibly 'the first great historical novel of the twenty-first century'.

Charles Lambert

Charles' debut novel, *Little Monsters*, will be published in Spring 2008 by Picador; a recent short story appeared in the British Council/Granta anthology *New Writing 15*.

Sam Llewellyn

Sam is a well-known writer of sea stories for adults and children. Born in the Isles of Scilly, he has sailed boats modern and traditional all over the world. He is enraged by the cynical rejection of sustainable fisheries policies in the EU and elsewhere.

Robert Minhinnick

Robert Minhinnick's book of essays, *To Babel and Back* (Seren) was Welsh Book of the Year in 2006. His novel, *Sea Holly* (Seren) appears this year, and Carcanet publish his next book of poems, *King Driftwood* in 2008.

Nick Parker

Nick's short stories have been published in many anthologies, and read on Radio 4. He is also the Deputy Editor of *The Oldie* magazine.

Jim Perrin

Jim is one of Britain's most-read writers on travel and the outdoors. His speciality is mountaineering. He has twice won the Boardman Tasker Prize for his biographies of Don Whillans and Menlove Edwards, as well as several other major awards.

James Scudamore

James Scudamore's first novel *The Amnesia Clinic* was published by Harvill Secker in 2006. It won the 2007 Somerset Maugham Award and was shortlisted for the Costa First Novel Award, the Commonwealth Writers Prize, the Glen Dimplex Award and the Dylan Thomas Prize.

Martin Stephen

Martin Stephen is the author of 17 academic books and 4 novels in the Henry Gresham series. He is High Master of St Paul's School.

Erica Wagner

Erica is Literary Editor of *The Times*. She published an acclaimed collection of short stories *Gravity* and *Ariel's Gift*, a commentary on Ted Hughes' *Birthday Letters*. Her debut novel, *Seizure*, was published by Faber & Faber in Spring 2007.

John Williams

John Williams lives and works in his hometown of Cardiff. His *Cardiff Trilogy*, set in and around the city's docklands, the former Tiger Bay, is published by Bloomsbury.

Evie Wyld

Evie Wyld graduated with a distinction in Creative Writing from Goldsmiths University in 2005. She is currently completing her first novel.

National Maritime Museum Publishing

At **National** Maritime Museum Publishing we pride ourselves on producing high-quality books exploring the sea, ships, time and the stars. *Sea Stories* is a collection of new short stories written to celebrate the 70th anniversary of the opening of the Museum in 1937.

- Trade orders: Bookpoint, 130 Milton Park, Abingdon, Oxon, ox14 4sb, T+44 (0)1235 400400, orders@bookpoint.co.uk
- To order any title directly from NMMP, please call T+44 (0)208 312 6700 or email shopweb@nmm.ac.uk.

To find out more about our titles visit www.nmm.ac.uk/publishing